"You lack subtlety,"

Roland told her. "Why not just simply tear off my
clothes and attempt a forced seduction?" He was
immediately more angry with what he'd just said than
he was with her. He saw the hurt in her eyes before she
covered it. "I'm sorry, Rhiannon. I didn't mean—"

"Of course you did. You'd prefer me to become what
you consider a true lady, to sit on an embroidered
cushion and bat my eyes until you take the initiative.
Hah! I'd be coated in more cobwebs than this great
hall by the time you did!"

Dear Reader,

We're ba-ck! And we've got another great month of reading in store for you, starting with *Lover in the Shadows,* by Lindsay Longford. This is an enthralling story about a man who is, well, not quite what he seems. And, of course, let's not forget the woman who loves him. In the hands of this masterful storyteller, their romance becomes a thing of "terrible beauty," as the poet said.

Then there's *Twilight Memories,* the second book of Maggie Shayne's irresistible "Wings in the Night" miniseries. This is another toothsome morsel (Sorry! I just couldn't resist) from a new author who's fast making a name for herself.

In months to come, look for books by more of your favorite authors when writers such as Diana Whitney, Marilyn Tracy and Jane Toombs—to name just a few— step into the shadows to bring you the best of the dark side of love.

Enjoy!

Leslie Wainger
Senior Editor and Editorial Coordinator

Please address questions and book requests to:
Reader Service
U.S.: P.O. Box 1325, Buffalo, NY 14269
Canadian: P.O. Box 1050, Niagara Falls, Ont. L2E 7G7

MAGGIE SHAYNE

TWILIGHT MEMORIES

Published by Silhouette Books
America's Publisher of Contemporary Romance

SILHOUETTE BOOKS

ISBN 0-373-27030-5

TWILIGHT MEMORIES

Printed in U.S.A.

Books by Maggie Shayne

Silhouette Shadows

Twilight Phantasies #18
Twilight Memories #30

Silhouette Intimate Moments

Reckless Angel #522

* Wings in the Night

MAGGIE SHAYNE

and her husband of sixteen years make their home in rural Otselic Valley, nestled in the rolling hills of southern central New York. Among her friends, Maggie is known for her quirky sense of humor, a tool she sees as essential to raising her five beautiful daughters.

Maggie has served for two years as secretary and conference coordinator for her chapter of Romance Writers of America. She has written articles for *Romance Writers Report,* and wrote features and humor for all but one issue of *Inside Romance.* In addition, she often writes for her chapter newsletter, *Prose and Cons.* More than anything else, she enjoys writing. She loves to create characters that come alive in her own mind and, she hopes, in the minds of her readers.

For Melissa and Leslie,
who recognized Rhiannon's potential
even before I did

INTRODUCTION

It's because I'm not good enough. Or, so he thinks. It isn't that he doesn't desire me, because we both know he does. And why wouldn't he? Mortal men fall at my feet like simpering fools begging for a crumb of attention. Immortals, as well, those few I've known. Why then, does the only man I desire reject me? Why does he feign indifference when I can see the lust in his eyes? Why has he asked me to remain away from him, to cease distracting him with my periodic visits? It isn't as if I bother him so often. Once every fifty years or so, when my fantasies of him no longer suffice—when my longing for him becomes too strong to resist.

My visits, though, do little to ease my discomfort. He only reaffirms his decision, each time, and pleads with me to stay away. He'd send me away himself, were he able. He'd banish me from his very sight, were it in his power to do so.

Just as my father did.

I know, I am not what most males expect a female to be. I am outspoken. I am strong. I fear very little in this world, nor would I, I suspect, in any other. But it is not my oddness that makes me so unloved by the males. Or should I say, unlovable? It can't be that, for my father rejected me before I'd had opportunity to display any of my strange tendencies. He rejected me simply for being his firstborn.

A great Pharaoh of Egypt, a god-king of the Nile, he fully expected the gods to bless him with a son as first-born. When he was given me, instead, he saw me as some sort of punishment for whatever sins he imagined himself guilty of. I was allowed to remain with my mother only until I saw my fifth year. It would have been more merciful to have tossed me at birth from the gilded halls of his palace, and left me as bait for the jackals. Yet he did not. At five, I was banished, sent to live among the priestesses of Isis at the temple. My brothers, when they came later, were treated as I should have been. They were welcomed as princes. Their arrivals were celebrated for months on end. Yet I, the one truly destined for immortality, was ignored.

I vowed then never again to care for the affections of any male, but I find I do now. Not that my emotions are involved. I am far too wise to fall prey to silly romanticism. I am not a simpleminded, gullible mortal, after all. No, it is not romance I want. It is only him. My desire for him is a palpable thing, as I know his for me to be, as well. It angers me that he denies it, that he sees me as unworthy.

This time, though, I will manage it. I will prove to him that I am the bravest, the strongest, the most cunning individual he's ever known.

I've come upon some information, you see. A while back, Roland had some serious trouble, along with two other immortals, back in the States. The details are not important. The gist is that the most precious being to Roland, right now, is a boy by the name of Jamison Bryant. He is one of The Chosen—that is, one of those rare humans who share the same ancestry and blood antigen as we immortals. One who can be transformed. He shares a special link with Roland, a closeness of which, I freely admit, I am envious. And the boy is in grave danger. So might Roland be. I am on my way not only to warn them, but to protect them both, in any way necessary.

Please, do not misinterpret my motive. I do not rush to his side because of any overblown emotional attachments. I've already made clear that my feelings for Roland are only physical in nature. It hurts enough to be rejected on that basis. Think how stupid one would have to be to open oneself up to more pain! No, I do this only to prove my worth. He will see, once and for all, that Rhiannon is not a bit of dust to be swept away at a whim. Not a mere limpid female, to be ignored as so much chattel. I am worthy of his affection, just as I was my father's. They are the ones who are wrong, to cast me aside.

They are the ones who are wrong.

Although...

There are times, when even I begin to doubt it. There are times when I hear my father's voice, echoing in those vaulted corridors, his condemnation of me. And I wonder. Could he have been right? Am I, truly, his curse? Nothing more than a pawn of the gods, to be used to mete out punishment to a sinful king? How could my father have been wrong, after all? He was pharaoh! Only a step below a god himself. Might he have been right?

Just as Roland might now be right in avoiding my touch? Perhaps he sees something that I have not. Perhaps he knows how unworthy I—

No!

I am Rhiannon—born Rhianikki, princess of Egypt, firstborn of Pharaoh. I am immortal, a goddess among humans, envied by women and worshipped by men. I could kill them all as easily as I could wish them goodnight.

I could!

I *am* worthy... and I intend to prove it.

I am Rhiannon. And this is my story.

CHAPTER ONE

He moved as one of the shadows beneath the overhung roofs, along the twisting, narrow streets. He detested the fact that he was here, walking among *them*. Some passed so near he could have touched them, simply by raising a hand. He felt the heat of their bodies, saw the steam of their warm breaths in the chill night air. He felt the blood pulsing beneath their skin, and heard the rapid, healthy patter of their hearts. He felt like a wolf slinking silently among timid rabbits. With his preternatural strength he could kill any of them without taxing himself. It frightened him to know he was capable of doing just that, if pushed.

For an instant, murky images of the distant past clouded his vision. Air heavy with dust and the scents of sweat and blood. Fallen men, like autumn leaves upon the damp, brown earth. Hooves thundering as the riderless horses fled in a hundred directions. One man, a boy, in truth, remained breathing. The lowly squire in ill-fitting armor sat high upon a magnificent, sooty destrier. The horse pawed the ground with a forefoot and blew, eager for more. Only silence came in answer. The silence of death, for it surrounded them.

The young Roland saw the blood-coated broadsword, the crimson tears, dripping slowly from its tip. As the red haze of fury began to fade, he let the weapon fall from his grasp. Stomach lurching, he tugged the steel helmet from his head, then the mail coif, and tossed both to the ground. Aghast, he stared at the carnage, too sickened just then to be thankful their faces were hidden by helmets, their wounds covered by their armor.

The boy felt no elation at what he'd done. No, not even later, when he was personally knighted by King Louis VII, for heroism and valor. He felt nothing but a grim and disgusting new self-knowledge.

For he had enjoyed the killing.

Roland shook himself. Now was no time for remembrances, or regrets. He reminded himself that despite his likening of them to rabbits, some humans were capable of ultimate deceit and treachery. Past experience had taught him that. And if the report he'd just had from the States were true, one of those humans, more treacherous than any, might even be a few yards from him. It was that possibility that had drawn Roland into the village tonight, in spite of his self-imposed solitude.

His plan was simple. He would slip unnoticed through the medieval-style streets of L'Ombre, and into the inn called Le Requin. He would listen, and he would watch. He'd scan their thinly veiled minds and he'd find the interloper, if, indeed, there was one to be found. And then he'd deal with it.

The night wind stiffened, bringing with it the scents of late-blooming roses, and dying ones, of freshly clipped grass and of the liquor and smoke just beyond the door he now approached. He paused as the door swung wide, and the odor sharpened. A cluster of inebriated tourists stumbled out and passed him. Roland drew back, averting his face, but it was an unnecessary precaution. They paid him no mind.

Roland squared his shoulders. He did not fear humans, nor did many of his kind. More that he feared *for* them, should he be forced into an unwanted encounter. Besides that, it made good sense to avoid contact. Should humans ever learn that the existence of vampires was more than just the stuff of legends and folklore, the damage done would be irreversible. There would be no peace. It was best to remain apart, to remain forever a myth to those endlessly prying mortals.

As the door swung once more, Roland caught it and slipped quickly through. He stepped to one side and took a moment to survey his surroundings. Low, round tables were scattered without order. People clustered around them, sitting, or standing, leaning over and speaking of nothing in particular. The smoke-laden air hung at face level, stinging his eyes and causing his nostrils to burn. The voices were a drone, punctuated often by the splashing of liquor and the clinking sounds of ice against glass.

Her laughter rose then, above all else. Low, husky and completely without reserve, it rode the smoky air to surround him, and caress his eardrums. His gaze shot toward the source of the sound, but he saw only a huddle of men vying for position near the bar. He could only guess *she* must be at the center of that huddle.

To push his way through the throng of admirers was out of the question. Roland had no desire to draw undue attention. No, nor indeed, any desire to renew his timeless acquaintance with her. To resume the slow torture. He ignored the surge of anger he felt at the idea that any of the humans might be close enough to touch her. He would not wish to witness the clumsy gropings of some drunken mortal. He didn't really believe he might break the fool's neck for such an offense, but there was no need pressing his temper to its limits.

He could learn as much by listening, and he did so now, attuning his mind as well as his hearing, and wondering what she was calling herself these days. For although he sought confirmation, he had no doubt about the identity of that seductive laugh's owner. No doubt at all.

"Do another one, Rhiannon!"

"Oui, cherié. 'Ow about zome rock and roll?"

A chorus of pleas followed, as the willowy, dark form extricated herself from the mass. She shook her head, not quite smiling in that way she had. She moved with such grace that she seemed to float over the hardwood rather than walk on it. The slightly flared hemline of black velvet swaying a fraction of an inch above the floor added to the illusion. Roland had no clue how she managed to move her legs at all, given the way the full-length skirt clung to them from midshin on up. She might as well have paraded naked before her gaping admirers for what the garment hid. The velvet seemed to have melded itself to her form, curving as her hips did, nipping inward at the waist, cupping her small, high breasts like possessive hands. Her long, slender arms were bare, save the bangles and bracelets adorning them. Her fingers were beringed, and tipped in lengthy, dagger-sharp nails of blood red.

Roland's gaze continued upward as she moved across the room, apparently unaware of his presence. The neckline of the ridiculous dress consisted only of two strips of velvet forming a halter around her throat. Between the swatches, the pale expanse of her skin glowed with ethereal smoothness. His sharp eyes missed nothing, from the gentle swell of her breasts, to the delicate outline of her collarbone at the base of her throat. Around her neck she wore an onyx pendant in the shape of a cradle moon. It rested flat on the surface of her chest, its lowest point just touching the uppermost curve of her breasts.

That swan's neck, creamy in color, satiny in texture, gracefully long and narrow, was partially covered by her hair. It hung as straight and perfectly jet as the velvet dress, yet glossy, more satin than velvet, in truth. She'd pulled it all to one side, and it hung down covering the right side of her neck, and most of the dress. It's shining length only ended at midthigh.

On her left ear she'd hung a cluster of diamonds and onyx that dangled so long they touched her shoulder. He couldn't tell whether the earring had a mate on her right ear, due to her abundance of hair.

She paused, and bent over the man on the piano bench, whispering in his ear, her narrow hand resting on his shoulder. Roland felt himself stiffen as the beast buried deep within him stirred for the first time in decades. He willed it away. The man nodded, and struck a chord. She turned, facing the crowd, one forearm resting upon the top of the piano. With the first rich, flawless note she sung, the entire room went silent. Her voice, so deep and smooth that were it given form it could only become honey, filled the room, coating everything and everyone within. Her expression gave the lyrics more meaning than they'd ever before had.

She sang as if her heart were breaking with each note, yet her voice never wavered or weakened in intensity.

She held the mortals in the palm of her hand, and she was loving every minute of it, Roland thought in silence. He ought to turn and leave her to make a spectacle of herself in this insane manner. But as she sung on, of heartache and unbearable loneliness, she looked toward him. She caught his gaze and she refused to let go. In spite of himself, Roland heard the pure beauty of her voice. And though he'd had no intention of doing so, he let his eyes take in every aspect of her face.

A perfect oval, with bone structure as exquisite and flawless as if she were a sculpture done by a master. Small, almost pointed chin and angling, defined jawline. The slight hollows beneath her cheeks and the high, wide-set cheekbones. Her eyes were almond-shaped and slanted slightly upward at the outer corners. The kohl that lined them only accentuated that exotic slant, and her lashes were as impenetrably dark as the irises they surrounded.

Against his will he focused on her full, always pouting lips as they formed each word of the song. Their color was deep, dark red, like that of wine. How many years had he hungered for those lips?

He shook himself. The fruit of those lips was one he must never sample. His gaze moved upward to her eyes again. Still, they focused solely upon him, as if the words she sung were meant for his ears alone. Gradually he realized the patrons were growing curious. Heads turned toward him to see who had caught the attention of the elusive Rhiannon. He'd fallen under her spell as surely as any of these simpering humans had, and as a result, he'd been unaware of the growing risk of discovery. Let her behave recklessly, if it pleased her to do so. He wouldn't risk his existence to warn her. More likely than not, his remaining here would result in trouble. Her nearness never failed to stir the beast to life, to bring out his baser instincts. That she did so deliberately was without doubt. Though if she knew the whole of it, she might change her mind.

He gripped the door, his eyes still on her, and jerked it open. He made himself step out into the bracing chill of the autumn night even as she held the hauntingly low, final note, drawing it out so long it ought to be obvious she was no ordinary woman. Yet, a second later, Roland heard no one questioning her. He only heard thunderous applause.

* * *

Rhiannon felt the sting of the slap she'd just been is-
sued. Her anger rose quickly, but not quite quickly enough
to prevent her feeling the hurt that came along with it. So
Roland could look her over so thoroughly and simply walk
away, could he? He could ignore the dress she'd chosen
simply to entice him. He could pretend not to hear the
emotion with which she'd sung or even to notice the song
she'd chosen. Well, she supposed she'd need more drastic
measures to get his attention.

She stepped away from the piano, quickly muttering that
she had a headache and needed to slip away without her
male attendants surrounding her. The piano player,
François, tilted his head toward a door in the back, and
Rhiannon made her way toward it. She paused only long
enough to grip the upper arm of the drunkest male in the
room. She pulled him, stumbling in her wake, out the
door.

She could only just make out the dark shape of Roland's retreating figure, farther along the narrow street.
She didn't call out to him. She wouldn't beg him for
something so simple as a hello, after decades of separa-
tion. She had a better idea.

She pulled the drunken man with her a few yards farther, then turned him, her hands supporting his weight
mostly by clenching his shirt front. She shoved his back
against a building.

For a moment, she studied him. He wasn't bad-looking,
really. Red hair, and freckles, but a rather nice face, except for the crooked, inebriated grin.

She hooked a finger beneath his chin, and stared into his
green, liquor-clouded eyes for a long moment. She focused her mental energies on calming him, and gaining his
utter cooperation. By the time she lowered her head to his

throat, the man would have gladly given her everything he owned, had she asked it. She sensed no evil in him. In fact, he seemed a perfectly nice fellow, except for his heavy drinking. She supposed everyone was entitled to one vice, though. She was about to indulge in hers.

She parted her lips and settled her mouth over the place where his jugular pulsed beneath the skin. She wished the man no harm. She only needed to get a rise out of Roland. Her willing victim moaned softly, and let his head fall to the side. She nearly choked on her laughter. She was glad one of them was getting some pleasure out of this. The act had lost its luster for her long ago.

"Dammit Rhianikki, let him go!"

Roland's hand closed on her shoulder, and he jerked her roughly away from the drunk's throat. The man sank to the ground, barely conscious, but from her entrancement of him, not from blood loss. "You could have killed him," Roland whispered harshly.

Rhiannon allowed the corners of her lips to pull ever so slightly upward. "Always so eager to think the worst of me, aren't you, darling? And it's Rhiannon, now. Rhianikki is too—" she waved a hand "—Egyptian." She gave the man on the ground a cursory glance. "It's all right, Paul. You may go now." With her mind, she released him, and he rose unsteadily. His puzzled expression moved from Rhiannon, to Roland, and back again.

"What happened?"

"You've had a little too much Chablis, *mon cher.* Go on, now. Be on your way."

Still frowning, he stumbled back into the tavern, and Rhiannon turned to Roland. "You see?"

"Why are you here?"

She lifted her hands, palms up. "Not even a hello? A how are you? A glad to see you're still drawing a breath? Nothing? How rude you've become, Roland."

"Why are you here?" His voice remained impassive as he repeated the question.

She shrugged. "Well, if you must know, I heard about a certain DPI agent, rather nasty one, too, who'd traced you here. They say he's already in the village. I was worried about you, Roland. I came to warn you."

He looked at the ground and slowly shook his head. "So, knowing an agent of the Division of Paranormal Investigations is in the village, you naturally flaunt your own presence here to the utmost possible degree."

"What better way to flush him out? You know how keen they are on vampire research."

"You might've been killed, Rhiannon."

"Then you'd have been rid of me at last."

He was silent for a moment, scanning her face. "I would find no joy in that, reckless one."

From beneath her lashes, she looked up at him. "You do have an odd way of showing it."

He placed a hand on her shoulder. She slipped one around his waist, and they moved together along the winding road, toward his castle. "You need to take more care," he went on, his tone fatherly...and utterly maddening. "You've no idea what DPI is capable of. They've developed a tranquilizer that renders us helpless."

"I know. And I know about your scrape with them in Connecticut, when they nearly took Eric and his fledgling, Tamara."

Roland's brows shot upward. "And how do you know all of that?"

"I keep track of you, darling." She smiled. "And for years I kept track of that scientist, St. Claire. He held me for a time in that laboratory of his, you know."

He sucked in a sharp breath, gripped her shoulders and turned her to face him. She could have laughed aloud. At last, some emotion!

"My God, I had no idea. When ... how ..." He broke off and shook his head. "Did he hurt you?"

Warmth surged within her. "Terribly," she confessed with a small pout. "But only for a short time. I had to break his partner's neck, I'm afraid, when I made my escape."

Roland shook his head, and closed his eyes. "You could have summoned me. I would've come—"

"Oh, posh, Roland. By the time you could have arrived, I was free again. No human can hope to get the best of Rhianikki, princess of the Nile, daughter of Pharaoh, immortal vampiress of time immemorial—"

His laughter burst from him involuntarily, she knew, and she drank in the beauty of his smile, wishing she could elicit its appearance more often. There was a darkness in Roland's eyes at times. Some secret that troubled him, one he'd never shared.

When his laughter died, he turned and began walking once more. "Tell me how you know about the DPI agent in L'Ombre?"

"Since St. Claire came so close to having me, I've kept a close watch on the organization. I have spies inside. They keep me informed."

He nodded. "Then you are a bit more sensible than I gave you credit for being. You know, of course, St. Claire is dead."

She nodded. "But his protégé, Curtis Rogers, is not."

Roland stopped walking again. "That can't be. Tamara shot him when he was trying his damnedest to kill Eric."

"Yes, shot him. And left him for dead, only he wasn't. He was found a short time later, and he survived. It is he who has come to France looking for you, Roland. He wants vengeance."

"On me?"

"You, Eric, Tamara . . . and the boy, I'm afraid."

She saw the pale coloring drain from Roland's face. She'd known already of his attachment to the child he'd rescued two years ago. The boy was one of The Chosen, a human with an unseen bond to immortals. DPI knew it, and attempted to use him as bait in their trap. No doubt, they would not hesitate to do so again. Rhiannon knew all of this, but seeing firsthand his obvious reaction to a whisper of a threat to the lad, brought home to her the intensity of his caring. She felt the rush of turmoil that coursed through him, and she placed a calming hand on his arm.

"Jamey," he whispered. "The bastard had him once. Nearly killed him."

"And so you know why I've come."

His brows rose inquiringly, and she rushed on. "To offer my help in protecting the boy."

"Noble of you, but unnecessary. I can protect Jamey. I won't have you putting yourself in harm's way for my sake. It would be far better if you left France at once."

"For your peace of mind, you mean?"

She searched his face and she knew when his gaze fell before hers that she'd hit on the truth. "Then you are not so indifferent to me as you pretend?"

"When have I ever been indifferent to you, oh goddess among women?"

She almost smiled. "Well, your peace of mind is of no concern to me. In fact, I find a certain pleasure in keeping you off balance. And I am staying, whether you like it or not. If you won't let me help you watch over the boy, I'll simply seek out this Rogers character, and drain him dry. That should solve the problem."

"Rhianik—Rhiannon, surely you are aware that the murder of a DPI agent would only serve to instigate further trouble." He drew an unsteady breath. "Killing rarely solves anything."

She shrugged, keeping him always in her sight with sidelong, lash-veiled glances. How she delighted in baiting him! "They'll never learn what became of him. I'll grind him up and feed him to my cat."

Roland grimaced and shook his head.

"Perhaps I'll torture him first. What do you think? Bamboo shoots under the nails? Usually effective. We could learn all DPI's secrets, and—"

"For God's sake, woman!" He gripped her shoulders hard as he shouted, but his horrified expression faded when she burst into helpless laughter.

He sighed, shook his head and eased his grip on her shoulders. Before he took his hands away, though, she caught his forearms. "No, Roland, don't."

He stood motionless, his face devoid of expression, as she slipped her arms around his waist, and drew herself to him. She rested her head upon his sturdy shoulder. With a sigh of reluctant compliance, Roland's arms tightened around her shoulders and he held her to him.

Rhiannon closed her eyes and simply allowed herself to feel him. The contained strength in him, the rapid thud of his heart, the way his breaths stirred her hair.

"I have missed you, Roland," she whispered. She turned her face slightly, and feathered his neck with her lips. "And you have missed me, though you are loath to admit it."

She felt the shudder she drew from him. He nodded. "I admit it, I've missed you."

"And you desire me," she went on, lifting her head enough so she could study his eyes as she spoke. "As you have no other... nor ever will. You disapprove of everything I am, and everything I do, but you want me, Roland. I feel it even now, in this simple embrace."

"Subtlety has never been your strong suit, Rhiannon." He took her arms from around him, and stepped away, resuming the walk without touching her.

"You deny it?"

He smiled slowly. "I want to walk in the sunshine, Rhiannon, yet to do so would mean my end. What one wants is not necessarily what one should have."

She frowned and tilted her head. "I hate when you speak in metaphors or parables or whatever you call those silly words you use."

He shook his head. "How long will you alight here this time, little bird?"

"Changing the subject won't make you feel better, you know."

"It was a simple question. If you cannot answer it—"

"Answer mine, and I'll answer yours. Do you want me?"

He scowled. "She is a fool who asks a question when she already knows the answer."

"I want to hear you say it." She stopped, and looked into his eyes. "Say you want me."

Roland's glance moved slowly down her body and she felt his gaze burn wherever it touched her. Finally, he nodded. "I want you, Rhiannon. But I will not—"

She held up her hands. "No more. Don't ruin it."

He chewed his inner cheek, and she felt his anger begin to boil up. "Now my question, temptress. How long will you stay?"

"Well, I've come to help protect the boy. I suppose I will stay until the threat is gone, and . . ."

"And?" His brows drew close and he scanned her face.

She tried not to smile as she answered him. "And until I've given you exactly what you want, Roland."

CHAPTER TWO

Roland felt as if he were the Bastille, and she the revolutionaries. For a single instant, he was certain he'd never stand a chance. He attempted to remind himself of all of her faults. She was impulsive, impetuous, and as unpredictable as the weather. She acted without first thinking through the consequences of her actions. And sooner or later it was going to cost her. Hell, it already had cost her, and dearly. He sensed she was glossing over the details of her time in St. Claire's hands. Yet he knew better than to press her for more. He'd have killed the bastard years ago, had he known. He'd kill him now, if the scientist were alive.

Studying her faults did little good. Already, the beast inside was wakening. Already, her presence had him thinking in terms of murder and retribution, had him fighting to control the violent side to his nature. He studied her and shook his head slowly. She was so much the way he'd been once, in his mortal lifetime. All the things he'd fought for years to suppress.

Perhaps he'd not succeed in dampening his desire for her by counting her faults. Perhaps instead, he ought to count his own. Even better, he should remind himself what had become of the other woman he'd lusted after.

"You're guarding your thoughts, Roland. Are they so unflattering?"

"I guard my thoughts out of habit. Do not take it personally."

"I think you lie. You don't wish me to see something."

He shrugged noncommittally. If she was determined to stay and taunt him, he'd resist her as best he could. For her sake, as well as his own. He would keep his distance. Never would the beast he held within be unleashed upon her. She'd done nothing to deserve that.

And perhaps while she was here, he'd teach her to act maturely and sensibly. He'd show her the differences between a true lady, and the untamed child she was now. Like changing a cactus flower to a rose, he thought. He refused to acknowledge that the results would benefit him, as well. For he could never be as inflamed with longing for the rose, as he'd always been for the prickly flower.

No, he told himself the lesson would be for her, to get her to exercise some caution from time to time. He liked Rhiannon, sometimes in spite of himself. He'd truly hate to see her come to grief because of her nature...the way he once had.

He frowned, and wondered briefly how long her visit would be. She hadn't told him. Her habit was to flit in and out of his life at will. She never remained long enough to do more than stir up a whirlwind, to pummel his senses— as well as his sense—with her vivacious nature, and then she would vanish. She was a desert sandstorm...a whirlpool from the Nile.

"Roland, darling, you are ignoring me."

He had been doing anything but that, though he would never admit it. Instead, he glanced down from the corners of his eyes, and gave her a sharp nod. "Precisely."

She sighed in exasperation. "I suppose if you refuse to discuss our relationship—"

"We have no relationship, Rhiannon."

"We'll simply have to discuss the boy." She kept on speaking as if she'd never been interrupted. It was another of her maddening habits. When speaking to Rhiannon, you either say what she wants to hear, or you are ignored. Maddening!

"What about the boy?"

"Where is he, Roland? Is he safe?"

He felt his spine relax a bit, now that they were on a neutral subject. "At first, he and his mother lived in the castle."

"That ruin?"

Roland stiffened. "The east wing, Rhiannon. It's perfectly habitable."

"For a monk, perhaps. Do go on."

He scowled, but kept on speaking. He had no desire to engage in verbal skirmishes. "Then Kathryn took ill."

"No wonder, in that drafty place."

Roland ignored the taunt this time. "It was cancer, Rhiannon. She died eight months ago."

Rhiannon's hand flew to her throat and she drew a quick, little breath. "Then, the boy is alone?"

"Not entirely. He has me, and there is Frederick, of course."

"Frederick?" She tilted her head slightly. "That bear of a man you found sleeping on the streets in New York? Roland, can he be trusted with the boy?"

Roland nodded without reservation. Frederick was slightly slow-witted, but he had a heart of pure gold. And he adored Jamey. "Yes. If I didn't trust him, he wouldn't be in my household. Jamey needs someone with him in those hours between school dismissal and sunset."

Still walking beside him, she stroked her long fingers across her forehead as would a Gypsy fortune-teller preparing to do a reading. "Mmm, you enrolled him in a private school, no doubt."

"He refused a private school. Said he was not a snob and had no intention of becoming one." Roland shook his head. "He does have a strong will. At any rate, he's known as James O'Brien. It's the closest I could come to Jamey Bryant."

"And where is this boy of yours, now? Tucked safely into his bed at your château?"

"He had a soccer match tonight. Ought to be arriving any time now." He glanced ahead of them, to the tall, gray stone wall that surrounded Castle Courtemanche, and the portcullis at its center.

"You provided Frederick with a car, as well? Can he maneuver one?"

He frowned, and turned to follow the direction of her gaze. "Damn it to hell." He gripped Rhiannon's arm and drew her nearer the cover of the brush along the narrow road's edge.

"Whatever are you doing?"

"Hush, Rhiannon." Roland moved slowly, silently, approaching the gate, and gazing toward the Cadillac that sat just outside it. "That car should not be here."

"It isn't..." She bit her lip, and her eyes narrowed as she stared hard at the dark colored vehicle. "There's a man behind the wheel."

Roland nodded. Already his mind scanned the intruder's but he found it closed to him. Most humans were so easily read it was child's play to scan their thoughts. This one had deliberately closed his mind off. Roland was certain of it. In the darkness, even with his preternatural vision, Roland couldn't see clearly enough to make a positive identification. The hard knot in his stomach was the only indication Curtis Rogers occupied the car, and that he was watching, waiting . . . for Jamey.

Rhiannon whispered. "But I get no sense of the boy." She shook her head in frustration. "Is that Rogers?"

"I don't know, but if it is, and it's truly vengeance he wants, then Jamison is in danger."

Rhiannon sucked in a breath. "You believe this Rogers would kill the boy simply to hurt you?"

Roland shook his head. "More likely kidnap him, and wait for me to come to his rescue. But while he had the boy, Rogers wouldn't hesitate to perform tests on him, experiments to discover more about the link between The Chosen, and the undead."

"I know about DPI and their love of . . . experiments."

Roland slanted a glance toward Rhiannon, sickened anew by the knowledge of what had befallen her while in DPI's hands. Truly, he felt an urge to protect her from them, just as he was forced to protect Jamison. Foolish notion, he knew. Rhiannon would never stand for being protected, not by anyone. Moreover, were she with him constantly, stirring his mind to such turmoil, she would need protecting not by him, but *from* him.

"Where is the boy? It's late."

Roland shook his head, freeing his mind of its distractions, focusing again on the matter at hand. "When they win, they usually stop for a meal on the way back. They are sometimes quite late." Even as he spoke, Roland searched for Jamey with his mind. It came as a blow when he found him, and realized he was ambling along the road from the opposite direction, completely oblivious to the threat that awaited him.

The man in the car saw the boy, too, for the door opened and he stepped out. Jamey drew nearer, and before Roland could decide on a course of action, Rhiannon shot to her feet and ran toward the man.

"Oh, thank goodness, I've finally found someone!"

He turned to face her, wary-eyed and suspicious. Roland had a perfect view now, of the man's face. Curtis Rogers had changed little in the past two years. His blond hair still hung untrimmed and too long in the front. His pale brows and light eyes gave him the look of a weakling, and Roland knew that was precisely what he was. Yet with the resources of DPI and their constantly innovative arsenal of weapons and drugs, he was an enemy not to be taken lightly.

And right now, Rhiannon was standing within his reach.

"Who the hell are you?"

"Just a woman in need of assistance. My car went off the road a few miles back. I've been walking forever, and..." She continued moving forward, affecting a rather convincing little limp as she went. "You simply must offer me a ride."

Get into that car with him, Rhiannon, and I'll remove you bodily! Roland made his thoughts clear to her, and his anger with them. Had the woman no sense? If she got herself killed, he'd...

Posh, Roland, you can be such a stick in the mud.

She smiled up at Curtis as she stepped closer. "You wouldn't dream of leaving me out here on my own, would you? I'd never forgive you if you did."

Her voice was a virtual purr now, and Roland felt his hackles rise. Rogers's gaze moved slowly, thoroughly down her body, not missing a curve, and lingering too long on the enticing expanse of cleavage her dress exposed.

"I'd like to help you, lady, but I have some business to take care of."

Roland began to step out of hiding. Enough was enough. If he let it go on much longer—if Rogers laid one finger on her—

No, darling! Her mind reached out to his with silent fingers. *Your Jamey is getting too near. Slip around us and intercept the boy. I'll keep this one distracted.*

If he realizes you're an immortal—Roland began to warn her.

Her low, husky laugh floated to him, and caused Rogers's brows to raise. *Look at him, Roland. He's far too busy noticing I'm a woman.* As if to prove her point, she stepped still nearer the man. Her hand floated upward and she traced the edge of his lapel with her nails. Rogers's attention was riveted. Roland thought he could have danced a jig around the fool and not gained his notice. Jealousy rose like bile into his throat to replace the fear for her that had been there before. He slipped into the trees along the roadside, and quickly emerged again when he'd passed them. Jamey approached him now, only a few yards distant.

"Jamison . . . it's Roland. Come here at once."

Without a moment's hesitation, Jamey ducked into the trees where Roland waited. "What's up?"

Roland frowned, noting the soon-to-form bruise under Jamey's left eye, and the slightly swollen lower lip. "What in God's name happened to you?"

Jamey shrugged in the carefree way only a fourteen-year-old can manage. "Soccer's a rough sport." He glanced farther along the road and the carefree demeanor left his face. "Who is that?"

He had a maturity that at times went far beyond his years, and he'd grown as protective of Roland as he had once been of Tamara. "I hate to upset you, Jamison, but the man in the car is—"

"Rogers!" Jamey recognized Curtis when the man moved into a more advantageous stance, and the boy lunged.

Roland caught his shoulders and held him easily. "What do you think you're doing?"

"That bastard almost killed me! When I get my hands on him, I—"

"You will watch your language, Jamison, and you will stay quiet and do as I tell you. You can't instigate a physical altercation with a grown man."

"I'm a lot bigger than I was two years ago," Jamey said, his voice dangerously low. "And you know he has it coming. I owe him." His milk-chocolate-colored eyes glowed with absolute fierceness.

Roland felt a shudder run up his spine. God, but Jamison was familiar. His rage, his anger—Roland had known all of it, at that age. It had nearly destroyed him. It had destroyed others. Far too many others.

"That he does, Jamison. But—"

Jamey's struggles suddenly ceased. "Who is *that?*" His eyes widened, and Roland followed his gaze to see Rhiannon, playfully tousling Curt Rogers's hair.

Roland felt anger prickle his nape. "A friend of mine. Her name's Rhiannon and I believe she thinks she's distracting Rogers so you can slip into the castle unnoticed."

Jamey swallowed. "She's gorgeous."

Roland just stared at her for an elongated moment. The moonlight played upon the satin skin of her shoulders like a caress. "Yes," he said softly. Then he shook himself. "Yes, and apparently Rogers thinks so, too."

Rogers's hand settled on one of Rhiannon's naked shoulders, and proceeded to stroke a slow path down her arm. Roland felt the fury leap to life in his veins in a way it seldom had. For just an instant, his palms itched to clutch the chilled hilt of a broadsword. Then he reminded himself he no longer needed one.

"Come, Jamey, before she decides to—" He stopped himself before he finished the comment.

Jamey looked up at him, then glanced toward Rhiannon again, a sudden understanding lighting his eyes. He said nothing, only nodded, and followed Roland into the woods and up to the tall stone wall. He put an arm around Roland's shoulders. Roland did likewise, then leapt, easily clearing the wall and landing with a thud on the opposite side. Jamey hit the ground and tumbled forward. He shook his head sheepishly, got to his feet and brushed the dust from his jeans. "One of these days, I'll get the hang of that."

Roland heard Rhiannon's deep laughter filling the night air.

"Is she . . . like you?" Jamey had never used the word vampire, but Roland thought he knew. The boy was too insightful not to make his own assumptions, and his assumptions were usually right. Roland looked at him, and simply nodded.

"She shouldn't be out there with Curt Rogers," Jamey said.

"You're right about that. Go on inside, and wait for me in the great hall." Roland spoke while gazing toward the portcullis. When Jamey didn't reply or move to obey, Roland sent him a sharp glance.

Jamey shook his head. "No. I'm not a little kid anymore and I'm tired of other people fighting my battles for me."

Roland very nearly barked at him, then closed his eyes and gave his head a shake. For an instant, he could have sworn he was looking at the image of himself, arguing with his father on the day before he'd left home for good.

Fourteen. Yes, he'd been just that. And a mere two years later . . .

He blocked out the memory of that bloody battlefield.

"There is no battle to be fought," he said calmly. "Please, just go inside so I can fetch Rhiannon. God knows what kind of trouble she'll get into on her own."

Jamey kicked at a stray pebble with undue force, and shoved a hand through his hair. "Why can't he just leave us alone?"

"Because he's still breathing." Rhiannon's voice startled Jamey. He jerked his head up in surprise. Roland only turned slowly and watched her approach. He'd heard her land when she'd vaulted the wall.

Apparently someone else had, too. A tall, beefy form lumbered forward from the shadows, placing himself directly between Rhiannon and Jamey. She stopped, her brows lifting.

"It's all right, Frederick. She's a friend."

Rhiannon's imperious gaze clashed with Frederick's untrusting one. Rhiannon took another step forward. "Don't you remember me, Freddy?"

He frowned, and tilted his head to one side. Then he nodded, smiling. "Rhia . . . Rhian—"

"Rhiannon," she supplied.

Frederick frowned, obviously remembering a slightly different version of her ever-changing name. Roland stepped forward, closing the gap between them, with Jamey at his side. He hoped the relief he felt at seeing her sound and without injury didn't show on his face.

"What have you done with Rogers?"

Rhiannon ignored Roland's question, and let her dark gaze linger on Jamey, who stared at her in turn as if she were made of chocolate.

"Hello, Jamison. I've heard a lot about you." She lifted her hand as she spoke, and Jamey took it at once, then looked down at it as if he wasn't sure what to do.

"Nice to, um, meet you." He let her hand go, after giving it a brief squeeze.

"Rhiannon . . ."

She met Roland's eyes. "Are you afraid I've killed him? Wouldn't we all be far better off, if I had?"

"I know we would," Jamey said softly.

Roland shook his head. "Killing is never justified, Jamison. It never makes anything better. It can destroy the killer just as surely as it does the victim. More so. At least the victim still has claim to his soul. The killer's is eaten away slowly."

Rhiannon rolled her eyes, and Jamey came close to smiling at her. She noticed, and bestowed upon him her devastating half smile, before turning back to Roland. "Well, if you're too kindhearted to kill the man, what do you suggest? He's obviously discovered Jamey's whereabouts. We can't simply sit here and wait for him to come and take the boy."

"I'm no boy," Jamey said.

"I think Jamison should go to the States for a while, spend some time with Eric and Tamara. It will be safer." Roland glanced at the boy to see what he thought of the idea.

Jamey widened his stance and lifted his chin. "I'm not running away from him."

Rhiannon's warm gaze bathed Jamey with approval. He felt it, and stood a little taller. Roland was beginning to feel outnumbered. "What have you done with Rogers?" he asked again.

Her gaze dropped before his. "I tired of his sloppy advances. The fool tried to put his tongue into my ear."

Jamey chuckled hard, shaking his head, so his longish black curls moved with his laughter. Rhiannon smiled at him, while Roland scowled at her.

"Rhiannon, you have not answered the question."

She shrugged delicately. "Monsieur Rogers is having a nap. I think he's been overworking himself of late."

"Rhiannon..." Roland's voice held a warning, but it seemed she was too busy exchanging secretive glances with Jamey, to take heed.

"Oh, Roland, I merely tapped him on the head. Honestly, he won't even bear a scar."

"Wonderful!" Roland threw his hands in the air. "Now he'll know you're in league with us. He'll hound your steps in search of retribution just as he does mine." It infuriated him that she constantly did things to put herself at risk. Then he realized how his concern for her would sound to her ears. If she knew of his true feelings, she would never let up on her attempts at seduction. And he would only hurt her in the end.

"And you've conveniently left him lying at the front gate, blocking our exit," Roland added, to give more severity to his complaints.

Rhiannon caught Jamey's eye and winked.

"All right, little bird, out with it. You haven't left him lying at the front gate, have you?"

"Well of course I haven't. I'm not an idiot." She placed a hand on Jamey's shoulder. "Come now, and pack yourself a bag or two. That lovely Cadillac is just sitting out there, all warmed up and ready to go."

"Go where?"

"My place. I have a little house just beyond the village. Rogers won't bother you there."

"No, Rhiannon. Jamey will be far safer here, with Frederick and I to watch over him."

She studied him for a long moment, and seemed deep in thought. "All right, then. I'll be back soon."

"Rhiannon, where are you—" Before Roland could finish the question, she was gone. He heard the sound of Curtis Rogers's car roaring to life a second later. Then it squealed away into the night.

CHAPTER THREE

She took the fine car. Not that she couldn't move much faster on her own. She drove for a long time, speeding past the tiny village of L'Ombre and over its twisting roads, taking sharp curves at excessive rates of speed, and laughing as she did so until gradually, the pavements broadened and traffic increased.

When she finally came to a grinding halt at the airport at Paris, she removed the keys and walked to the rear to open the trunk.

Rogers moaned, holding his head in two hands as he sat up. His narrow, angry eyes raked her but he didn't attempt to move.

"You carry a syringe in your breast pocket," she said softly. "Take it out."

He straightened, one hand slipping beneath his jacket toward the pocket. She watched him, and when that hand tensed, hers shot forward entraping it at the wrist before he'd had the chance to move it. He probably hadn't even seen her movement.

"Now, I'll stand for none of that. Roland tells me this drug of yours actually works." She pulled his hand from beneath the jacket, his resistance so puny in comparison to her strength that it was almost laughable. When the syringe was in the open, she took it with her free hand. "Perfectly awful, this little needle. Still, I suppose it's better than St. Claire's former methods. Draining our blood until we become too weak to fight him, leaving him free to perform his sadistic little experiments."

Curtis looked up suddenly, still rubbing the wrist she'd just released. "You're the one, aren't you?"

"Which one would that be, darling? Certainly not one of the two fledglings he held. The ones from whom he drained a bit too much blood? The ones he murdered? No, I'm not one of those. Not at all, as you can see."

"You're...Rhiannon. You escaped. You killed one of the finest scientists DPI has ever—"

She waved a hand. "Scientist? I say he was a twisted little pervert. He enjoyed the pain he inflicted." She tilted her head to one side and fought not to let her face reveal what the memory of that pain did to her insides. She'd been tortured to the point of near madness. To an immortal as old as she, pain was magnified incredibly. It was felt thousands of times more keenly than by a human, hundreds of times more keenly than by younger vampires.

"Then again, that night I must say I understood. I did enjoy what I did to him." She kept her voice cold, her tone without inflection. "Tell me now, Curtis Rogers, has this drug been tested on human subjects? What, I wonder, would be the effect should I inject it into you, for example?"

His face lost all color and she felt his rush of fear. "The drug has absolutely no noticeable effect on human beings."

She tilted her head back and laughed, the sound bubbling up from deep in her throat. "Oh, how you amuse me. You know I can read your thoughts. You're far too frightened right now to mask them, and yet you lie determinedly. The drug would kill you, would it not?"

He shook his head in denial.

Rhiannon held the needle skyward and depressed the plunger, sending a small spurt of silvery liquid into the air. Curtis lunged, landing on his feet on the concrete of the parking lot and immediately ready to flee. Rhiannon closed her hand over his nape and squeezed.

"It's no use, you know. I'm as strong as twenty grown men, and you with all your research of my kind, are aware of it. I'm older and more powerful than any of us you've encountered. I could kill you now without breaking a sweat, Rogers, my pet."

Still holding his nape in an unshakable grip, she dragged one nail lightly over the short hairs there. "How do you want it, I wonder? Would you like me to simply snap this neck of yours? It would be the quickest, the most merciful way. Or I could, indeed, inject you with your own creation. Any drug powerful enough to tranquilize a vampire would probably kill an elephant in its tracks, to say nothing of a puny mortal such as yourself."

She turned him to face her and she saw his fear. She could feel it, and she could smell it. She shook her head slowly. "No, I think those methods are not nearly poetic enough to suit me, Curtis, dear." She depressed the plunger farther, squirting the contents of the syringe down the front of his shirt, splattering his jacket. She tossed the empty needle to the floor. "I think, perhaps, for you—" she gripped his necktie and jerked him nearer "—the old-fashioned methods are the best."

"No," he whispered. "For God's sake, no!"

She went so far as to actually rake her teeth across the tight skin of his throat, even drawing a bit of blood, which tasted so delightfully wonderful she nearly forgot to behave herself. But then she took a firm grip on her thirst, and she lifted her head from his throat.

"Oh, *mon cher,* you are delicious. But Roland has warned me I mustn't kill you. Only delay you until their flight—" She bit her lips, as if she'd let some important bit of secrecy slip through them. "No matter. They are far from your reach now." She released her hold on him and he staggered backward. One hand lifted, palm pressing to his throat. When he saw the blood it came away with, he nearly fainted, such was his distress. She could have seen it even with mortal eyes, but in her vampiric state, she felt and sensed his every thought.

"Bother the boy again, *monsieur,* and I will delight in finishing you. And I assure you, despite your protests to the contrary, you shall delight in it, too. Right unto the moment of your death."

His eyes shifted frantically right and left as he sought assistance. None was to be had. "You'll pay for this," he shouted when he felt safer, farther from her. He edged toward an approaching vehicle. "I'll make sure you pay. All of you."

"Yes, I know you will try. One final word, my dear, and then I must go. The taste of you on my lips has left me with a powerful appetite."

"You're an animal!"

She smiled slowly. "Quite right. A predator, to be precise. And if you go near Roland again, you will become my prey. Believe me, if it is Roland I avenge, your experience will not be a pleasant one. I will hurt you, Curtis Rogers. I will make you writhe!"

With a single burst of speed, she left him there, knowing to his human eyes, it must have seemed she'd simply vanished. He wouldn't go to the castle. Not right away, at least. She thought she'd convinced him that Roland and the boy had boarded a jet bound for parts unknown. He'd fallen so easily. He would search elsewhere first. They'd be safe during the approaching dawn. Yet, there were still precautions to be taken. Rhiannon sped toward the small rental house outside L'Ombre, to accomplish these, and of course, to fetch her cat.

Roland had no idea where she'd gone, or when she'd return. That was the thing about her. Flighty. Volatile. Unstoppable. Damn near irresistible. He groaned under his breath. He couldn't forget his desire even in his anger.

When she'd looked at Jamey earlier, Roland could have sworn he'd seen the stirrings of genuine affection. Of course, she would have to feel something for the boy. He was one of The Chosen. A human with the same two rare traits all vampires had as humans, the single combination that allowed them to be transformed. The line of descent, including, but surpassing, Prince Vlad the Impaler—yes, despite all of Eric Marquand's theories, it went back farther than that. And the blood antigen known as belladonna. A human with these traits, though he may never be aware of it, becomes the ward of the undead. Vampires watch over such ones, especially the children. They cannot do otherwise. And all preternatural beings can sense the presence of such ones, or the hint of a threat to them. Yet rarely are these Chosen ones transformed, or even contacted. Mostly, they simply go through their lives never knowing of their psychic link to a society they would believe a myth.

The situation with Jamey was unique. In order to protect him, Roland had been left with little choice but to arrange things as they now stood. DPI knew of Jamey's traits. They knew of his connection, not to one, but to three—now four—vampires. They placed a great value on the boy, his worth to them greater than would be his weight in gold. They would stop at nothing to possess him, to hold

him in one of their diabolical laboratories, to run countless, torturous experiments upon his fragile young body
while they awaited the inevitable arrival of his protectors.

And with all of this on the line, Rhiannon had played
another of her vanishing acts.

But he knew better than that, didn't he? Unpredictable,
she was, but not disloyal. Her carelessness only applied to
matters of her own safety. Not to that of others. He
wanted to be angry with her, but instead, found himself
worried. She was gone, yes, but where was Rogers? With
her? She'd been captured by a man like him once. Would
she be reckless enough to end up in their hands again?

As soon as Jamey was safely installed in his modern-
ized apartment in the east wing with Frederick at his side,
Roland made the decision to search for her. She'd resent
it, no doubt. She liked to do as she pleased without inter-
ference. But he felt she might be at risk, and he couldn't
ignore that possibility.

Before he made it to the door, he sensed her presence.
He realized a moment later that he'd felt an overwhelming sense of relief along with it. But that was ridiculous. He
hadn't been *that* worried about her.

She entered the great hall through the tall, arching door
of ancient hardwood, which was banded with black iron
straps. At her side lumbered a panther, sleek and black as
the velvet gown she still wore. The beast's green eyes glittered like emeralds, and as it gazed steadily at Roland, it
stilled utterly, and emitted a deep-throated growl.

"What in God's name is that?"

"My cat. Her name is Pandora, and I would appreciate
it if you would treat her with the respect she deserves."

"Rhiannon, for God's sake—" Roland took a single
step forward, and froze when the cat crouched, snarling,
teeth bared, about to spring.

"Pandora, hush!" At her stern command the animal relaxed, straightening rather lazily, still watching Roland's every move. "Roland is a friend," Rhiannon said softly, stroking the cat's big head with her long, dagger-tipped fingers. "Come, Roland, stroke her head, so she'll know you mean no harm."

Roland swore under his breath, but knew Rhiannon adored the beast, simply by the light in her eyes. He would indulge her, this once. It wasn't as if the cat could harm him. He moved nearer the animal, and stretched out one hand.

In a lightning-fast move, Pandora batted his hand away with claws extended, and a short angry snarl.

"Pandora!" Rhiannon smacked the cat on the nose, and reached out, gripping Roland's hand and frowning at the single scratch the cat had managed to inflict. A tiny, narrow path of beaded red droplets.

"I'm sorry, Roland. She is so protective of me, you see, and you did raise your voice." Then she lifted his hand, brought it to her lips, and, very catlike, herself, ran her damp tongue over the mark, from knuckles to wrist. She closed her eyes at the erotic impact of the act. Roland knew, because it rocked him, too.

Tongues of flame licked at his groin, and Roland winced at the force of it.

"Come, darling," she whispered. "Show Pandora how close we are. That will work to calm her. I know it will. Come, take me in your arms. Just this once. Just to calm the cat."

"Rhiannon, I don't think—"

"Why must I work so hard to earn each little touch you bestow?" She shook her head, glancing at the cat, who again, began to snarl menacingly. "Surely you won't die from my kisses, Roland, toxic though they may be. Our embrace will reassure Pandora. She will keep Rogers out of the castle while we rest, by day. She is well trained, I assure you. Now, please, just take me in your arms. Hold me to you. Kiss my lips. It will be all the evidence she requires, I promise you."

Without quite meaning to, Roland stepped closer. He slipped his arms around Rhiannon's slender waist, and she immediately pressed her hips against him. Waves of desire raced through his veins. Her deceptively fragile-looking arms linked around his neck. Her scent was unlike anything human. An exotic mingling of the preternatural blood flowing beneath her skin and the spiced juices of her arousal dampening her interior, the henna she insisted on rinsing through her hair and the mysterious incense she burned regularly.

A mortal man would notice none of it. Nor would he see the subtle change in the light refracted in her black eyes, and know it signaled the onset of the powerful lust only immortals can feel or understand. It borders on violence, this lust. It mingles with the thirst for blood until the two entwine and become inseparable.

His arms tightened around her, until her proud breasts pressed hard against his chest. Their stiff little nipples—twenty times more sensitive than a mortal woman's might be—poked into his skin, even through the dress she wore, and the shirt covering him.

He looked down into her face, his eyes feasting for a moment on her parted lips. He could still catch the faint trace of his own blood on her tongue. Slowly, he sunk into the madness only she could create within him. He lowered his head until his face, his lips, moved over her smooth cheek. He traced the high cheekbone, and then the shape of her finely arched brow. His lips nibbled a path down the straight, narrow bridge of her nose, then danced over the bit of flesh between nose and upper lip.

She made a tiny sound, like a purr, in her throat, and tipped her head back slightly, to lift her lips to his. Driven beyond restraint, Roland took her mouth the way a man dying of slow starvation takes his first crumb of food. His hands twisted themselves into her hair and his tongue swept inside her. Her taste was intoxicating, an aphrodisiac, certainly, for he throbbed with wanting her.

She felt his arousal, pressed her hips closer, and murmured his name into his mouth on a low, husky exhalation.

Roland put her from him, stepping back, though it took more effort than lifting this castle above his head could have taken. The lust in him roared loudly in his ears, but he dared not give in to it. No. He could too easily lose his sanity in Rhiannon. He could be swept completely away on a mindless journey of passion. He could forget what was important.

The boy, in the east wing preparing once again to face a fight not even a grown man should have to endure. The tiny *cimetière* in the forest beyond the castle's outer walls. The five graves, so old now they would be invisible had he not kept them up, replacing the headstones every few years, and always with more ornate and expensive pieces. His mother lay there, beneath the cold earth. His father, and his three hearty brothers who had once scoffed at his desire to become a knight. Truly, he knew, they'd only been afraid to see their youngest sibling thrown into bloody battle. They'd loved him. And he'd returned their love with hatred, and betrayal, and finally, with abandonment. No, he could never forgive himself that.

Most important of all was that he never forget the beast that lived within him. It had lurked in the depths of his black soul even when he'd been a mere mortal. It must be contained, for were it loosed now, the destruction it might wreak would be irreparable.

Rhiannon made him careless. She brought out the impulsive, irresponsible lad he'd once been. The one foolish enough to let that beast escape. She made him, at times, long to free the animal inside. To allow it to take over. She filled him with such hunger that all else seemed unimportant.

"Roland, darling? What is it?" Rhiannon stood alone now, a yard of space between him and her. She appeared composed, but he felt the confusion, the thwarted passion frustrating her. "Don't stop now," she whispered. "We must convince Pandora . . ."

Roland shook himself. What he felt for her was nothing but lust. He wanted no companion at all, let alone one as uncontrollable and explosive as she. Her very presence was a danger to his sanity.

He felt the huge cat's heavy, silken body pressing to his leg, first the head, then a long, slow stroke of its neck and side over Roland's calf.

"I believe the cat is convinced, Rhiannon." Roland lowered his hand and scratched the feline's head. It arched to his touch and purred like a motorcar.

"Pandora, you traitor! I told you to wait until later to be friendly!"

Roland's brows shot up. "You mean she didn't need convincing at all, only your command?"

Rhiannon's lower lip protruded ever so slightly farther than her upper one, looking as plump and moist as a ripe plum. "I have to go to great lengths, sometimes, to get any cooperation from you, you stubborn man."

"And the cat?"

Rhiannon shrugged. "I haven't figured her out yet. Only that she can read me, and I her. We connect on a psychic level neither of us can understand. I don't need to speak to her, only to send her mental messages. Not words, mind you. Images. And she obeys me without question."

"So she snarled at me because you told her to do so?"

She shrugged, trying for a look of innocence and failing. "Just as I shall tell her to guard Jamey as we rest. No mortal shall set foot inside these walls with Pandora about. Not and live, at least."

"Suppose she makes the boy into a light snack?"

"She would no more do so than you would, love."

The remark stung, but Roland ignored the barb. "You're certain?"

"Do you think I would risk the child you adore so blatantly?"

He pursed his lips, then shook his head. "No. I suppose you would not."

"You suppose." She tossed her hair over her shoulder and strode away, toward the crumbling, curving stone stairs that spiraled upward along the circular keep's wall. "Come, Pandora. I'll introduce you to your new friends."

As she moved up the stairs, the huge cat leaping to catch up with her, Roland scanned her mind. He saw her envisioning Jamey and Frederick, envisioning herself embracing them, and the cat being lovingly stroked by their mortal hands. He wondered at it, but he didn't question it.

He had enough on his mind at the moment. He wouldn't waste time worrying about her true motives in wishing to help the boy. She was sincere, he knew. Yet still, it baffled him; for in all the time he'd known Rhiannon, he'd never thought her capable of feeling much for any mortal. Her thirst for adventure, and constant excitement came above all else. He'd never understood her, the risks she took.

No. He'd do better to assess his own ridiculous responses to her. Naturally, she excited him. What man, mortal or immortal, could remain indifferent to her touch, her scent, her vibrancy? He didn't constantly resist her advances because he didn't want her. Quite the opposite, in fact. He wanted her too much... physically. To copulate simply for lust's sake was to lower oneself to the level of an animal.

Moreover, she would only flit out of his life when it was over.

Not that he cared.

And there was the constant fear of losing control. Rhiannon inspired that tendency in him like nothing else could.

Roland composed himself after several moments of pondering, and went to the worn stone stairs. He slipped along the darkened corridor, and paused outside the vaulted door to the apartment. He opened it only slightly, and nearly cried out at what he saw.

Jamey lay on his back upon the floor, with that black beast over him, front paws pressed to Jamey's chest. The boy's hands cupped the panther's huge head, shoving it left and right roughly. The cat made deep, threatening sounds, its tail swishing in agitation. Roland tensed, about to launch himself upon the cat, but he stopped in his tracks as he realized that Jamey wasn't crying out for assistance. He was laughing!

Before Roland's stunned eyes, Jamey threw the cat over, onto its side, then Pandora rolled herself onto her back and lay still, head turned, watching the boy. He got to his feet and rubbed the animal's glossy underbelly vigorously, while the cat arched her neck and closed her eyes, emitting a loud purr.

Roland forced his gaze beyond the spectacle, to where Rhiannon stood with Frederick. She gave him a half smile. "She's just an overgrown kitten, you see?" She crossed the room to Roland's side. "It's odd, I thought I would have to introduce them...give them time to become acquainted. Yet, it's as if she recognized Jamey the moment she saw him." Her dark gaze reached out to Frederick with intensity. "You must take care with her, Freddy. She may not be as receptive to you."

Frederick licked his thick lips and moved slowly forward, his limp more pronounced now than earlier. "Pandora," he called in his baritone voice. He moved slowly toward the two on the carpeted floor. "Pandora, come here, kitty."

The cat looked up, then slowly rolled onto her stomach. She lay with paws extended, head up, still as a sphinx, eyeing Frederick. He glanced up at Rhiannon. "Can I pet her?"

Rhiannon nodded, her own gaze fixed on the panther, sending silent messages. Frederick reached out, gently touched Pandora's head, and stroked it slowly. He continued until, finally, the cat's deep purr came once more. The glittering eyes closed, and the big head pressed upward against Frederick's hand.

Frederick laughed, tipping back his big, blond head as he did. "Thank you for bringing her."

"Thank you for trusting her," Rhiannon replied. "Rogers likely won't bother us here today. I led him to believe you'd all left the country. Still, she will keep him out should he attempt anything."

"I bet she will," Frederick said softly.

"And tomorrow evening, we'll see about getting Jamey somewhere safe."

"No." Jamey stood, and faced both Rhiannon and Roland.

Roland sighed. "I know this is difficult for you, Jamison, but—"

"No. It's impossible. I'm not going anywhere tomorrow. I have one more practice, and then the big match." He faced Rhiannon. "It's the championship, Rhiannon. We can't leave until after that."

Roland opened his mouth, but Rhiannon held up her hand. "This game of yours... soccer, isn't it?"

Jamey nodded. "I've worked all season for this. I'm not letting Curt Rogers cheat me out of it. He's taken enough from me. We're playing in the dome stadium, under the lights. It's the biggest match of the year."

Rhiannon nodded. "The game, what time—"

"Seven tomorrow night." Jamey's eyes lit with hope.

Rhiannon seemed deep in thought. "It is dark by seven, is it not?"

Roland was unable to hold his silence any longer. "Rhiannon, we cannot protect the boy in a stadium crowded with spectators. Do not even suggest—"

"It is important to him, Roland. Surely you can see that."

"I have to make the practice after school tomorrow. If I miss it, I can't play in the match. Coach's rule."

"No. That I cannot arrange," Rhiannon said softly. "This practice session is by day, Jamey. We could not protect you there."

"I can protect myself."

"It is simple, really," Rhiannon went on as if he hadn't spoken. "I will simply pen a note to this coach, telling him you've twisted your ankle, and must rest it for the entire day or else not be capable of playing in the game. If he requires a note from a doctor, I will, of course, write one. I will deliver this note, along with a check, a donation, if you will, to the athletic department. I'll make it a hefty enough sum that the man will be only too happy to excuse you from practice. There, you see how simple?''

Jamey smiled slightly. Then frowned. "I shouldn't take your money—"

"Posh," Rhiannon said with a wave of her hand. "I have more than you can imagine." She looked at Jamey, her eyes glowing with affection. "Besides, I can't remember the last time I watched a soccer match. So, it is decided."

She strode out the door, the picture of elegance in her black velvet gown.

Roland dogged her steps.

She stopped on the stairway and turned to face him, daring him to argue with her.

"I do not have any intention of attending this soccer match."

She shrugged delicately. "Well, we'll miss you, of course, but if that's your decision—"

"Jamison isn't going either. It's too great a risk."

She rolled her eyes. "What is life without risk?"

"I forbid this, Rhiannon."

"Forbid all you like. Jamey and I are attending the match. And believe me, darling, no mere mortal is going to harm that boy while I am near. You forget who I am."

He shook his head. "There will be, perhaps, over a hundred mortals in attendance. We'd be spotted immediately. Recognized for what we are. Have you no sense?"

She only turned and resumed walking down the stairs. "Just as I was recognized the other night at Le Requin? Roland, there are ways to disguise ourselves. A bit of flesh-toned makeup on our pale skin, a pair of shaded lenses if you fear the glow in your eyes will be seen. A bit of powder to those blood-red lips. It is so obscenely simple to fool them, you see. Besides, they are modern humans. They wouldn't believe what we are, even if we walked up to them and announced it.''

"This is utter foolishness,'' he muttered as he watched her proceed down the stairs. How could one disguise one's nature, one's violence? How could Roland allow the two people he most wanted to protect to place themselves in such a vulnerable position?

She reached the bottom step, and waited for him to join her there. "You've lived as a hermit far too long, Roland. You deny yourself the simplest luxuries.''

"I have all I require.''

"Nonsense. If you could see some of the places I've lived. Mansions in the countryside, penthouse suites in the finest hotels. I have a delicious condo in New York. When I choose to drive, I only travel in the height of luxury. I attend the opera, the ballet, the theater. Roland, there is no danger. Not to us. Who could hope to harm us?''

"DPI, as you well know.''

"Ah. I make one mistake in all my centuries of existence, and you cling to it like Pandora with a steak.''

"They nearly had Eric, too. It can happen.''

"Eric is young…a mere two centuries old, Roland. You have triple his strength and powers. Besides, what is the use of endless life if one lives it like this?'' Her hands moved to encompass the great hall.

He sighed. Arguing with her was an exhausting venture. "I live here because I want to do so.''

"No. I think you cling to the past. I think you fail to embrace your immortality, to relish it, as I do, out of some misguided sense of family loyalty, or something.''

"And I think you seek out danger deliberately, as if daring death to claim you. Why do you do it, Rhiannon?"

Her face quickly became shuttered, showing not a trace of emotion. Even her mind closed to him, a heavy veil dropping instantly over it. He knew he'd hit on something, but had no idea what.

"Even if that were true, you must believe I wouldn't include your Jamey in my challenge. I would not risk him, Roland."

"Why not? What is he to you?"

"It is what he is to you that matters." Her ebony gaze fell to the floor, and for an instant, Roland glimpsed stark agony in her eyes. "I know how he feels. I know just the kind of pain there is in his young heart. The loss of his mother—" She blinked rapidly, and stopped speaking as her voice grew hoarse. She whirled away from him, and headed across the stone floor toward the heavy doors.

"Where are you going?" His mind reached out to hers. He felt as if he'd been shown a part of Rhiannon no one had ever before seen. He wanted to know more, wanted to identify the source of the pain he'd just glimpsed. Wanted to end it.

"To my lair, of course. It's nearly dawn."

He found himself at a loss. He hadn't expected her to leave the castle today. "I...I thought you'd stay here."

"And sleep where? I suppose you have some spare box of polished hardwood I could use, stored in those dank dungeons of yours?" The cynicism returned to her voice.

He didn't answer.

"I prefer a soft bed, Roland. I prefer satin sheets to shrouds. A fluffy down comforter and a plump soft pillow beneath my head. I prefer fresh air, rife with the fragrance of incense."

"Sounds very lovely. But where is your protection?"

"Come to me some dawn, darling, and I will show you." With a swish of her velvet dress, she turned, strode to the door and was gone.

CHAPTER FOUR

Roland woke at full dark, feeling the rush of tingling awareness sizzling in his every nerve ending. He quickly unfastened the complex locks on the inner lid, using his mind to scan the immediate area, before throwing it wide. He leapt to the floor with ease, landing soundlessly on the cold stone.

His rest had not been peaceful. Often he'd found himself hovering on the verge of consciousness, while images flitted to and fro in his mind. He was troubled, and not just on Jamey's behalf. The images had been of Rhiannon, more often than not. Beautiful, desirable, reckless Rhiannon. Had he no more sense than a rutting mortal? Could he not distinguish common, vulgar lust from true feelings of affection? Could he not banish the temptress from his mind?

He moved slowly through the crumbling passages of the dungeons in utter darkness, his extraordinary vision showing him the way. Blind, he'd have known the way. It was embedded in him. Every niche of this castle was. It had been his home in boyhood, his curse in adolescence, his prison as a young man. It had become the purgatory of the immortal, the place in which he would serve the sentence for the sin he'd committed against the family he'd adored. Yes, adored, but adored too late.

And what earthly good was done by dwelling on it now?

He tugged at an iron ring mounted in what appeared to be an immobile stone wall, using a great deal of his vampiric strength to move it. No mortal could hope to achieve the same feat without the help of some explosive or other. He slipped into the passage, and mounted the perpendicular spiral stairs of rusting iron. His every step echoed a thousand times in the darkness. There had once been a ladder here as the sole entrance to the dungeon's lowest level from the castle keep. When the ladder had needed replacing, the set of spiral stairs had seemed more apropos.

At the entrance to his chambers on the castle's ground level, he opened the door and emerged into his wardrobe, shoving hangers and suits of clothes aside. These, of course, he carefully rearranged to cover the entrance. Then he chose a fresh suit, and emerged into his chambers in the west wing.

He moved directly to the antique desk and took a long wooden match from the holder there to light the oil lamp. He repeated the ritual, lighting several more until the room glowed with a soft, golden hue. Looking around him now, he supposed Rhiannon would scoff at the place he called his home. The draperies that covered the tall, arched windows were heavy and faded with time. They smelled of dust and age. Their color was green, once brilliant as emeralds, but now dull, as if one were seeing them through a heavy fog. The windows themselves, a concession to modern times and added long after the deaths of the castle's rightful barons, were streaked and dirty. Looking through them was like looking through the filmy eyes of an old man. But wasn't that what this castle was, after all? An old, old man, whose every beloved friend had left him to wither and die alone?

The brocade upholstery on the antique settee had lost its luster long ago. The fireplace was a cold, dark cavity, holding the ashes of a fire long forgotten. The hardwood chairs, once thronelike and imposing, sat like sad witnesses to the end of an era, their wood grain and hand-tooled designs barely discernible through the years of neglect, their embroidered cushions worn and faded. High above, the chandelier, with its tier upon tier of candles, hung dark and brooding like a ghost of the past. Draped with cobwebs and shrouded with dust, it watched in silence as Roland served his eternal death sentence in the rooms below.

Rhiannon would hate these rooms.

And what did he care what Rhiannon thought of anything?

She's here, now.

The realization came to him with sudden clarity. She was here, on the grounds. He felt the vivid colors of her aura, and sensed the mad vibrations in the air, the snapping electricity that always announced her presence. In spite of himself, Roland hurried through his nightly bathing and dressing. Not because he was eager to see her again, he told himself. Not that at all. He only wished to be present to keep her in check. God only knew what she might do left to her own devices.

He followed his sense of her, moving soundlessly and quickly through the echoing corridors and finally into the great hall. Still she was not in sight. He sensed Jamey's presence now, as well, and Frederick's...and the cat's. Not within the keep, but without, in the courtyard.

Beyond the heavy plank door, he saw her in the darkness. Surprising him was something she did well and often. Why had he not grown used to it by now?

She raced over the grassless brown earth, her path illuminated by silvery moonlight, keeping a spotted ball moving along between her feet. She was clad in a pair of black denims, which had been cut off midway up her shapely thighs. Small white socks barely covered her ankles and her feet were encased in black, lacing shoes with garish red stripes and mean-looking cleats protruding from their soles.

As Roland stood, transfixed, Jamey raced toward Rhiannon thrusting one foot between her two and snatching the ball away. Rhiannon tripped and tumbled head over heels in the dirt, rolling to a stop with a cloud of brown dust rising around her. Roland lunged, but stopped himself when he heard her deep laughter. She stood and brushed the dirt from her derriere.

"Very good, Jamey." Again she laughed. She pushed the ebony hair from her face, leaving a dirt smear on her cheek. "Show me again, I want to learn this."

Roland cleared his throat, and Rhiannon turned, spotting him. "Don't look that way, love," she cooed. "I'm not going to hurt him."

For a shocking instant, Roland realized he'd been more concerned about her hurting herself. Imagine! He'd been afraid the most powerful immortal he knew might hurt herself playing soccer with a young boy. Damn strange. True enough, immortals felt pain more keenly than mortals did, and Rhiannon would be especially sensitive. But any injuries Rhiannon might sustain would heal as she rested by day. Still, it stunned him that the thought of seeing her in pain should shake him so.

"See to it you don't," he told her, unwilling to admit the true path of his thoughts. "He does have that match tomorrow night."

"Does this mean you've decided to stop arguing the point?"

He nodded, but reluctantly. Rhiannon strode baldly up to him and threw her arms around his neck. Her embrace resulted in his starched white shirt and tailored jacket becoming as dirty as she was. Yet he withstood it well enough, even though her body pressed tightly to his that way sent his pulse racing and caused his eyes to water.

"There are conditions, Rhiannon."

She gazed up at him, for though she was tall for a woman, he was still a good deal taller. "Conditions?" Her eyebrows furrowed, showing her displeasure.

He cleared his throat. He was about to anger her. Seemed to him everything he said angered her. Still, he had to speak his mind. A ball of foreboding about this excursion had lodged somewhere in his stomach and he couldn't shake the feeling that she was about to put herself at risk . . . yet again. "At this match, you will behave with a modicum of decorum."

"Oh, will I?"

"You will try, for once in your existence, not to draw undue attention. You will be polite, soft-spoken and unobtrusive."

Her eyes glittered. "And just why will I transform myself this way?"

Roland sighed. He only wanted to keep her from being discovered by Rogers or another one like him. Why did she have to be so defensive? "Because I have asked you to, Rhiannon. And because it is the wisest course to take. Rogers isn't stupid, nor is he the only agent in the area. Anyone who's learned Jamey's identity will know enough to look for him at that match."

For once, her chin dropped rather than thrusting upward into his face. She gave an almost imperceptible nod, and Roland felt a mingling of surprise and relief. He'd been certain she would argue. Protecting Rhiannon was going to be as much a challenge as protecting Jamey, he thought grimly.

* * *

"Ready?" Roland asked the following evening, an hour before the match was to begin. He stood near the huge, empty hearth in the great hall. Rhiannon closed the heavy door, causing its hinges to groan in protest, and crossed the cold, dusty stone floor to join him.

She chewed her lower lip. "I'm not sure. I don't have the benefit of a reflection by which to judge my appearance."

He fought the urge to smile. "Must be a damned nuisance to a woman of your vanity."

She met his gaze, her own flashing. "Quite right. You ought to paint my portrait, so I can see what I look like when I wish it."

"You know I don't paint anymore."

"Perhaps it's time you started." She glanced around her, and he knew she was noting the absence of any decoration adorning the gray stone walls. There were only torches mounted in brackets, and here and there the mounted antlers of one of his brothers' kills. "This place could use it. Whatever became of the portraits you'd done of your family?"

He shook his head. The subject was not open to discussion. Having the faces of those he'd failed looking down at him would be too much agony to bear. "In answer to your initial question, Rhiannon, you look fine."

"That, my dear Roland, is no answer at all." She stood before him, hands at her sides. "Look at me, darling. Describe to me what you see. I am so tired of going out and about wondering if everything is in place." She waited a moment. Roland's gaze moved over her, and he found himself unable to form a coherent thought. "I'll help," she offered. "Begin with my hair. Is it all right?"

She turned slowly and Roland nodded. "It gleams like satin, as you well know." His eyes traveled the length of it. She wore it long, and unencumbered by barrettes or dressings of any kind. She'd combed it all to one side, as she was prone to do, thus leaving the bare length of her swan's neck visible to the point of distraction. She had braided a tiny, silken lock on the left side of her face, from the crown of her head all the way to her waist. It had a petite charm that lured one to touch it.

Rhiannon, catching his gaze, lifted the braid in two fingers. "You like it?"

"Yes." He licked his lips, then caught himself. "Yes, it's just fine. Are you ready to go now?"

"But you haven't finished." Her pout was utterly false. She leaned forward. "What about the blouse? Does it show too much cleavage?"

Against his will, his eyes were drawn downward to the plunging neckline of the satiny, emerald-colored garment. The swell of her creamy breasts filled the lowest part of the V, and Roland felt a twisting sensation in his stomach. "When do you not show too much," he asked, trying for a sarcastic tone.

She shrugged, straightened and struck yet another pose, this time hands on her hips. "And the skirt? Do you think it's too short?"

It was tight, molded to her hips like cling wrap, black and made of suede. It buttoned down the front, and as if the garment had not already been daring enough, Rhiannon had left the bottom two buttons agape. Her thighs, shimmering beneath silk stockings, extended from the skirt's edge. As she stood there, turning first to one side, then the other, Roland's gaze affixed itself to her legs. "Perhaps it's simply that your legs are too long," he suggested. But instead of sounding dry and uninterested, his voice came out hoarse and none too loudly.

"These stockings are wonderful, don't you think?" She stepped nearer and bent one knee, propping her foot on a low stool. "So soft against my skin. Touch them, Roland, and you'll see what I mean." She caught his hand in hers and pressed his palm to the front of her thigh, then rubbed it up and down over the smooth, cinnamon-tinted silk.

He swallowed. "As I've mentioned before, you lack a certain degree of subtlety. Why do you not simply tear my clothes off and attempt a forced seduction?" He snatched his hand away, more angry with his own responses than with her childish attempts to lure him.

He saw the hurt in her eyes before she covered it, and he regretted his words at once. She truly couldn't help herself, he supposed. She was simply being Rhiannon. He'd allowed his anger at himself to spill out onto her. "I'm sorry, Rhiannon. I didn't mean—"

She tossed her hair. "Of course you did. You'd prefer me to become what you consider a true lady, to sit on an embroidered cushion and bat my eyes until you take the initiative, and ask me to dance. Hah! I'd be coated in more cobwebs than this great hall by the time you made up your mind."

She turned her back to him. "I was going to the match with you, but now I believe I will ride in the car with Frederick and Jamey. Enjoy your walk, Roland. And for God's sake, change into the clothes I brought for you before you leave. If you think attending a school-boy's soccer match in such formal attire is inconspicuous, you'd better think again."

He glanced down at the bag she'd dropped near the door as she whirled and walked through it.

He did not enjoy his walk. It turned out that he wasn't quite hard-hearted enough to hurt Rhiannon and take any sort of pleasure from it. He hadn't meant to insult her, but she was getting to him, dammit. Any man would be less than cheerful and charming when feeling as frustrated as he'd been. To resist her overt sexual overtures took every bit of will he possessed. But to give in to them would be foolhardy, to say the least. Not only would she never let him forget that she'd won this particular battle of wills, but she'd probably flit away like a summer breeze when the act was done. He might not see her again for years. And in the process, she'd have loosed the beast he'd battled for so long.

No. This... thing that sizzled between them was purely physical in nature. It's overwhelming potency... well, he could attribute that to the vampiric state. Every sensation was felt more keenly by immortals. Desire was simply magnified by his nature.

That explanation firmly established in his mind, he used his preternatural speed to arrive at the stadium before the little car he'd purchased for Frederick. He much preferred travel by his own power or by horse, to being helplessly hurtled through space by three thousand pounds of man-made scrap metal.

At the stadium, he felt more conspicuous in the attire Rhiannon had chosen for him than ever he had in his own overly formal clothing. The blue denim hugged his backside and clung with unaccustomed tightness to his groin. The sweatshirt was black. That part did not disturb him. But the blaze of neon paint across his chest, proclaiming him a fan of something called the Grateful Dead, had him at the end of his patience. He was not amused by the skull and crossbones, or by the not so subtle irony in her choice. At least he blended in with the crowd.

In contrast, Rhiannon, seated just to his left, was anything but unnoticeable. She shouted encouragement, not to mention a few obscenities when the opposing team made progress. She was in constant motion, wriggling in her seat, leaning forward or standing or both, when she wanted a better view, much to the delight of the males in the seats near her, Roland noted with a rush of inexplicable anger.

Still, in the seats below, near the team's bench, he saw that Frederick was nearly as animated.

Jamey, looking fierce in his uniform and with black smudges under his eyes to fight glare from the overhead lights, raced across the artificial turf with the ball. Rhiannon shouted encouragement, getting to her feet as he neared the goal.

Roland scowled. Was this supposed to be unobtrusive behavior? My God, he couldn't take his eyes off her, nor could several other men in the immediate area.

Roland forced his gaze back to the field of play, just as another lad thrust a leg in Jamey's path, tripping him so he tumbled head over heels, hitting hard. Roland caught his breath. Jamey got to his feet, though, and charged after the brat. When Jamey regained possession of the ball, Roland stood. He had no idea he'd done so, but there he was, upright. When the bully approached, Jamey skillfully passed the ball to a teammate, and when the teammate was similarly accosted, he passed back to Jamey.

A moment later, Jamey planted one foot and slammed the ball with the other, driving it into the goal with impressive speed. Roland applauded as loudly as anyone. Rhiannon released a piercing whistle that probably damaged some human ears. He touched her arm. She looked at him, her half smile a full-blown one for a change.

"You're forgetting yourself." He nearly didn't remind her. He didn't want to see her brilliant smile die.

"So are you," she told him. But she did sit down again.

Jamey's team won by a slim margin. Rhiannon felt drained from the excitement of the match. She and Frederick walked to the parking lot, while Roland waited outside the locker room to escort Jamey out. Rhiannon was certain no DPI operatives had been in the stadium. She'd kept her mind attuned throughout the match, and had caught not the faintest sense of a threat. Still, she remained watchful, and she scanned the minds of everyone who passed, in search of belligerent thoughts.

Frederick got into the car and started the engine, letting it idle as they waited for Roland and Jamey. Rhiannon stood near the driver's door, one arm propped on the car's roof. Others began to leave, a few at a time.

Within a short time, the lot was deserted. The moon's light this evening was more often than not obliterated by inky clouds. The concrete field became eerily silent, save the occasional sounds of vehicles passing on the street nearby. Time passed with leaden feet.

"The game was wonderful, wasn't it, Freddy?"

He nodded enthusiastically. "I practice with Jamey sometimes. But I'm not much good at running."

Rhiannon frowned slightly. "Your leg?"

Again, he nodded.

"Do you mind if I ask what happened to it?"

"No, it's all right. It happened when I was in the city, when I didn't have anyplace to live. It was wintertime, and I guess it just got too cold."

Rhiannon suppressed a shudder at the thought of gentle Freddy, freezing his limbs on a frigid winter's night. "Does it hurt you very much?"

"Oh, no. It hardly bothers me at all, anymore."

"I'm glad." She looked toward the rapidly darkening building. "They're taking too long."

"Maybe we better go back and check on them."

A warning prickle of danger danced over Rhiannon's nape. She sent the probing fingers of her mind in search of the source, but there was nothing tangible. "I think you should wait here, in the car." Rhiannon shook her head, still unable to pinpoint the source of her precognition. "Lock the doors," she added.

"Rhiannon, is somethin' wrong with Jamey?" Fear made Freddy's voice hoarse. "'Cause if there is, I'm going with you."

"I don't know," she said truthfully. "But it really will be better if you wait here. In case Jamey comes out and I miss him. Okay?" She tried to sound unconcerned, and for a moment it surprised her that she should care to ease the mind of a mortal. Then again, Freddy was no ordinary human. When she saw the car doors were locked, she gave him an encouraging nod and hurried across the blacktop toward the entrance.

The thrill of foreboding grew stronger and her fear for Roland and the boy grew with it. Her quickened steps snapped loudly over the lot, and then the sidewalk. She rounded a corner and reached for the doors.

A heavy arm came around her from behind, jerking her off balance and into the shadows.

Fool! Did this human think he could hope to do battle with her and win?

She prepared to pull free, turn around and wring the idiot's neck, when pain split through her consciousness like a piercing cry. The blade tore the flesh at her waist, only a small cut, surely. Yet the scalding pain paralyzed her. And when she felt she could move again, his voice gave her pause.

"I know your weaknesses, Rhiannon. Loss of blood, exposure to sunlight, direct contact between your flesh and an open fire... and pain." The blade pressed to her rib cage, but didn't cut. "Pain," he went on, his voice a rasping serpent in her ear, "The more severe, the more it weakens you. Isn't that right?" The blade's point pressed into her sensitive skin. "And the older the vampire, the more keenly she feels it." More pressure on the blade. A trickle of blood ran beneath her satin blouse, over her abdomen. She sucked breath through her teeth. "So this must be just about maddening, isn't it?"

Teeth grated, she forced words through her lips. "What do you want?"

Again the blade poked, twisting this time. She cried out, then bit her lip. She wouldn't summon Roland, not until she knew what he would be facing. "What do you think?" he rasped.

He was not Curtis Rogers. He was not anyone she'd ever encountered before. He was strong for a human, and unstintingly cruel. The first wound, the one in her side, still pulsed hot spasms of pain as well as blood. She felt herself weakening. A vampire as old as Rhiannon need lose very little to meet her demise. She needed help. Damn, but she hated to admit that. She'd never found herself less than able to deal with adversity. It infuriated her that this human had identified her few weaknesses, and used them so skillfully against her.

Her knees began to tremble and she forced them rigid once more. "Who are you," she growled, "and why do you court death so eagerly?"

"Not death, Rhiannon. Life. Eternal life. Immortality. You have it. I want it."

The man was insane! "You have no idea what you're talking about. You're not..." She paused, dizziness swamping her brain. She blinked it away. "Release me. I must...sit." She pressed her free hand against the hole in her side, hoping to slow the flow of her life from her body.

"If I release you, lady, you might just find enough strength to kill me. That is not my goal."

"If I die, so does your chance of getting what you want."

"Not really. There are others." His grip on her tightened. His pinpoint blade pressed harder, and the end twisted slowly. She was breathing hard now, in broken, ragged gasps. A response to the pain. Tears blurred her vision. "Give me what I want and I will let you go."

"And if I refuse, you'll let me die?" The words came slowly, and her speech was slurred. "I choose death, then."

"Not death, Rhiannon. Something far worse. There are DPI agents all over this place tonight, waiting for that boy of yours. But they'd consider you a greater prize, don't you think? The vampiress who murdered one of their most highly valued researchers all those years ago? I'll just give a shout and bring them running. You're too weak to fight them. Getting weaker all the time."

She closed her eyes and focused her thoughts on Roland. *Take Jamey out of here. Be careful. They're watching, and...* Before she completed the thought, the bastard twisted his blade again, and Rhiannon couldn't stop the gasp of pain that escaped her. "Well? Are you going to give me what I want?"

Her legs gave out. The loss of blood combined with the pain was simply too much. She went to her knees, causing the man's blade to rake up over her rib cage, and nick her throat.

At that moment, the man flew backward for no apparent cause, landing with a heavy thud on the ground. "You've just ended your life, human." It was Roland's voice, and it was quivering with a rage she'd never heard in him before. He reached for the man, who lay on his back, staring defiantly up at him.

"Here!" the mortal yelled at the top of his lungs. "They're here! Hurry!"

"That won't save you." Roland lifted the man by the front of his shirt, and Rhiannon knew he was about to crush his larynx. She'd never seen Roland so angry. He'd forgotten his well-schooled caution, his carefully cultivated calm. She felt it in his every thought, saw it in every line of his face. He would kill the man, and anyone who tried to stop him. The force of his anger shook her to the core. She hadn't known he was capable of such explosive violence.

"Roland, they're coming," she managed to say. "We must go. Think...of Jamey."

He pummeled the man's face with his fist, and slowly lifted him again. "Let them come. They'll soon wish they'd kept their distance."

She put every ounce of strength she had into her voice. "Roland, please! I'm bleeding—"

All at once, it seemed, his fury dissipated. Roland dropped the limp form to the ground. Then he whirled, bending over Rhiannon and lifting her easily into his arms. He searched her face, his eyes wide with fear now, rather than narrow with a barely suppressed rage. She felt him stiffen as he realized the extent of her blood loss and the weakness of her body. In a burst of preternatural speed, he left the parking lot and the sounds of running feet behind.

"Where...is Jamey?"

"We had to sneak out a window and duck through the brush. There were DPI agents watching all the exits. I put him in the car with Frederick and saw them safely off. They're fine."

She sighed, but it was broken by pain. "Good."

"You're still losing blood." He stopped, and settled her on the ground. She glanced upward, seeing only the black outline of gnarled tree limbs against the paler gray of the night. They were in a wooded area.

She heard the tear of fabric as Roland hurriedly opened her blouse. Then there was more pain, even at his gentle touch, as he pressed a handkerchief firmly to the wound. "Hold it there," he instructed. "Hold it tightly. Ignore the pain."

She did, but cried out. "Easy for you to say. You're less than ten centuries old. I'm more than twice that."

"With age comes strength," he replied in a hoarse voice as his fingers touched the smaller wound. She winced.

"And weakness." She drew a shaky breath. "You well know that I'm far more vulnerable to pain and blood loss, sunlight and fire, than you are." Her head fell backward, her neck suddenly incapable of supporting it. "I'm not certain I'll make it to dawn, Roland."

Again, he slipped his arms beneath her, lifted her. This time, he pressed her face to the crook of his neck. "You will, Rhiannon. I won't allow it to be otherwise. You only need to drink."

She stiffened, unsure of his meaning. His hand at the back of her head pressed her nearer, his fingers moving softly through her hair as his palm held her to him. Her lips touched the skin of his throat, tasted its salt.

"Drink," he said again.

And she did.

CHAPTER FIVE

Roland closed his eyes as her lips moved against his throat. The blood lust came alive at her touch. The sexual desire pummeled him until he felt too weak to fight it. God, but he wanted her. And what she was doing now only trebled the already powerful longing. Slowly the restraint he'd been struggling to hold in place shuddered beneath the assault of desire. Roland drew a strangled breath.

"Enough!"

He hadn't meant the single command to sound so harsh. She immediately lifted her head, blinking. Roland saw the passion in her eyes, even through the pain clouding them.

"Any more and I'll not have the strength to carry you home, Rhiannon," he lied in a much softer tone. He still feared for her well-being, but in truth if she didn't stop right then, he'd have dropped her into the tangy scented leaves at their feet, and made frantic love to her, pain or no pain.

"Put me down, then. I can walk."

He only shook his head and began again, in the direction of the castle.

"I said put me down. I've never needed any man to help me, and I never will. I can manage on my own."

"You needed the help of a man tonight, Rhiannon. No doubt if you continue in your reckless life-style, you'll need it again. And you need it now, whether you'll admit it or not, so rest in my arms and be quiet."

She did settle more comfortably against him, but the set of her lips told him the argument was far from over. "I will, but only because I know the truth. You're carrying me because you like it. You like the way my body feels so close to yours. As for my needing the help of a male, you are completely wrong. I was only waiting for the right moment to rip that fool's head from his shoulders. I'm as capable as any male, mortal or immortal, young or old, and you ought not forget it."

Roland rolled his eyes. "I thought at least to get a word of thanks for saving your life. Instead, I get scolded for daring to assume you were in need of assistance."

She was silent for a moment, considering his words, he thought. "All right, I suppose I owe you my thanks, then. Only don't dare think of me as inferior."

"I never have, Rhiannon."

"That is purely a lie."

Roland frowned, searching her upturned face as he continued carrying her through the thickening forest. Crisp leaves and fallen twigs crackled beneath his hurried steps. "Why do you say so?"

"Foolish question."

Roland focused on the bite in her tone, rather than on the weight of her hip, or the way it slid over his abdomen with his every step. He forcibly ignored the feel of her head nestled upon his shoulder, and the softness of the rounded breast that pressed to his chest. "I believe being assaulted by DPI operatives makes you decidedly cranky."

He saw her part her lips to reply, then she stopped herself, frowning. "I'm not sure he was DPI. At least, if he was, he was more concerned with his own interests than theirs."

"What do you mean?"

"Roland, the man was uncommonly knowledgeable about our kind. He listed our weaknesses. He called me by name."

Roland stopped walking, glancing ahead to the dark stone wall that completely surrounded the Castle Courtemanche. He could hear the violence of the River Tordu to his left as it splashed and roiled its way to fuse with the older, calmer waters of the River Loire. To his right, past the edge of the woods, a cool, green meadow rolled like a carpet from the outer wall to the winding dirt road. But the aromas of the grasses, of the rivers, of the very night, faded beside the scent of Rhiannon's hair and skin.

Roland shook himself and honed his senses, searching for the presence of others. They'd made excellent time, but he feared DPI forces would be on their way.

"Roland, you aren't listening. I scanned, and found no sign of this man, though he was lying in ambush. He can mask his presence, block us out."

Roland nodded. "It was only a matter of time before they learned that simple trick, Rhiannon. It shouldn't alarm you."

"He ordered me to transform him."

Roland froze, a chill of precognition tiptoeing up his spine. "That's ridiculous. He couldn't be transformed unless he was one of The Chosen. Anyone working for DPI would know that—"

"Which can only mean he *is* one of The Chosen. Roland, we should have felt his presence. He has somehow sharpened his psychic abilities. The man is dangerous."

Roland recalled again the shock of pain that had lanced through him when he'd felt Rhiannon's mind reaching out to him back at the stadium. He recalled the rage he'd felt when he'd seen the bastard holding her, that knife piercing her sensitive skin, the blade twisting as she gasped in pain, the tears shimmering over her eyes.

"You ought to have let me kill him."

She stilled utterly, searching his face. "You very nearly did, Roland. I've never seen you like that."

"With good reason." He glanced down at her. He wished to God she hadn't witnessed the ugliness inside him. But now that she had, there was little use in denying it. "I'm a man capable of great violence, Rhiannon. There lurks within me a demon, one who thrives on blood-shed."

She frowned, sable eyebrows bunching over her small, narrow nose. "I've known you from the first moment of your preternatural existence, Roland. I've never seen a sign of this demon."

"I keep it in check, or I have, until now." He gazed at her beautiful, flawless face. Why was control so much more difficult when she was near? She was like a magnet, drawing the beast from its hidden lair, stirring it to life by her very presence. "It was in me before, Rhiannon, when I was yet a mortal."

"You were a knight! One known far and wide for cour-age and valor and—"

"All pretty words for bloodlust. I was talented in the art of battle. A skillful killer. No more."

She stiffened in his arms. "You're wrong about your-self. This demon you claim possesses you is no more than the will to live. Those times were violent, and only the vi-olent survived. In battle, a man must kill or be killed. You did what was necessary..." She winced all at once, and clung more tightly to his neck.

His knowledge of her discomfort was as acute as if the pain were his own. "Press the handkerchief more tight-ly, Rhiannon. The bleeding is beginning again." He strengthened his hold on her and ran the last few steps to the wall, leaping easily over it. Now was no time for recriminations or confessions. Not while her very life was slowly seeping from her body. Oddly enough, Roland felt as if his vitality were draining away, as well, keeping perfect pace with hers.

He carried her over the barren courtyard, past the crumbling fountain that marked its center and through the huge, groaning door. He set her on her feet to pull the door closed.

The cat lunged gracefully from the lowest stair, stopped in front of her mistress and seemed almost to study her, eyes intent and intelligent. Pandora lifted her head, and sniffed delicately at Rhiannon's blood-soaked blouse, and the sound she emitted from deep in her throat could have been a snort of alarm.

"There, kitty. It's not the end of me." Rhiannon stroked the cat's head with one hand, still holding the hanky to her waist with the other.

Jamey came bounding down the stairs with Frederick on his heels. The boy stopped a yard from Rhiannon, his face setting into a granite mask no child of his age had any business wearing.

Frederick came forward, dropped to one knee in front of her and moved the handkerchief aside briefly before pressing it tight again. "It's bad. You need stitches."

"Not necessary," Roland stated, hoping to hide the effect of those words on his equilibrium. Stitches. It brought to mind the image of a sharp object piercing her sensitive skin, an object held by his hand. The pain would be incredible.

Frederick looked again and shook his head. "It isn't gonna stop bleeding."

Roland swallowed hard. Frederick had been a medic in the army before he'd succumbed to the mental illness that kept him so childlike. The man knew a bit about injuries. Still, the thought of the pain... "She needs only rest."

"Nonsense," Rhiannon said softly. "I can rest, but the regenerative sleep will only come with the dawn. I doubt I can keep from bleeding to death until then."

At her words, Roland felt a fist in his stomach. Reckless and irritating though she was, he could not see her die. Even the thought was too much to bear. He glanced once more at Frederick. "Can you do it?"

Frederick's blue eyes widened and he shook his head. It was obvious the very idea scared him to death.

"You'll have to stitch it up, Roland." Rhiannon's voice was steady and firm, but he heard the underlying weakness. "There must be a needle somewhere in this place. You can use the silk thread from my blouse. It's ruined, anyway."

He met her slowly clouding gaze and knew she was right. The specterlike image of the needle, wielded by his own hands, inflicting what would be agonizing pain on her sickened him. He stiffened his resolve. He would do what must be done.

"I'll bring a needle," Frederick said softly. He turned and lumbered up the curving stone stairs, hugging the wall as if afraid of falling should he walk too near the open side.

Roland swept Rhiannon up once again. He turned toward the vaulted corridor to the west wing. Jamey's voice, low and trembling, stopped him. "It was Rogers, wasn't it?"

Rhiannon's head rose from his shoulder as Roland turned to face the angry boy. "No, Jamison," she told him. "It was not. It was a man I've never seen before."

"Was he DPI?"

She sighed. "I can't be certain."

Jamey's gaze met Roland's then. "Did you kill him?"

"No."

"He would have, though," Rhiannon put in quickly, as if defending him. "I had to insist he drop the man and leave before the others discovered us there."

"Killing him would have solved nothing, Jamison. It would only have brought more trouble."

Jamey shook his head slowly. "Not good enough." His gaze again met Roland's and there was an intensity burning in the young eyes that gave him cause to shudder. Like looking into a mirror and seeing his own youth. "Doesn't matter," Jamey said. He glanced back at Pandora, and simply tilted his head. Then he walked ahead of them down the corridor, with the cat leaping to keep up with him.

Roland frowned. "Did you see that?"

Rhiannon, still staring down the dim corridor after the two, shook her head. "He is communicating with my kitten."

She sounded as if she disliked the idea.

Rhiannon grated her teeth and squeezed her eyes tightly. Roland's hands trembled as he poked the needle into her skin, and pulled another tight knot in the thread. He snipped the thread with tiny scissors, and bent over her to begin again.

She wore a cream-colored camisole, stained with her own blood. Roland had deftly removed her ruined blouse and her skirt. She lay on her back on Roland's bed. Of course, it wasn't really his bed. He only kept one in his chamber for appearance's sake. She'd had a brief moment to be grateful he kept it made up with fresh linens and a fluffy down comforter, before this torture had begun.

Roland sat upon the bed's edge, grim-faced. Jamey stood at the opposite side. After the first stitch and Rhiannon's breathless reaction to it, the boy had gripped her hand. She squeezed it harder with each jolt of pain, then reminded herself not to crush his mortal bones to dust.

"This is my fault. I shouldn't have made you take me to that game."

Rhiannon shook her head quickly. "I was the one who insisted you go, and I don't regret it a bit." Her teeth clamped down on her lower lip as the needle was plied once more. She felt beads of icy sweat upon her forehead. "You played wonderfully, Jamey. I thoroughly enjoyed myself."

"You could have been killed."

"No danger of that with Roland around." Again a jab, and again she sucked in a sharp breath. "Of course, protecting helpless women is old hat to him."

"You are hardly helpless, Rhiannon," Roland stated, but his lips were set in a thin line as he worked.

"He was a knight. Did you know that?" She had to say something, anything to distract Jamey from the bitter fury she sensed overwhelming him, and to distract herself from her own suffering. It was unfair for one to be so strong and yet so weak. And though she tried to disguise her agony from both of them, she knew she was failing utterly. Roland's face grew more pale and the hatred in Jamison's eyes increased with every gasp she drew.

Her effort to distract the boy seemed to work, for Jamey's eyes widened. For once, he lost the look of a haunted young man, and looked like a boy, filled with wonder. "A knight? With armor and swords, and all that?"

"Yes. He was knighted by King Louis VII, for heroism. But he's never told me the entire story." She squeezed her eyes tightly against hot tears as the needle poked again. She wanted to hear the tale, she realized. It would alleviate some of the pain. More over, she sensed Roland needed to tell it.

He shot her a look meant to quell her, but she responded with a quick shake of her head.

"Will you tell us now, Roland?"

Roland glanced quickly at Jamey.

"Yes, I wish you would," a deep voice boomed from beyond the open door. Rhiannon looked up quickly to see a large, handsome man, and a petite woman with a head of long, dark curls and perfectly round, doe's eyes. Immortals, both of them.

"Eric." Roland stood at once, dropping his implement of torture to the bedside stand. The two men met in the center of the room and embraced as if they were brothers. Jamey ran to the woman, who wrapped her arms around him and began sniffling like some simpering human.

From the corner of her eye, Rhiannon saw Pandora crouch. The cat's teeth became visible as her lip curled away from them in a menacing snarl. Her claws extended to a dangerous length, and her haunches tensed as she prepared to spring upon the woman holding Jamey.

There was no time to shout a warning. Rhiannon lunged from the bed, landing awkwardly upon the cat, clinging tightly to her neck. The stitches Roland had painstakingly administered tore free, and she cried out in excruciating pain.

The soft-looking female flung herself away from Jamey, and fell to her knees beside Rhiannon. Pandora struggled free of Rhiannon's weakened grasp, but was firmly caught again by Jamey. Then Roland was scooping her back into the bed, swearing under his breath.

"Mind telling us what the hell is going on, old friend?"

Roland didn't look at Eric. His tortured gaze remained on Rhiannon's face. He swept her hair out of her eyes and smoothed it back. "We had a little run-in with DPI. I'll fill you in later." Roland searched for his needle, and tried to thread it without success. Through the burning tears, Rhiannon saw the violence with which his hands trembled.

The small woman touched his shoulder. "Let me."

Sighing in unmistakable relief, Roland surrendered the implements, and got to his feet. The woman took his place on the bed at her side. "I'm Tamara."

"Rhiannon," she said through grated teeth. "And I'll have no more of that needle."

Tamara frowned and glanced down at the wound, bending to push the camisole up, out of the way. "Doesn't look like you have a choice." Her head swung around sharply when the cat stepped up and sniffed at her hand. Jamey still held the panther by the diamond-studded collar.

"Pandora, my cat," Rhiannon supplied, her voice weakening by the second.

"What are you doing here?" Roland's voice was clipped as he addressed Eric. "The village is swarming with DPI agents."

"Yes, that's why we've come. We thought you might need reinforcements."

"But how did you know?"

Tamara bit her lip as she applied the needle. "I have a friend, Hilary Garner, who still works for them. She's kept us informed. DPI knows you're in the area, but not about the castle. Not yet, anyway."

Rhiannon shook her head. The woman worked swiftly, and steadily. It would soon be over, at least she could be certain of that much. "Curtis Rogers knows. He was at the front gate only last night."

"Curt is here?" Tamara's skin paled, and her hand stilled briefly.

"Not at the moment. I sent him on a wild-goose chase."

"If Rogers knows, he's keeping it to himself," Eric said, his voice low and dangerous. "No doubt he wants to exact his revenge single-handedly."

Tamara looked up suddenly, her gaze meeting Jamey's across the room. Her eyes took on a troubled expression. "Enough talk about Curt and DPI. I, for one, am dying to hear this medieval tale. Roland, a knight? No wonder you ooze such chivalrous charm."

Rhiannon shot a narrow look toward Tamara. She disliked this fledgling's open flirting.

"I was a knight. There is little else to tell." Roland's expression was guarded.

"I doubt that is the case, Roland," Eric said.

"Doubt all you like. There is little else I care to tell, then. Leave it."

His clipped tone left no question as to his stand on the topic. Eric's brows rose, but he nodded. "If that's what you wish."

Tamara put one final stitch into Rhiannon's side, tied the knot and set the needle aside. Rhiannon sighed loudly. "Thank God that is over."

"Lie still until dawn, Rhiannon. If you tear them out before then, I'll have to do it all over again."

Rhiannon was stunned. Was this mere fledgling threatening her? Her? Rhiannon? Princess of Egypt?

Then the slip of a thing glanced down at her and winked. "It's late. Jamey, you ought to be getting to bed."

To Rhiannon's surprise, Jamey didn't argue with Tamara. He nodded, and glanced toward a chair in a corner, where Freddy already slumped, snoring.

Eric had a crackling fire blazing in the hearth, behind the protective screen. Rhiannon lay still in the oversize bed, and Roland thought even she looked small in its billowing folds and covers. He hadn't seen Tamara since the death of Jamey's mother, eight months ago. Tamara and Kathryn Bryant had been friends before Tamara's transformation, so the young one had taken it hard. He still saw that pain lingering in her eyes. Along with it, he saw her worry for Jamey.

"He's so different. So... full of anger."

"Most of it aimed at DPI, and Curtis Rogers in particular," Roland told her. "It troubles me. And it troubles me still further to leave the boy unguarded by day. Except for Frederick, there is no one to watch over him."

"Well, we can solve that problem, for the moment at least."

Roland frowned at Eric's statement. "What on earth do you mean?"

"I've been experimenting with a new drug, a sort of a supercharged amphetamine. By using it, I can remain awake and alert by day."

"In sunlight?" Roland was amazed. True, he'd known of Eric's passion for test tubes and chemicals, but he'd never dreamed of results such as this.

"No, I need to remain shielded from the sun."

Rhiannon sat up slightly only to have Tamara, ever attentive, sit beside her and help her into an upright position. As she bent to tuck more pillows behind her, the young one said, "There are side effects, Roland. Without the benefit of the regenerative sleep, he gets weak, tired, not to mention damned irritable."

"Never mind that," Roland said quickly. "You'll give me this drug, and I'll be able to guard Jamey by day."

"I'll guard him myself, Roland. Until we think of a better solution."

Roland shook his head quickly. "No. It is my responsibility—"

"You can both do it," Tamara interrupted. "Take turns, for heaven's sake."

Rhiannon sighed hard and shook her head. "A fine solution, but a temporary one. I believe you are all overlooking the obvious."

Roland moved nearer the bedside. Her face still twisted with pain whenever she moved, but besides that, she seemed to be holding her own. "What is it, Rhiannon?"

"Somewhere on the planet, the boy has a father, does he not?"

Her words were a blade in his heart. "A...father?" He shot a questioning glance at Tamara.

"Kathryn's husband left her before Jamey was born. He might not even know he has a son. His name was James. James Adam Knudson." She shook her head. "I wouldn't know where to begin searching for him."

"Not that it matters. A man who would abandon a wife and child has no right to reclaim either one of them." Roland stalked away from Rhiannon. She didn't argue the point. And no one again suggested that Jamey might be better off with his natural parent.

Roland filled his friends in on what had happened at the stadium, and Rhiannon told them of the strange man who'd attacked her, and his demands.

* * *

Toward dawn, Eric took Tamara down to the dungeons, to one of the hidden resting places Roland had at the ready. After hours of discussion, Eric had finally agreed to allow Roland to take the drug, and remain awake through the daylight hours to watch over Jamey. He'd given Roland three vials of fluid, to be taken at four-hour intervals, beginning well before the lethargy began to steal over him.

Roland swallowed the first of them, grimacing at the bitter taste. He tucked the empty vial into a pocket, and climbed the stairs to check in on Jamey and Frederick. Pandora lay at the foot of Jamey's bed. Jamey slept peacefully.

He returned to his chambers. There was still an hour before dawn. He found Rhiannon still in his bed, though she'd obviously been up briefly. Long enough to "borrow" one of his white shirts, and shed the bloodstained camisole, along with every other scrap of clothing she'd worn. She lay on her side, giving him an optimum view of the long, slender leg exposed beneath the shirt's hem.

"When dawn approaches, I'll take you below."

She rolled onto her back, wincing slightly with the action, and bending one knee. "I've no desire to rest my bones in a dungeon."

"Rhiannon, it isn't safe here." He turned to pace away from her. "Hasn't this incident taught you a thing about caution?"

"Posh, Roland, this is a perfectly secure place to rest. Draw those musty old drapes of yours, bolt the door, and there you are. Indulge me just this once. I promise I won't make a habit of napping here and disturbing your precious solitude."

"With everyone milling about the castle, my solitude has long since been shot to hell, as the expression goes. Here, my dear, is the only place you'll be napping in the foreseeable future. I want you where I can be sure you're safe."

She bit her lower lip as if to think it over. He knew the tone of command in his voice would rankle her. Still, he wouldn't have her in some insecure little house so near a village overrun with DPI operatives.

"It's true that my main source of security is Pandora. With her guarding Jamey, I might be vulnerable in my usual place. I might consider staying here..."

"There is nothing to consider. You're staying."

"There are conditions, Roland."

He lifted his brows. "Conditions?"

"For one, I will sleep here, in the bed. If you're so worried about my well-being, you can simply climb in beside me. Should anyone attack me as I rest, I have no doubt one of us would rouse enough to summon Pandora, who would make them into catnip. Besides, if this new drug of Eric's works, one of you will be awake, anyway."

Roland shook his head slowly. "I will concede to that request, so long as you will give it up should there be an added threat, or reason to believe DPI can reach us here."

She nodded once. "I'm not finished. I simply cannot rest in a place that looks like this. So, you will allow me to spruce it up a bit."

Frowning, he moved nearer, and sat on the edge of the bed. "Your conditions are piling high. Surely you do not envision yourself a chatelaine."

"I envision myself comfortable, Roland. Nothing more." She lifted an arm in a sweeping gesture. "Surely you cannot mind if I wish to remove a few cobwebs and a bit of dust."

His eyes narrowed. "I know you too well to believe that is all you will do."

She shrugged, lowering her lashes over downcast eyes. "Well, I was thinking new drapes might be of use. After all, I want to be sure the sun can't penetrate by day."

He gave her a curt nod. "Drapes and dusting, then. That is the extent of it. Agreed?"

"And I wish to keep the fire." She met his gaze again, and the look in her eyes should have warned him. "It gives me that warm, cozy feeling I had when you carried me through the forest in your arms."

"You press your advantage, Rhiannon." His voice had little force behind it. He, too, was remembering the feel of her in his arms, and of her lips upon his throat.

"Oh, but I'm not finished yet." She sat up carefully, and took his hand in two of hers, tracing invisible patterns on his palm with her nails until he shuddered. "I want you to tell me about your life before I met you. I want to know how you became a knight."

"That is not a subject I wish to discuss."

She stared so intently he felt her tugging at the curtains that veiled his mind. "Roland, you've kept your past inside you for a very long time, and a great deal of pain along with it, I believe. You've twisted events until you've branded yourself a devil. Don't you think you might benefit from an objective opinion?"

He felt, oddly enough, an urge to tell her everything. But he feared even that Rhiannon might be repulsed if she knew the entire tale. Then he asked himself if that wouldn't be a good thing. Let her see the blackness in his soul for herself, and perhaps she would finally understand why he kept himself from her. She might even decide she no longer wanted him.

Some time later, he wondered how he had capitulated so easily. What was there about her that usurped his will?

Still, he found himself sitting with his back against the headboard, his legs stretched out over the mattress. Rhiannon snuggled down, her head resting on his thighs. He absently stroked her hair as he spoke.

"I was the youngest of four sons. It was my parents' fondest wish that I enter the monastery. In those times, there was little else for a younger son to do. My becoming a monk would bring prestige and influence to the family name."

Her hand stroked his thigh. Her silken fingers left a fiery path. "You, a monk?" She said it as if it were laughable.

"I felt the same. So, at fourteen, I ran off, determined to make my own way. I wanted nothing more in the world than to become a knight. After two weeks of scrounging myself enough to eat, I came upon a small babe, not yet a full year of age. He sat upon a blanket on the grass, while his mother and her ladies gathered berries nearby. None of them saw the wolf. But I did."

"A wolf?" Rhiannon's eyes widened and her hand stilled upon his thigh. "Stalking the child? What did you do?"

"Froze with fear, at first. Then the babe looked toward me and smiled. He made this gurgling, cooing sound and waved his chubby hands in the air." Roland shook his head. "I don't know what possessed me, but I drew my knife, the only weapon I had, and I leapt on the wolf as it went for the child. It was a fool's errand. I was nearly torn to shreds."

She sat up slowly, facing him. It surprised him to see her blink fast against a moisture building in her eyes. Her face was so near to his he could feel the quickening of her breaths. "Did you kill this wolf, Roland?"

"Yes, apparently so. I don't remember much after the first few bites." She closed her eyes and shuddered visibly. Her hair fell over one eye, and without thinking, Roland reached out, and moved it aside. His fingers lingered on her face, so soft. He thought he might be absorbed in her eyes, those huge, exotically slanted, jet orbs. "When next I woke, I was in a fine bed, being tended by servants. The child was the grandson of a great baron, and the son of a knight, Sir Gareth of Le Blanc. He took me as his squire when I was healed. For two years, he treated me almost as a son. He taught me all he knew, and allowed me to train with the knights in his outer bailey."

"And you, with your stubborn determination, which I know so well, took to that training with a vengeance. You grew stronger and more skilled with each passing day."

He shrugged. "I did pick up some basic skills."

"Tell me the rest." She was like a child asking for a story, he thought idly, his fingers still stroking her hair.

"I was traveling with Sir Gareth one day. There was a tournament he was to attend. Of course, there were others along, knights and their squires who rode with us. A band of knights loyal to a sworn enemy of Gareth's father were waiting in ambush."

She said nothing. But she lifted her hand to touch his face, almost as if she could see the pain of the memory there. "Gareth and the others fought fiercely, and killed several of them, but they were outnumbered." He shook his head slowly, and the past resurfaced as if it were yesterday. The clang of steel upon steel. The shouts and groans of the fallen men. The frantic shrieks of the horses. The pounding hooves.

"When Gareth fell...something happened to me. I don't know what. I found myself dragging him off the battlefield, into the brush, and pulling the helmet and mail coif from his head. With his last breath, he pushed his sword into my hands, and bade me fight on."

"But you were just a boy!"

He shook his head. "Sixteen was near enough to manhood in those times, Rhiannon. You know that. I demanded the other squires assist me as I removed Gareth's breastplate and hauberk, and put them on. It seemed to take forever, but we accomplished the task in minutes. I donned his coif and helmet, and pulled Gareth's gauntlets onto my hands. With his sword in my grip, and a layer of ice coating my heart, I marched straight into the melee. I was driven by a force I didn't know. It was the demon I've since discovered in my soul.

"I found my master's horse, a massive destrier with a taste for battle, and mounted him."

"And you fought in his place," she breathed.

"More than fought. I was enraged. I remember little, other than the endless swinging of the broadsword, and the shattering impact of it when it hit home. I remember the sounds, the screams of the fallen, and my own battle cry. I was a man possessed, Rhiannon. When the battle ended, I alone remained. Dead men surrounded me."

He shook himself of the memory, and gazed into Rhiannon's eyes. He was shocked to see a single tear roll slowly over her face. He leaned forward, for some inexplicable reason, and pressed his lips to it, absorbing its salty taste.

"I've never told this story to another living soul, Rhiannon." His lips moved against her dampened cheek as he whispered the words, and her fingers threaded in his hair.

"Nor will I," she promised. "Not on pain of death." She lowered her head to his shoulder. "What happened next?"

"The squires had scattered, but not far enough that they hadn't witnessed the battle. When we returned to the castle of Gareth's father, they told of what they'd seen. I was treated as some sort of hero. It wasn't long before I was summoned to the court of King Louis, who was a second cousin to Gareth's father, the baron. I was knighted as a reward for what they called valor. I had my wish. But I no longer wanted it. I wanted only to return to my family, and never experience such violence again."

"And did you?"

He forced a smile for her. Her eyelids were drooping. Apparently, Eric's potion was working, for he felt no hint of tiredness. "I'll save the rest of the tale for another night, Rhiannon. You need to sleep now. And heal."

She shook her head as she lifted it from his shoulder. "You loved this Gareth. It is no wonder you fought as you did. Your grief gave you this rage, not some demon."

He closed his eyes, and wished he could believe it were the truth. "Rest, Rhiannon. We'll talk more when you wake."

She lowered herself into the bed until her head again lay in his lap, and her arms encircled his waist. It was exceedingly strange, he thought, that he felt comfortable with her there so close, rather than disturbed. Moreover, the weight on his heart seemed somehow lighter than it had before.

CHAPTER SIX

As she felt herself falling steadily into the leaden, replenishing sleep, Rhiannon felt the hard length of his thigh beneath her head. For once, she had no desire to seduce him. In fact, she felt closer to Roland than she ever had, and he hadn't so much as kissed her.

A strange turn of events, since she knew full well her feelings for him were only physical in nature.

Still, it was nice, this closeness, this sharing. It felt right, in some way.

It also troubled her. She'd been determined to demonstrate to him that she was as worthy as any male on the planet. She'd been ready to show him she could be just as brave, just as fierce, just as strong. She'd wanted to be certain he could no longer reject her on grounds similar to those her father had used. That she was not good enough.

Now, knowing of his unstinting courage and ferocity in battle, even as a boy, she would have to try harder than ever. A man of such valor would not be easily impressed. A man who, as a mere boy, had thrown himself upon a wolf to save a babe . . . this was pure heroism, whatever he chose to call it. This would require some thinking.

Before the cloak of blackness settled completely over her mind, she felt the wonderful sensation of his hand cupping her face, his fingers tracing its shape. She smiled . . . and then she slept.

* * *

Roland studied her as she rested, but he couldn't see well enough from his present position. He slid himself from beneath her, and rose. Standing beside the bed, he could gaze down at her face to his heart's content. God, but she was a beauty. Every delicate bone beneath her satin skin delineated and shaped her face to sheer perfection.

He was suddenly, overwhelmingly, besieged with the urge to paint her portrait. He longed all at once for a brush in his hand, and the smooth feel of oils as he spread them over canvas.

Ah, but that was foolish thinking. Painting was a mortal pursuit. Something best done beneath the sun's golden rays and caressing warmth. It was not the pastime of undead, restless souls.

What was it about her that brought out such urges? By the gods, he'd actually stood in a crowded stadium and cheered on a school soccer team last night! He'd dressed in denims and a sweatshirt, and he'd placed himself into a crowd with countless DPI agents milling about. When was the last time he'd participated in anything so foolish?

He shook his head. She did have a way of reducing a man to the role of willing servant. Even him.

He knew it beyond any doubt, when, a few seconds later, he gripped her shoulders and rolled her from her side onto her back. She was so perfect. He had to see her, just see her. Though he had no intention of indulging himself in the luxury of reproducing her image on canvas, he could at least appreciate what was here before him.

He reached for the shirtfront, and hesitated. Was it wrong to look at her this way, as she rested, helpless to object?

He closed his eyes. No. Rhiannon wouldn't object in the least.

He released the buttons, the few she'd bothered to fasten. Slowly, very slowly, he parted the garment until her body was revealed to him. His sigh was involuntary, and indicative of how much he'd longed to look at her this way.

His gaze traced her arching, graceful neck to the delicately etched collarbones. Lower, to her small, proud breasts, perfectly round and lily-white. Their centers were the subtle color of the meat of a sweet melon. Their nipples pouted. He wouldn't paint her that way, though. If he were intending to capture her image, he'd tease them taut first, so they thrust outward, tempting a man's lips to touch them.

The way he was tempted now. Just to capture one soft bud between his lips, to suckle it until it became hard, until it throbbed against his tongue.

He swallowed hard against the onslaught of desire, and resumed his perusal of her form, letting his gaze move lower, over the gentle swell of her belly, the dark hollow of her navel, the narrow curve of her waist with the painful wound on one side, the soft flare of her hips. The triangle of sable curls. God, it gleamed like satin. He wanted to touch it, to see if it could truly be as soft as it looked.

Before he could tell himself not to, he was doing just that. His fingers settled themselves into the silken nest. Yes. It was as soft as it appeared. Softer. And though he knew he should not, he moved his fingers lower, parting her secret lips, delving into her. When he felt the answering moistness coat his fingers, he closed his eyes and groaned aloud. He sunk onto the bed, leaning nearer. Her subtle scent reached him and he shuddered. He moved his fingers deeper, then slowly drew them back. Her body trembled, and he looked up quickly.

She lay exactly as she had, perfectly still. But her nipples stood stiff and aroused now. He brought his fingers to his lips, his eyes closing involuntarily as he sucked the taste of her from their tips. He wanted her. More than wanted her, he had to have her. If not physically, then at least . . .

Roland stepped away from the bed, but his gaze remained. He had to capture her on canvas. There was no other way to rid himself of this all-consuming lust. True, he hadn't painted in a very long time. He'd lost the desire, or perhaps the ability to pour his soul onto a rectangle of canvas. Suddenly, now, that desire returned. He'd never thought to feel it again.

Today, this once, he would put brush to canvas. And when his little bird took wing, he'd have a bit of her here, with him.

In the hours of earliest dawn, behind the tightly drawn draperies and beneath a cobweb-draped ceiling, Roland worked with materials that had long ago been packed away in trunks. The oils were newer. He'd been unable to resist buying the new, modern paints whenever he'd seen them. It had become a ritual of self-torment, knowing they were at hand, and wondering if he'd ever feel moved to use them. Now, the smell of the paints in his nostrils was like a drug, and his brush flew over the canvas as an extension of his soul.

He didn't sketch her first. He didn't need to do so. He needed only to look at her, stretched upon the bed like an offering to the gods, and allow his image of her to transfer itself from his eyes to his mind to his hands.

He worked feverishly, losing himself utterly in the act of creation in a way he had not done in years. His hands moved the brush with a touch as gentle as if he were caressing her skin.

And then, almost before he'd been aware a minute had passed, he sensed movement in the castle. Jamey was awake, and Frederick. Even now they were making their way down to the great hall, and then off to the lower east wing, where the kitchens awaited them.

He sighed, saddened at having to give up so soon. He'd forgotten the delight he could feel in such a simple act. He'd accomplished so little. The shapes and colors on the canvas were not recognizable. But he knew they'd take form, gradually, over the next several days.

He reluctantly cleaned his brushes and put his paints away. The canvas, he left, to allow it to dry. He'd be sure it was stored safely long before Rhiannon stirred tonight. Not that he thought she would mind him so closely studying her nude form as she rested. He rather thought the idea would please her.

Lastly, he went to the bed, gazing once more at her nakedness. The length and firmness of her legs enticed him, with flickering images of those shapely limbs wrapped around his body, those curving hips pumping against him.

He was aroused. Painfully so. He realized that he had been the entire time he'd been painting. He closed his eyes and tried not to think that he could strip off his clothing and slip into the bed with her. He could fondle her, touch her, taste her to his heart's content, and she would never know. He could bury himself inside her. He could find release in her succulent moistness, and she'd never be the wiser.

He bent over, blowing a cool breath of air across her breasts, to see the nipples stand hard once more. Her response was immediate. Perhaps he could even bring her to climax without her being aware of it.

The thought was enticing—no, maddening. To elicit the ultimate response from her body without the awareness of her mind. By night, he could remain as resistant to her charms as he wished. By day, she could be his to pleasure.

The temptation was great, nearly too great. He took a firm grip on his mind, realizing that once again the beast inside was trying to take over. To use Rhiannon in such a way would be rape. Whether he knew she wouldn't object or not was not the issue. To take her without her consent would be unforgivable. Was this the way he would repay her for the sheer joy she'd given him?

Joy?

Roland blinked, replaying his own thoughts. Yes. Joy was what he'd felt for those brief hours this morning while he'd been painting. And earlier, when he'd watched Jamey fight his way to victory in the soccer match. He'd felt joy then, too. Absolute pleasure. Delight.

He hadn't thought himself capable of feeling any of those things anymore.

He looked at her face, and shook his head. Who'd have thought a reckless, out of control, renegade vampiress like Rhiannon could instigate the return of pleasure in his life?

He pulled the shirt together, and fastened the buttons. He tugged the comforter over her, then bent low, and pressed his lips to hers. They were moist and pliant and sweet, even in sleep. He slipped his tongue inside her mouth, tasting every part of it, only stopping when he felt madness trying to engulf him.

"Thank you, Rhianikki, princess of the Nile."

Roland was nowhere about when she rose. But she wrinkled her nose at the very slight scent in the air. She sniffed again, and frowned. It smelled a little like paint.

Unable to positively identify the lingering odor, she rolled out of the bed before she gave the wound at her waist a thought. She stiffened as she remembered it, half expecting to be pummeled by pain at any second. She wasn't, though, and when she parted the shirt she wore, she saw that the wound was gone without a trace. Only the tiny stitches remained. The area wasn't even sore.

She got to her feet and strolled about the chambers, whipping open wardrobes and peering into closets in search of something to wear. She didn't find anything, but decided not to let it dampen her spirits. She felt good this evening.

After hearing him talk last night, she'd come to the conclusion that Roland was suffering from a ridiculously prolonged state of depression and a severe guilt complex. But since he'd opened up that painful wound and allowed her to see a little of what caused it, he might be better able to heal. And that thought brought her pleasure. She hated to see him tormenting himself over things long past. It was a waste of his time and his energies. Besides, he ought to be spending both on her. It would be a far more exciting exercise.

The door opened and he entered then, bringing with him a heavy decanter made of lead crystal and filled with crimson liquid. He placed it on a stand, and a glass beside it.

She frowned. "What is this?"

"Nourishment. You need it, after last night."

"What I need is warm, and drawn straight from some innocent throat, Roland."

"Rhiannon, that is murder."

"Still perfectly willing to believe the worst of me, I see." She strode toward him, the shirt gaping in a way he could not fail to notice. "I never murder them. I only taste. A sip here, a sip there. It isn't missed." She was teasing him, and delighting in it as she always did.

His gaze seemed drawn to the swell of her breasts the shirt revealed, so she stepped closer, and bent low to reach for the decanter.

"But if they remember—"

"I take from men as they sleep, Roland. Most of them recall it as an erotic dream." She filled the glass, straightened again, and brought it to her lips.

"And the marks you leave on their throats?"

"It isn't necessary to mark the throats. Blood can be taken from any number of places, some that are difficult to examine too closely." She drained the glass and set it down, licking her lips. "Would you like me to show you?"

He averted his gaze, she hoped, to hide a sudden surge of passion. "No, Rhiannon, I wouldn't. And I would strongly suggest that you feed as we do, from our own supply here. It will not do to rouse undue suspicion with so many DPI operatives in L'Ombre."

She stepped closer, and ran her fingernails up the column of his throat. "Or is it that you dislike the thought of my lips touching another man's flesh?"

He met her gaze and held it for a moment.

She licked her lips. "I had the most interesting dream as I rested."

He quickly looked away. "Did you?"

"Mmm. It isn't often I dream, you know. The sleep is too deep. But this time . . . I felt things."

"What sort of things?"

She shrugged. "It was very brief. A touch, an incredibly intimate touch. And later, a delicious kiss."

He turned from her, and she knew he was guarding his thoughts. "Very strange, indeed."

"Perhaps it is only that I so long for such things." She walked up behind him, so when she spoke, her breath would fan the back of his neck. "If only you would oblige me, I might sleep more soundly, Roland."

His back went rigid. "I'm sorry, Rhiannon. I don't think it would be wise."

She sniffed. He still wasn't impressed enough with her. He still thought her unworthy of his attention. She stepped around in front of him. "My wound needs attending. Will you at least assist me with that?"

His brows bunched with immediate worry, and when she strode away, toward the bed, he followed on her heels. "What is it, Rhiannon? Hasn't it healed yet?"

She sat on the bed's edge, then leaned back, flipping the shirt open to reveal her waist, her hip, and the lower edge of one breast. "It's healed, but I wish you would snip away the threads. They itch."

Roland closed his eyes briefly. When he opened them again, he seemed to have become a mannequin. No emotion showed in his eyes. "Of course." He located the scissors on the nightstand, and pulled up a stool, sitting so his head was more or less level with the mattress. His hand touched the spot on her waist, and stilled. Slowly, he stroked his fingers over the area.

She closed her eyes. "It feels so good when you touch me."

He drew his hand away, and brought the tiny scissors to her flesh. Carefully, he snipped the threads.

"Even when I was asleep, it felt good. You did touch me, Roland, didn't you? It wasn't a dream."

He finished the job, set the scissors aside, and got to his feet. "I'm going out to check the grounds." She felt waves of frustration emanating from him. Why was he so determined to resist her?

"I'll come with you."

"I'll go alone. Jamison is with Eric and Tamara in the great hall. You might ask him for something to wear. Eric and I will fetch some of your own things for you, later on."

She was immediately angry. "I am capable of fetching my own things, Roland. Furthermore, I'm not about to stay where I am so obviously not wanted. Perhaps I'll rest in my own bed tomorrow.''

He said nothing, only walked out of the room. Rhiannon picked up the glass from the stand and hurled it against the wall, where it smashed to bits.

She heard a small laugh and then Tamara appeared in the doorway Roland had just exited. ''You find my anger amusing, fledgling? You wouldn't, were it directed at you.''

Tamara shook her head and stepped inside. ''I'm not laughing at you, Rhiannon. Don't be so defensive. It's just that Eric has made me feel like throwing things a time or two.''

Rhiannon tossed her head. ''He could never have been as purely maddening as Roland is.'' She strode to the hearth and bent to toss a log onto the barely glowing sparks.

''He wouldn't make love to me when we both wanted it so badly we were going slowly insane,'' Tamara confided.

Rhiannon straightened, but didn't turn. ''What was *his* reason?''

''He thought I would be repulsed when I learned what he was.''

''And were you?''

''I loved him. It took a while, but I finally convinced him of it. Be patient with Roland. Don't give up.''

Rhiannon whirled to face the little thing. ''You don't think I'm in love with him, do you? My God, Tamara, I am not nearly so foolish as to allow that to happen.''

Tamara smiled. ''Of course not. Then, you're only interested in a fling?''

Rhiannon's gaze fell. ''I want him. There is nothing wrong in that.'' She frowned. ''Except for his exceeding stubbornness.''

"Does he give you some well thought-out reason for abstaining?"

Rhiannon shook her head. "Only some nonsense about what one wants not always being what is good for one. I know the true reason. He thinks I'm not good enough. He'll soon learn better." Rhiannon searched the room for her skirt, and shed Roland's shirt, only to reach for a fresh one.

"Why on earth do you say that?"

"Because it is true." She found the skirt and stepped into it, fastening a few of the buttons, and then tucking the shirttails into it.

"That's crazy. You're the most attractive woman I've ever seen."

Rhiannon turned to face her. Perhaps the little fledgling wasn't as bad as she had first thought. "And you are indomitably cheerful."

She smiled. "Why shouldn't I be? I get to spend eternity with the man I love."

Rhiannon rolled her eyes. "Must you be so human?" She hunted for her shoes, found them and slipped them on. "Tell Roland I'll return before dawn."

She felt Tamara's rush of alarm at her announcement. "Rhiannon, where are you going?"

"To my house, to fetch some clothing."

"You shouldn't. It isn't safe, there are DPI—"

"Too bad for them if they get in my way. I'm in no mood for it tonight."

She moved toward the door, but the bold little thing grabbed her arm. "Rhiannon, please wait. There's something I need to say to you."

Rhiannon tilted her head to one side. "Say it, then. I'm in a hurry."

"It's about...the man who held you prisoner, in his lab in Connecticut."

"Daniel St. Claire?"

Tamara nodded. "Yes. He...he was my guardian. He adopted me after my parents were killed." Tamara swallowed hard as Rhiannon frowned. "I learned later that their deaths were planned. He only wanted custody of me to try to lure Eric in for live research. I know what happened to you—I read about it in his files, after he died. And, those other two he held, as well. I'm...I'm sorry."

Compelled by Tamara's honesty, Rhiannon reached out one hand to ruffle the young one's curls. "You have nothing to be sorry for, Tamara. These things happened before you were born. You're lucky you survived."

"I don't know if I would've, if it hadn't been for Eric." She licked her lips. "I loved Daniel like a parent for a long time, even after Eric tried to tell me the truth about him. I hope—"

"That I do not hate you for it," Rhiannon finished, reading the young one's thoughts. "Rest assured, I do not."

Tamara smiled, her eyes slightly damp. "I'd like to be your friend."

Rhiannon blinked fast, angry at the ridiculous lump that came into her throat. "I don't believe I've ever had one of those."

"Not even Roland?"

Rhiannon laughed. "No, most especially not him. He doesn't even like me."

"I think you're wrong about that. When we came in last night, it looked as if his seeing you in pain was killing him."

"Really?" Rhiannon's brows lifted and she felt something silly warm her insides. She caught herself. "Listen to us, gibbering about males like a pair of giggling teenage mortals. We are above it, Tamara. Goddesses among women."

"But women, all the same," Tamara replied.

Rhiannon frowned, considering that. Then she shook her head. "I must go. I have much to do tonight. Some shopping, even."

"Shopping? But, Rhiannon, the DPI—"

"Posh, let them chase me through the stores if they think they can keep up. I extracted permission from Roland to clean these chambers up a bit, and hang new drapes. I further intend to purchase enough candles to keep that chandelier glowing nightly for a year. It's like resting in a graveyard this way."

Tamara chewed her lower lip. "I don't blame you for wanting to spruce things up. This is like something out of an old horror movie."

"Precisely. Besides that, my efforts will drive Roland to the point of murdering me. And I do love to torment him. Unless I hurry, the stores will close. So, farewell."

Rhiannon hurried out a rear door, leapt the wall without an effort and raced to her rental house outside L'Ombre. She wasn't a complete fool. Though she saw no sign of anyone watching the house, she took the precaution of slipping around the back. She scaled a wall, and entered through a second-story window.

She turned on no lights at all, only lit a few candles. Her night vision was excellent. She picked through her clothing until she found a short little skirt that flared when she moved, and a blouse to go with it. She packed other items into a suitcase, to take back to the castle when her errands were finished. Then she ran a hot bath until the tub was brimming, and spent a heavenly, albeit all too brief time soaking. She would have loved to linger, to burn some incense and relax, but with Roland's warnings still echoing in her mind, she didn't dare.

She'd return later for her suitcase. For now, she went over to the hidden safe and took out some of the credit cards she kept on hand. She had one more errand, an important one. She would show Roland how worthy she was before this night ended. She lifted the receiver and dialed a number she knew well.

Her agent in France, Jacques Renot, was highly paid, and utterly trustworthy. He also was an ex-DPI operative who knew how to break into their computers.

He recognized her voice at once, and she could almost hear him smiling through the phone lines. Whenever she woke him at night, it always meant a large bonus in his next check. He was worth every penny she paid him. How many others could keep track of her many aliases, her countless bank accounts? Her need for anonymity was making Jacques a very rich man.

"I need to know the name of the hotel where Curtis Rogers is staying, in L'Ombre," she said simply. "Can you get it?"

"*Oui*. It might take awhile, but—"

"I'll call you back in twenty minutes." She hung up.

It wouldn't take long to do the shopping. After all, she knew exactly what she wanted, and price was no object, so why waste time? She had important things to do.

CHAPTER SEVEN

"She said she was going shopping."

Roland felt as if he would explode. Shopping! By God, Rhiannon was more than reckless. She was utterly insane! "Why the hell didn't someone come and let me know?"

Eric pulled Tamara aside and stepped in front of her, as if to guard her from Roland's anger. "I've been looking for you for two hours, Roland. I had no idea where to find you, and you ignored my summons. What more could we do?"

Roland pushed one hand through his hair, and let his eyes fall closed. "We have to find her. There are DPI operatives all over the village. And if Curtis hasn't told them about the castle, you can bet he's told them about her. They'll spot her in a second. She stands out from other women like a swan among crows."

He ignored the meaningful glance Tamara shot Eric. "Might be nice if *she* could hear you say so." Roland only shook his head. "Honestly, Roland, I don't know why you're so worried. She isn't going to do anything risky," Tamara said.

"Hah! She likes nothing better than to risk her pretty neck at every opportunity. If you knew her at all, you would be worried, too." He was racked with worry. Why on earth had he let her out of his sight after she'd been nearly killed? Why in the name of God had he thought she'd exercise some caution after that incident? Didn't he know her better? He ought to have been watching her every move. Instead, he'd deliberately closed off his mind so she wouldn't be able to track him down while he visited the little *cimetière* in the small woodlot near the castle. He'd felt a sudden need to be there, to remind himself what he'd done to his family, and to the only other woman who'd ever stirred him to this kind of madness. He'd come close to letting those sins slip his mind yesterday, and doing that would only doom him to repeat them.

As he started for the door, Eric gripped his shoulder. "I'll come with you."

He glanced through the window where Frederick and Jamey frolicked with Pandora in the safety of the courtyard.

"And leave only Tamara to watch over Jamey?"

"What do you suppose Rogers would do if he found her here with only gentle Freddy and a cat for protection?"

Tamara tossed her head, flipping her hair behind her shoulders in exactly the way Rhiannon always did. "I'm no helpless mortal," she declared. "I can take care of myself."

Eric bit his inner cheek to keep from smiling, Roland noted. "You've been around Rhiannon too much, fledgling," Roland said.

"And you haven't been around her enough," she snapped. "Either that, or you're a blind fool. She thinks you dislike her. She thinks you believe she's not good enough for you. If she does do something crazy, it will probably only be her way of trying to show you how wrong you are."

"Where on earth do you get these notions? Rhiannon believes herself good enough for God himself, to say nothing about me."

"It's not what *she* thinks that matters, it's what she believes *you* think." When he only frowned and shook his head, she fumed. "I could just shake you!"

Eric caught her shoulders and drew her back against him. "Easy, my love. You might hurt him." He glanced up at Roland. "Go on, go find your rebel. I'll keep things secure here."

Roland left the castle, but he couldn't help wondering about Tamara's words. Was there the slightest chance that Rhiannon felt she had to prove herself to him? It was utterly ridiculous, of course. But then, Rhiannon had made that remark about his seeing her as inferior. Perhaps there was some truth to Tamara's theory.

Now, though, he had no time to worry about theories or motivations. Rhiannon was out on her own, and there were at least two potentially lethal enemies lurking in the village. He needed to find her right away.

He began at the house she'd told him she was renting, just outside the village. That she'd been there was without question. The bloodstained skirt and his white shirt lay on the floor, and the tub's interior was coated in droplets announcing its recent use. The room still smelled of the scented candles she'd burned. The candle wax was still warm.

A suitcase lay on the bed, laden with clothing. He assumed she was planning to bring it back to the castle with her on the return trip, but wondered if he was assuming too much. She'd been fairly angry when he'd last seen her.

He shook his head, and checked the room thoroughly. He saw the notepad and pencil near the phone and he hurried to it. She'd written something on the top sheet, obviously. But she'd torn it off. He licked his lips, lifting the pad to the light to try to make out the indentations of the pencil. No luck. Angry, he turned to fling the thing at the wastebasket . . . and he saw the small bit of yellow paper, crumpled and resting atop some other rubbish. He picked it up, and smoothed it out.

There was an address, and a room number. Beneath those, underlined, one word: "Rogers."

Rhiannon saw the two men silhouetted by the lamplight. They sat in the hotel suite's front room. She clung to the windowsill, fifteen stories up, peering in at them as the sounds of traffic and mortal activity filled the night. She was at the window of a bedroom, but she could see them both clearly through the open door. For once, she wished she were older, more powerful. She longed for the power to transmute herself into a mouse, and crawl about the room that way. She'd heard there were a few who could achieve such a thing, the very ancient ones. She'd tried it herself a few times, but always only managed to give herself a walloping headache for her trouble.

She did have the ability to entrance humans. She could, possibly, lull them into a state of catatonia, and then dance through the rooms at will without arousing a response from them. But there was a chance her efforts would only result in alerting them of her presence. For the man with Curtis Rogers was the one who'd attacked her at the soccer match. And she already knew he could guard his mind from hers.

A little shiver raced over her spine as she studied his face. He was mean-looking, with a wide, pugnacious nose and a thick coating of dark stubble. He was heavy, his arms big, but not fat. He looked like one of the professional wrestlers she'd seen on cable TV a time or two. He wore his dark hair cut close to his head, in short bristles. His lips were too thick.

She listened intently, and heard little other than their voices, speaking low. She sniffed the air, and smelled the big one's sweat, and Curtis's cologne, and expensive whiskey.

Silently, she hauled herself over the edge.

"We understand each other, then?"

Curtis shrugged. Rhiannon slipped to one side, out of their range of vision should they look this way. "I don't need to understand you. If you can help me capture one of them, you can name your price."

The man shook his head. "Not just *any* one of them. Her. She's the oldest, the most powerful. It's her I want." He slugged back the whiskey in his glass and licked his lips with a fat tongue. "I want you to tranquilize her, and leave me alone with her, for as long as I need."

Curtis shook his head. He got to his feet, crossed to the bar and gripped the amber-filled bottle by its neck. "You want to screw her. You're not fooling me. Hell, I can't blame you. She's a hot one."

The other man pursed his lips and said nothing. He held his glass up when Curtis approached, and whiskey splashed into it. "Maybe I will, but that isn't my main goal. You're certain she'll be absolutely helpless?"

"Absolutely. This drug has been tested. It works." Curtis filled his own glass and paced away. "You mind if I ask why you think you can capture her when the rest of us have failed?"

"I have certain abilities. And I know their weaknesses."

"So do we."

"I know how to use them."

"Yeah, well, I can't say I have much confidence in your chances. But if you can do it, you can have her as helpless and as often as you want her."

Rhiannon shuddered at the image. She recalled too well the last time she'd been helpless at the hands of a DPI operative. Weakened from the blood they'd drained away, she could only lie there, hands and feet restrained, as they tortured and touched her.

"Then you'll tell me where they are."

She stiffened, listening.

Curtis hesitated. "There are others that interest me, besides her. They're mine. Mine alone, you understand?"

"Perfectly." He chuckled and the sound made her shiver. "You have special plans for them, no doubt. I wouldn't dream of interfering."

"And you can tell no one else. If their locale gets out, the entire DPI body will be staked out around the place. I'll never get my hands on them," Curtis said.

The man nodded. "Agreed."

Curtis sighed long and hard. "They're at a castle called Le Château de Courtemanche, south of L'Ombre."

His accent was terrible. The name of the village had sounded like "lumber." Rhiannon wished she could simply kill the both of them. God knew it would be justified. Unfortunately, Roland would never forgive her. He and his noble, knightly ideas about honor. And he thought he had a demon in him. Ha! If he had a demon, then *she* must be one.

"It might be of help if I were to take a sample of the drug—"

"Forget it, pal. That formula is top secret. No one has it but me, and that's the way it's going to stay."

So you think, Curtis, dear, Rhiannon thought.

"All right. I don't need it." The man rose and turned toward the door. Curtis turned to a table, out of Rhiannon's sight. She moved to a more advantageous angle and peered at him. He snapped the lid on a briefcase, and she glimpsed rows of test tubes, with rubber stoppers, inside.

The drug.

"Aren't you going to tell me how to reach you? I don't even know your name."

The man opened the door and paused. "I'll contact you, when it's necessary. As for my name, you may call me Lucien, for now."

He left the room, leaving the door wide. Curtis hurried to close it, shaking his head. He carefully fastened the lock, and then came toward the room she was in. She flung herself beneath the bed, and peered out to watch him. He kept going, right through the door that led to the bathroom. She pulled herself out, and hurried to grab the briefcase. In seconds she was out the window once more, and clambering carefully down.

She reached jumping distance and leapt elegantly to the ground, landing with a little bounce, and fighting to stave off laughter. She was nearly giddy with her success.

Arms came around her from behind and pulled her into a darkened alley. She struggled, but the strength in them was unbelievable, and for just an instant, she fully expected to feel the jab of Lucien's blade in her side once more.

"What the hell do you think you're doing?"

"Roland!" She turned in his grip, and went nearly limp with relief. "You frightened me half to death. I thought you were that hunk of beef who tried to knife me before."

"I could very well have been. You take less care than a whirling dervish."

"I daresay, I've known more dervishes than you have Roland, and I take a good deal more care than they." His arms still imprisoned hers, and she shook free. She lifted the briefcase, and thrust it at him. "Maybe you'll stop being so angry when you see what I have."

"I don't care what you have, you could have been killed or captured trying to get it. When are you going to listen to me, Rhiannon?"

"Just look at it, Roland. I know you'll be pleased."

He thrust the case back into her hands. "Not here." He gripped her arm and began striding away, down the alley.

She tugged free once again, sorely hurt that he didn't even care to see what she'd accomplished. "I have a car waiting. A rental."

"Leave it," he barked.

"Go to hell, Roland. My packages are inside."

She raced away from him before he could grab her again. In seconds, she'd settled herself behind the steering wheel. She was surprised when the passenger door jerked open and he slid in beside her.

"You detest automobiles."

"I'll put up with one tonight."

A little of her anger faded. "Just to be with me?"

"Yes."

She very nearly grinned.

"Because if I let you out of my sight, there is no telling what kind of foolish thing you'll do next."

He could have slapped her and hurt her less. She refused to let him see it, though. She started the engine and pulled away from the hotel. The case rested on the seat between them. He didn't make a move to look inside and she wouldn't ask again.

She pulled to a stop right in front of her rental house, and Roland scowled. "Keep going, Rhiannon."

"I only want to fetch my suitcase."

"Then park somewhere else and we'll walk back for it. No sense announcing our presence."

"Stop telling me what to do."

"Someone has to. You haven't sense enough to act responsibly on your own."

She got out and slammed the door. "That's enough. I am staying right here. I wouldn't go back to that musty old castle of yours if there were twenty DPI men waiting for me right now."

She dragged the briefcase out of the car as Roland jumped out the opposite door. She threw it at him, putting a good deal of force into it. The case hit him squarely in the chest, and he staggered backward. "Give it to Eric. It's the tranquilizer. I thought he might like to examine it, see if he can come up with an antidote, or something."

"Rhiannon, don't be ridiculous." He tossed the case back into the car and came around it. He caught up with her, gripped her upper arms and made her face him. Then his eyes widened, and he looked at her in disbelief. "You're crying."

She ripped one arm free of him, even though doing so hurt considerably, and dashed the tears from her face with her hand. "No, I'm not."

He shook his head slowly. "Rhiannon, I didn't mean to hurt you—"

"You? Hurt me?" She released a bark of laughter. "I am the daughter of a Pharaoh, a princess of Egypt. Men fall at my feet if I wish it. Mortals and immortals alike. Do you really think I can be hurt by the likes of you?" Her throat burned. "I hate you, Roland de Courtemanche. I detest you, and you will not have the opportunity to reject me ever again."

Roland returned to the castle alone. He drove the car, for the simple reason that he didn't want DPI to see it outside Rhiannon's house and realize she was inside. He wasn't even certain they knew it was her house, but it would seem likely. Her description would have been bandied about L'Ombre, and questions asked. Someone would know the elusive Rhiannon had rented the cottage.

He entered through the front door, and found no one about. He stalked to his chambers and stopped in the doorway, unable for a moment, to draw a breath.

Frederick glanced down from the ladder where he stood, polishing the silver chandelier that winked and sparkled. Tamara stopped swiping the bare windows with the wet cloth. Eric glanced up from the hearth where he knelt with a wire brush, scrubbing the stones. Jamey lowered the broom with which he'd been attacking cobwebs.

"Where's Rhiannon?" the boy asked.

Roland looked at the floor, rather than into Jamey's eyes. The cat came toward him, tail swishing, a similar question in her feline eyes. "She's at the house she rented. She wanted to stay there."

"Roland..." Tamara's voice carried a warning, but Eric stopped her with a glance and came forward.

"What's in the briefcase, my friend?"

He looked down, having nearly forgotten what he carried. "It's the drug, the tranquilizer Rogers used against you before."

Eric lifted one eyebrow. "How did you—"

"Not me. Rhiannon. She slipped into Rogers's hotel suite and stole it."

Eric's jaw dropped for just a moment.

Jamey smiled and shook his head. "Man, she's got guts."

"Guts?" Roland scowled at the boy. "It was an idiotic thing to do. Rogers was in the room at the time, not to mention that other fellow. The one who nearly killed her."

"And she went in there, anyway," Jamey insisted. "That took guts."

"She is reckless and self-destructive."

Tamara threw the washrag she'd been using onto the floor and stomped across the room. "She is brave, and cunning, and absolutely beautiful. I wish I were more like her."

Eric looked at her, a hint of alarm on his face. "I like you the way you are, Tamara."

"Rhiannon is far too sure of herself. She should be more careful." Roland slung the briefcase onto a stand and sunk into a chair.

"She's not at all sure of herself. Roland, you hurt her again, didn't you?"

"What on earth do you mean, 'again'?"

"Tamara, leave him alone. Roland is right about this. Rhiannon takes far too many risks." Eric touched her shoulder and she whirled on him, glaring in a way Roland had rarely seen her do. "If one of you had done what she did tonight, you'd be congratulating yourselves until dawn. Why on earth can't you give the woman some credit?"

"Did Rhiannon get the new drapes?" Frederick called down from the ladder.

Roland lifted his head. He felt a heavy burden of guilt lowering itself upon his shoulders, and Tamara was only adding to it. He'd wanted to protect Rhiannon. Instead, he'd somehow hurt her. "Out in the car, I believe." He looked once again at the rooms around him, and shook his head. "You've all been working nonstop all night, haven't you?"

"Don't thank us," Tamara snapped. "We did it for her, not you." She hurried out of the room with Jamey on her heels. Frederick limped down from the ladder and went after them.

Eric sat in a chair opposite Roland. "A car? Care to tell me how that came about?"

Roland did, beginning with the luggage in the cottage, and ending with the scene outside it. As he spoke, Jamey carried in a package containing the new drapes, and took his place on the ladder to hang them. Frederick came in to help, setting a box containing no less than a hundred candles, on the floor.

Roland and Eric largely ignored the two, and soon they trooped out again to return with more packages. It was a full thirty minutes before Eric frowned hard and looked up. "Where is Tamara?"

Frederick only shrugged and limped out once more.

Jamey went to follow, but Eric gripped his arm. "Jamison, tell me where she is."

Jamey licked his lips. "She went to Rhiannon's. Don't be mad, Eric. She made me promise not to say a word."

Eric grimaced and whirled to go out the door. He nearly collided with Tamara and Rhiannon. Roland swallowed hard, relief welling up that she was here, safe. She looked around the room with ill-concealed surprise. Roland thought she deliberately avoided his eyes.

"Your drapes are perfect, Rhiannon. The color of sunshine, and still heavy enough to keep it out. They look wonderful." Tamara's hand rested gently upon Rhiannon's arm.

"Tamara, you scared me half to death." Eric pulled her into his arms and squeezed her hard. "Next time you get the notion to go off on your own, would you check with me, please?"

"Why should I?" She thrust her chin up at him, but slanted a glance toward Roland.

"Because I love you, Tamara. If anything should happen to you..." He closed his eyes and shook his head. "It would kill me. You know that."

Again she looked at Roland, her glare as piercing as a blade. When she faced Eric again, her expression softened. "I know. I'm sorry I worried you." She kissed him lingeringly, and Roland averted his gaze. He noticed Rhiannon had turned away, too.

Frederick had mounted the ladder and was fitting candles into the holders. Tamara turned to him. "It's late, Frederick. Why don't we leave the rest for another time?"

He nodded, fit one last candle into place, and climbed slowly down. Rhiannon picked up her case and walked through the double doors into the bedroom. She put it on the bed, and began unpacking.

Eric went in behind her. "Getting those vials was quite a coup, Rhiannon. I might be able to find a way to nullify the drug's effects, given time."

"I was hoping that would be the case." She cleared her throat. "I learned a bit while I was in the hotel room. The man who attacked me is not with DPI. He calls himself Lucien."

Roland's attention was caught. As Tamara hustled Jamey and Frederick toward the door, shooing Pandora out with them, Roland moved into the bedroom.

She didn't look at him, only kept removing things from her case, sorting them into neat stacks on the bed. "No one in DPI knows about this castle. Only Curtis Rogers and this Lucien. He convinced Curtis to tell him while I was listening in. He offered to help capture me, in exchange for certain... privileges."

"What sort of privileges?" Roland couldn't keep quiet any longer.

Rhiannon barely spared him a glance. "He asked if Curtis would tranquilize me to the point of absolute helplessness, and then let him have me alone for as long as he needed."

Tamara gasped from the doorway. Roland swore fluently.

Rhiannon shook her head. "He wants to be transformed. I imagine that is the only thing he would force me to do. Not that I intend to give him the chance."

Roland paced toward her. "Why you? Why doesn't he target one of us?"

"He said because I was the oldest. He wants high-proof blood, Roland." It was the first time she'd addressed him directly. Her eyes still looked like those of a wounded animal, and he realized all over again how deeply he had hurt her.

Eric put a hand on Rhiannon's shoulder. "We all care about you, Rhiannon. For that reason, we hope you won't take any more unnecessary risks."

She faced him head-on. "I will not cower in a corner and wait for them to come for me. They will be the ones cowering before I finish. They will wish they'd never heard my name."

Tamara touched Eric's arm, and tilted her head toward the door. He sent Roland a sympathetic glance before they left. Alone with Rhiannon, Roland had no idea what to say.

"I, um . . . I'm glad you came back."

"I am only here because of Tamara. She is frightened for Jamey and she asked me to stay, and help protect him."

He nodded. She opened the drawer of an empty dresser. "They might be rather stale-smelling. Haven't been used in a while," he said.

She drew a small package from her case. "I brought some cedar chips." She sprinkled some of them into the drawer. "You haven't said anything about the drapes. How much do you hate them?"

He drew a deep breath. "Actually, I'm beginning to feel glad you convinced me to allow it. The entire place feels ... warmer."

"Then you won't mind that I bought a bedspread and some throw pillows to match."

He shook his head slowly. "No. I don't mind." He felt his eyelids growing heavy, his body slowing gradually. He reached inside his jacket and removed a vial of Eric's revivifying potion.

Rhiannon frowned. "Perhaps you shouldn't. You look tired."

He only shook his head. "Rhiannon, do you feel as if you need to prove something to me?"

Her gaze lowered all at once. "No, Roland. Not anymore."

There was a finality in her tone that hit him with staggering force. Was she giving up on her relentless pursuit of him, then? Why on earth should that make him feel so utterly miserable?

He shook off the feeling of desolation, and downed the potion. "Good. Because you never did, you know." She said nothing, only continued piling clothes into drawers. "I've never doubted your abilities, Rhiannon. Your strength, your courage, your utter boldness in facing danger."

She stopped in the act of sorting nightgowns, holding a sheer black peignoir out before her. She frowned over it. "For a woman, you mean?"

"That is not what I mean. I wouldn't have wished to face you in battle as a human. I still wouldn't."

She draped the gown over the back of a chair, and Roland's mouth went dry when he realized she probably intended to wear it. He couldn't help envisioning her pale, smooth limbs beneath the translucent gauze. She scooped up a handful of clothing and moved toward the wardrobe, to begin hanging them.

Standing with her back to him, she shook her head. "I don't understand you at all, Roland. If you don't think of me as inferior, then why do you dislike me so?"

"I do not dislike you. I dislike thc things you do."

She finished hanging clothes, and turned, tilting her head. "Which things?"

"Outrageous things, Rhiannon. Things that put you at risk. Like...like singing in that tavern, for example."

She smiled fully, and her eyes sparkled. "Ah, but Roland, it was such great fun. And you have to admit, I'm not bad." She frowned then. "Was that it, you think I sing horribly?"

He closed his eyes. Truly, she was exasperating. "You have the voice of an angel."

She seemed to glow with his praise. "Really?"

He nodded. "It's that you were drawing so much attention to yourself. I only want you to be careful."

"The only attention I wished to draw was yours."

"Then you ought to have come here, and sung to me in private." She opened her mouth to reply, but he continued speaking. "It's not only the singing. It's all the other risks you take. Flirting with Rogers that first night. Slipping into his hotel room tonight." He lifted his hands in a helpless gesture. "Can't you see that my anger at you was because I was afraid for you?"

She studied him so intently that he had a brief surge of hope she might actually be listening. Then, "If I had come to the castle, to sing to you in private, would you really have listened?''

He clapped a hand to his forehead. ''You haven't heard a word I've said, have you?''

She waved a hand. ''Of course, I have. You dislike my risky adventures. You dislike my every behavior. No doubt, you dislike the way I dress, as well.''

''In public, Rhiannon, it wouldn't hurt to try a bit harder to blend in, for your own protection.''

''I knew it. Well, Roland, where shall I begin? Shall I fashion a dress from a feed sack?'' Her voice grew louder, her words tumbling out in a rush of anger. ''Would that please you? Shall I slouch when I walk, so my height isn't so noticeable? Or maybe I should begin by hacking off my hair. It's probably my most conspicuous feature, wouldn't you say?'' She strode away from him, and began a frantic search of the chambers, opening every drawer and cupboard and chest.

Roland gripped her shoulders and turned her to face him. ''Stop it.''

''No. There are scissors here, somewhere. I know there are. I'll even let you do the honors, Roland. Just—''

He shook her. ''Stop it! You know that isn't what I meant.''

''No, I don't. I don't understand you at all. If I dress and behave as a widow in mourning, will that make you want me, Roland? If I suddenly become a blushing wallflower, will you find me desirable then?''

''You want to know how desirable I find you?'' He glared at her, his rage blending with his passion to overwhelm his common sense. He knew he should release her, leave the chamber this instant before she drove him too far. The beast within, taunted to wakefulness by his anger, his fear for her, and his desire, was on the rampage.

But her scent twined through his brain, eliciting the memory of her the previous day, lying all but naked before him. The taste of her seemed to come to life upon his lips. The way her breasts had looked, and how they'd responded to his touch. His lips had been so close to them. His hunger for her whipped the beast to a frenzy and he shuddered with the force of it.

"You want to know how much I desire you?" he repeated. He looked down into her blazing eyes, and knew it was too late to battle the beast inside.

CHAPTER EIGHT

There was something in his eyes, something that should have warned her. But she couldn't curb her anger. "I already know. You don't desire me at all. You want someone who looks like me, but who is timid and quiet and withdrawn. You touched me while I rested, Roland. While my body could respond but my mind could not." She shook her head in frustration. "It isn't me you want."

Roland's grip on her shoulders eased, and his hands slipped slowly down her arms. His gaze stabbing into her eyes, he reached her wrists, encircled them and drew her hands forward. Then he pressed her palms flat to his groin, and moved them slowly up and down over the solid, throbbing length of him. "You're wrong." His words were nearly a growl.

Rhiannon felt a shudder of absolute longing move through her. She closed her eyes at the force of it. Then his mouth was crushing hers, his arms were around her, pinning hers immobile. He pressed her lips open and thrust his tongue into her mouth, licking its roof, and her teeth and her tongue.

She wanted to put her arms around him, but his crushing embrace prevented that. Her hands worked, all the same, at the button of his trousers. In moments, she was able to close them around the silken, rigid evidence of how very much he did want her. She squeezed, and stroked, and ran the pad of her thumb over the tip.

He moaned into her mouth, and suddenly gripped the front of her blouse and tore it open. He was frantic, a man possessed, she thought, as he ripped the bra away, and bent her backward, bowing to suckle her breast. Ruthlessly he tugged and bit, ravaging her sensitive nipple until her knees quivered and her hands buried in his hair to urge him on.

He fell to his knees then, and yanked the skirt until its seam gave way. He pressed his lips to the front of her panties, hands gripping her buttocks, and she felt his breath and the moistness of his kiss right through them. A second later he ripped them aside, and kissed her there again.

She couldn't stand up much longer. Her legs were jelly. Her knees had dissolved.

Then his tongue parted her folds, and lapped a hot path inside. She fell to the floor, but he came right with her. Growling deep in his throat, he pressed his palms to her inner thighs, and shoved them apart. He buried his face between them.

It was torture, sweet, succulent torture, and he applied it like an attack. His mouth devoured, his tongue assaulted. His hands fought to widen the gate of her fortress, and he mercilessly deepened his invasion.

She screamed aloud when his conquest was complete, and still the siege continued, rendering her no more than a quivering, panting captive. When her hands tried to push his head away, he caught her wrists in a grip of iron, and plundered on, until every bastion of sanity had been rendered useless.

Then he was moving upward, over her body. Her newly freed, trembling hands shoved his trousers lower, and he plunged himself inside her without a second's hesitation.

His size and the force of his thrusts made her gasp. His mouth covered hers again, and the sweep of his tongue into her throat matched the rhythm of his body, pounding into hers. She pressed at his shoulders once, as a signal he should slow down. This wasn't as she had envisioned it. This wasn't the lovemaking she craved from him. But his hands only caught hers, and pinned them to the floor at her sides. His pace, if anything, became more demanding.

And in moments, her hips arched in response to that demand, and her tongue swirled around his in a savory dance. Harder and harder he rode her, until his lips left her mouth to slide down to her throat. She tipped her head back as he drew her skin into his mouth. She was approaching a second, shattering climax, and she reached for it, eagerly.

She knew he was there as well when he reared inside her, and she felt the hot pulse of his seed. Then his teeth sank into her throat, and he growled once again. She moaned in a hoarse voice as the climax held her endlessly in its grip, then shook all over as it released her.

Her muscles slowly untwined, and relaxed. His mouth was still fastened to her throat. She felt the movements of his lips and knew he still drank. Her essence flowed into him, and her body began to weaken. The lethargy that crept around her senses was tempting her, calling her to embrace it. But it would be brief, she knew. He would stop at any moment, and her head would clear.

But he didn't. On and on, he took from her, and the ecstasy she felt became tinged with fear.

She pushed at his shoulders. "Roland..."

He lifted his head with some reluctance. His eyes still glowing with passion, he stared into hers. "You're delicious," he whispered. "All of you."

She felt a sudden confusion inside her. She thought she ought to smile up at him, but instead she felt like crying.

Why? For God's sake, why? Wasn't this what she'd wanted?

He rolled off her, stood and righted his trousers. He reached a hand down to her. "Come, it's nearly dawn. You're feeling it already, aren't you?"

She swallowed the lump in her throat. He hadn't even taken off his clothes. His eyes were hot with lust, but devoid of feeling. "Yes, I suppose I am." She allowed him to take her hand, and pull her to her feet. But her knees refused to support her, and she swayed away from him. She caught herself on the arm of the settee, leaning over it like a drunkard. Her head fell forward. Her hair veiled her face like a dark curtain, through which she could not see. Rather, she heard his ragged breathing slowly take on a normal rhythm. She felt the gradual ebb of his mindless lust.

Roland caught her shoulders, tugging her upright, turning her to face him. "What is it?"

She lifted her chin to see confusion in his expression. My God, he wasn't even aware . . .

His eyes narrowed, then focused on the fresh wound at her throat. The heightened color left his face all at once. She heard him curse roughly, and that was all. She felt herself falling, but oddly, there was no sense of landing at his feet. Instead, it was as if she simply continued a downward spiral into utter blackness.

The knowledge of what he'd done was like a blade thrust through the mists of passion to plunge into his heart as he caught her in his arms, and lifted her. Her head fell backward, her endless satin hair trailing down his legs as he carried her to the bedroom, and laid her down. He smoothed the ebony locks away from her face and pulled the covers over her pale body. He had to close his eyes tightly for the burning that assailed them. Certainly not tears. He had none. Hadn't had for centuries. What use were tears to a beast?

God, that he'd thought he might someday conquer the bloodthirsty demon within him was a joke. But to have found the proof of it like this...

Mentally, he called to Eric. She wouldn't die. As he recalled the way he'd ravaged her, second by second, he knew he hadn't taken enough to kill her. But he might have, had she not stopped him when she had. There'd been no logic in his brain at that moment. Only sensation. The feel of his body possessing hers, of her climax milking the seed from him, of her blood filling him, had chased every vestige of morality from his mind, and given free rein to the monster that lurked inside.

He heard the door creak open, but didn't turn. Instead he clasped her limp, slender hand in both of his, and brought it to his lips. "I'm sorry, Rhiannon. God, I'm sorry."

"Roland, what..." Eric's steps approached from behind, then stopped. Roland released her hand and turned to face his friend. Eric wasn't looking at him, however. His gaze fixed upon Rhiannon's white face, and then upon the two tiny wounds at her throat. "What the hell have you done?"

Roland parted his lips but found himself unable to speak. Then he was shoved roughly aside as Eric went to the bed, leaned over it and touched Rhiannon's face. Roland turned his back. Shame engulfed him. Remorse filled his every pore. "I didn't mean—I lost control, Eric. I nearly—"

Eric gripped Roland's arm and drew him from the room. He closed the bedroom door. His anger struck like a fist, and Roland couldn't blame him for it. "What the hell were you thinking? How could you allow yourself to—"

"I don't know, dammit!" Roland lowered his head, pressing a palm to his forehead. "Is she all right?"

Eric sighed hard. "She'll be weak when she wakes, and more than likely, she'll feel like hell. She'll need to feed right away. All in all, I'd say she's in better shape than you right now." He shook his head. "Tell me what happened, Roland. This is so unlike you."

"Oh, but it isn't. It's exactly like me."

"That's ridiculous. You're the most controlled man I know."

"Am I?" Roland paced away, toward the fire. He stared into the glowing coals, inhaled the pungent aroma of the smoldering wood. "Have you ever wondered why I remain such a staid, quiet individual? Have you ever once considered what fiendish qualities I might be holding in check?"

"I don't know what you're talking about." Eric came nearer.

Roland faced him, pointing one outstretched finger toward the bedroom. "That is what happens when I ease the reins of control, Eric. The lust for blood, be it in battle or in passion, takes over. It's time you knew your dearest friend is no more than evil given form and substance."

Eric frowned. He touched Roland's shoulder, then gripped it hard. "I've never seen you like this."

"What you've seen of me is a veneer, my friend. Today, you've met me for the first time. Perhaps it would be best if you took your fledgling and the boy, and went as far from me as possible, before I contaminate all of you."

"Don't be ridiculous." Eric let his hand fall away. "We'll talk more tonight. The sun is already cresting the horizon. You ought to go below."

Roland shook his head. "No need. I availed myself of your potion."

Eric's frown deepened. "When?"

Roland shrugged. "An hour ago. Perhaps less. What does it matter?"

"Why didn't I realize...Roland, sit down. Crawl out of this well of self-loathing and listen to me." Without waiting for Roland's compliance, Eric shoved him toward a chair.

Roland sat, but he wasn't concerned with what Eric had to say. No words could alter the truth.

"It wasn't you, you fool," Eric all but shouted. "It was the drug. If anyone is to blame for this debacle, it's me." He pulled a chair close to Roland's and sat down. "The drug has a tendency to increase aggressive behavior. At least it did in the animals I initially tested it on. When the same symptoms didn't occur in me, I assumed immortals were immune to that side effect. That was a grave error, obviously."

Roland shook his head slowly. "What a genuine friend you are to try to accept blame for my true nature. It wasn't the drug, Eric. It was me."

"No. Roland, use your brain and listen. I should have realized that older vampires would be more susceptible to adverse effects than younger ones. Just as they're more susceptible to other elements. Sunlight. Pain. Don't you see? The drug caused this."

Roland faced Eric without blinking. "You truly do not wish to see me for what I am. If the drug did anything at all, it was only to weaken the tenuous grip of my control. The beast within is mine alone. I know it well."

"You're a damned fool if you believe that."

Roland stood. "This conversation is senseless. Go below and rest before the sun fries your wits any further."

"I've been below. I took Tamara down not thirty minutes ago. But, like you, I imbibed the drug this dawn. I understood we would take turns at this day shift of ours. And this conversation is not senseless. It makes perfect sense, and if you were not so stubborn, you would know it."

Roland could stand no more of Eric's rationalizing. He started for the great hall. But his persistent friend followed on his heels. At the foot of the worn stone stairs, Roland turned. "You want a turn guarding the castle, be my guest. But stop hounding me, Eric. I need to be by myself for a time."

Roland hurried up the stairs. Thankfully, Eric remained at the bottom.

He moved past the second level, and the entrance to Jamey's apartment. He continued upward, beyond the third level, and the decaying chambers that hadn't been used since his time as a mortal. The stairs ended abruptly at a heavy wood door, and Roland shoved it open. He stepped into the weapons room, a huge, circular tomb, without windows. It was black as pitch, but he could see clearly.

Suits of armor stood like dust-coated specters, the darkness within them eyeing him with what felt to him like condemnation. Well deserved, Roland thought. Broadswords hung upon the stone walls, tarnished with neglect and time. Their finely detailed scabbards were barely discernible through the filth. Crossbows lined the floor in one section, likely inoperable by now. Bolts stood in a short, wooden box. Hundreds of them, bunched together like a porcupine's quills. Shields leaned against the wall, the faded remnants of the Courtemanche family crest upon their faces.

Roland felt bitter irony when he glanced at the black, rampant lion, teeth bared, upon a field of red.

The beast and the blood. How appropriate.

He tore his gaze from the grim reminders of his past, of his family, and strode toward the ladder at the far end of the room. As he neared the top, he shoved at the trapdoor above him, and climbed through it to the tower room. He found the long, wooden matches upon the table where he'd left them, and struck one against the rough stone wall. Then he lit the candles until the entire room was aglow.

Like the chamber below, this one was circular. The walls had been lined with slits, from which the archers of old could shoot at intruders if the castle came under siege. Roland had sealed the slits only recently. There were times when he rested here, by day, rather than in the dungeons beneath the earth.

He wouldn't do so again. The dungeons were fitting enough for a man such as he.

For a moment, he stood in the room's center and turned slowly. His paintings stood all around him. Those he'd done as a boy, all but ruined by the ravaging hands of time. Once they'd been fanciful images of dragons and knights and heroic dreams. Then there were the portraits, which had come much later. The faces of his mother, and father. The accusing eyes of his brothers.

Upon an easel, the unfinished portrait of Rhiannon drew him nearer.

He'd come to this room to destroy it, to destroy all of them. He intended to slice them to shreds. He was no painter, no artist. He had not the heart of a poet, but the heart of a villain. What right did he have to hold to these memories of a human with a soul? They were false. Utter lies, all of them.

He drew a dagger from a sheath at his hip, and lifted it. He strode up to the portrait.

But something stopped him. He knew not what, only that it was a force stronger than his anger. He gazed at the image, that was now only a jumble of vague shapes and outlines. In it, he saw Rhiannon, her almond eyes reaching out to him, filled with warmth, and light. With a strangled sob, he dropped the dagger to the stone floor.

He turned his back to the painting and faced instead a small table where his paints and pallets and brushes stood at the ready. Beside it, stood another ladder. He looked slowly upward, to the trapdoor at the top. Above was the top of the castle.

He used to go up there as a boy, and look out over the woods to the spot where the two rivers joined. Narrow, rapid Tordu, laughing as it bounded into the broad, calm waters of the Loire. As one, the two rivers continued their unending journey southward in a glistening, glittering strand.

Beyond the trapdoor was daylight by now. The warm rays of a golden sun, with nothing overhead to prevent its touch. He started forward, placed his hands on the rungs.

Then he paused, and looked again toward the painting. He moved as a blind man, guided by unseen hands. He grabbed up the brushes, and a pallet.

Her head throbbed, and her stomach seemed alive, the way it twisted and writhed within her. She felt slightly stronger now than she had when she'd first stirred, to find Tamara in worried attendance. She'd fed, and gradually, her strength had begun to filter back into her.

"Where is he?" She saw Tamara's face tighten when she asked the question.

"I don't know. Eric said he'd holed himself up in the tower room all day. Then at dusk, he went outside. He hasn't come back." The young one searched Rhiannon's eyes. "You were hoping he'd be here when you woke."

Rhiannon shrugged, hoping to hide her disappointment. "I was only curious."

Tamara touched her hand. "Don't be too disappointed in him, Rhiannon. Eric said he was pretty distraught over what happened." She frowned, her pretty face puckering. "Not that he doesn't deserve to be."

"Oh, posh, Tamara, I'm fine. And don't tell me you don't enjoy a small sip or two in the throes of passion."

Tamara blushed. "Well, yes . . . but—"

"I like to think he was so overwhelmed with desire for me that he took leave of his senses. It's rather flattering, actually."

Tamara shook her head. "Eric thinks the drug was to blame. He feels terrible about it."

Rhiannon tilted her head to one side. "I know little of chemistry. Do you think he's right?"

"Oh, yes. Eric is a genius about those things." She glanced at Rhiannon, then lowered her lashes. "Was it . . . very nice?"

Rhiannon almost smiled. Perhaps would have, if not for the lingering pain lodged in the center of her chest, for which she had no explanation. She'd never encountered a vampiress so embarrassed to discuss sex. "My body nearly exploded at his touch," she said frankly. "I've wanted him for a very long time, you know."

Tamara faced her fully then. "So, why do I see such sadness in your eyes?"

Rhiannon blinked and turned away.

"Come on, Rhiannon. If you aren't going to talk to me, then who?"

She met the younger woman's gaze once more. She sensed only genuine caring emanating from her. "My body was sated."

"But?"

Rhiannon sighed. "It was almost as if he were alone as he plunged himself into me. Almost as if I weren't even there."

Tamara nodded sagely. "You wanted tenderness, some cuddling, some talking. I understand."

Rhiannon lifted her brows. "Cuddling? Where do you come by such ideas, fledgling? Do I honestly look to you like the type of woman who needs cuddling?"

Tamara grinned. "He'll come around. Give him time."

Exasperated with the young woman's nonsense, Rhiannon flung back her covers and got to her feet. She didn't miss the sudden widening of Tamara's eyes, before she turned her back. Imagine, being so bashful with another woman. Well, Rhiannon certainly had nothing to be embarrassed about. She went to the dresser, tugged out a pair of designer denims and slipped them on. At the wardrobe, she removed a thin silk blouse in a stunning electric blue, and poked her arms into the sleeves. As she fastened the onyx buttons, Tamara faced her again.

"You're going out, aren't you?"

Rhiannon nodded. "Yes, and it will be useless for you to tell me to stay here and rest. I'm immortal. Granted, I feel like a brisk wind could blow me away right now, but it will pass." She knelt near the closet and searched for a suitable pair of walking shoes.

"Eric said Roland headed for the woods, just beyond the wall."

Rhiannon turned. "Reading my mind, are you?"

"I don't have to. I'm a woman."

* * *

She'd rested too long, Rhiannon told herself as she crossed the grassy meadow, its dew dampening the hem of her jeans. Cool, moist breezes bathed her face, and the full moon lit her way. She wouldn't try to summon Roland, or to track him down by honing her senses to his. She had a feeling he would only go out of his way to avoid her if he knew she sought him.

At the meadow's edge she leaped the wall, and stepped into the darkness of the woods. Twisted, dark-skinned trees and thorny bushes surrounded her, but she pushed steadily onward, determined to find him. She had no idea what she wanted to say to him, but she knew she had to say something. Tamara had been wrong about her wishing to be cuddled, but right about the talking. She needed, desperately, to talk to Roland. More important, she needed him to talk to her.

The scents of the rivers grew stronger as she neared them, and a fine, silvery mist hung at knee level. Decomposing limbs and plants made the earth beneath her feet like a sponge. It sank with her every step.

She took her time, moving slowly, inhaling deeply to experience every aroma the night had to offer. The spinning in her head eased a bit with each passing moment, and eventually she came upon a well-worn path, meandering among the trees. She followed it, stepping in and out of the abstract patterns the moon's light painted on the ground. A small gust caused the elms to sway and groan as if in agony... or in ecstasy. Their deep tenor harmonized with the soprano voice of the breeze rushing over the smaller branches high above.

She approached a wrought-iron gate, with an elaborate C twined around its bars. It creaked as she pushed it open. The wind stiffened. Huge limbs parted, bathing the tiny cemetery in moonglow. Markers stood in uneven rows, most crumbling with age. Five stood apart, large and elaborate.

Roland stood with one hand braced against an obelisk taller than he. On the face was carved a crest, with two crossed swords above it.

Without turning, he spoke. "So, you've found me."

"So I have." She stepped nearer. The crest on the stone was one she knew well. She'd seen the same rampant lion on Roland's shield when she'd found him all those years ago, lying near death on a field of battle. "A relative?" she asked softly.

"My father." He straightened and waved a hand to the man-size crucifix beside him. "And my mother."

Rhiannon came forward until she stood very close to him. He didn't look at her. She glanced at the stone, at the likeness of the Savior painstakingly chiseled into it, every detail of his face clear in the swirling white marble. "The stone is breathtaking."

"In deference to her devotion." He shook his head. "I shudder to think what she would say, could she see what I've become."

She wanted to argue, but sensed it would best be put off for another time. She moved to the three nearly identical stones in the next row. Tall blocks, arched at the tops and made of obsidian. They differed only in the scenes etched into their faces.

Roland came behind her and pressed a palm to the proud stag depicted on the first. "Albert, the hunter," he said softly.

She could feel the pain emanating from him in waves as he moved to the next marker and touched the knight, seated upon a rearing destrier. "Eustace, the warrior," he told her. He then glanced toward the third, with the warship at full sail upon a choppy sea. "Pierre, the sailor. My brothers. Meet Rhiannon, the latest victim of my cruelty."

"Roland, no—"

"Ah, but you wish to hear the rest of the story, do you not?" He faced her with bitter hurt in his eyes. "I believe I left off after the first appearance of the beast that lives in my soul. You remember, how I butchered the men who'd murdered Sir Gareth?"

"You were little more than a boy, and enraged by your grief."

He nodded. "So you said before. No doubt, after a firsthand encounter with my violent side, you've reformed that opinion."

She studied his face, noting the puffy circles beneath his eyes, the haggard features, the tight jaw. "Eric believes it was a side effect of the drug."

"Eric would rather believe anything than the truth." He turned away from her. "Can you stomach the rest of the tale, Rhiannon, or would you prefer to leave now? I've no idea why, but some demon drives me to tell it to you. All of it. Perhaps I need to see your face when you finally realize what I am."

"I know what you are. If you want to tell me, I want to hear it."

His eyes narrowed, and one hand shot out to grip her upper arm. "You'd best be certain, Rhiannon. Once I begin, you will hear it all, whether you wish to or not."

She stared up into his face, aching for the pain he felt. "Are you trying to frighten me, Roland? To drive me away so you won't have to release this pain or exorcise these demons?"

"There is no exorcising these demons. They are a part of me. And if you are not frightened of me after what I did, then you are a fool."

She jerked her arm from his grasp, and drew herself up to her full height. "Then I am a fool." She walked past him, away from the markers to a small, grassy knoll beneath a giant of a tree. She sat down there, leaning her back against the rough bark. "Tell me."

CHAPTER NINE

She was a fool. She must be, to be here with him like this. Even with the remorse flooding his mind, he was aware of her. His body ached to join with hers once more, to find that blissful release that had nearly shattered the ice coating his heart. Just looking at her hands reminded him of how they'd felt stroking his arousal; like silk and firm and strong. So strong. The sight of her lips elicited the memory of the heat and moisture he'd found beyond them, the taste of her tongue. Beneath the thin silk blouse, she wore nothing. He found himself wondering if the brush of the fabric over her breasts would arouse her nipples to the hard tautness of pebbles, and if it did, whether he could stop himself from tearing it off her, and sucking at them until she begged him to stop.

She wore tight-fitting denims, damn her. They were pressed as snugly between her silken thighs as his body had been. He wanted to put his face into her lap and inhale her bittersweet fragrance. He wanted to taste her again, to become drunk on her own potent brand of spirits.

"Roland." Her voice was but a whisper. He saw her hand reaching up to him, and he took it. She tugged until he sat beside her against the tree trunk. "Tell me," she urged again.

He nodded. "The tale is not a pleasant one, Rhiannon." Roland drew one bracing breath and prepared himself for her reactions. "After the battle of which I told you,

I longed only to return home. To put aside my sword and my lust for violence forever.'' He paused, looking for a long moment into her fathomless eyes. She would, no doubt, detest him when he'd finished the tale. All the better. Perhaps she'd finally get some sense and leave him alone for good.

''But when I did, it was to find my father's enemies at the castle. The Baron Rosbrook and his clan had taken it.'' He closed his eyes at the memory. The first sight to welcome him upon returning home had been the crumbled outer wall, then the charred, blackened section of the castle that had been burned.

Rhiannon's hand touched his face. ''Your family?''

''Murdered.'' The single word carried little emphasis. But words could not describe what he'd felt that day. Looking like a man, but with the fears and the heart of a boy, he'd crossed the barren courtyard in time to see them cut his father's limp body down from the gallows, and toss it atop the others in a rickety wagon. He'd stood motionless, unable to believe that what he saw was real as the wagon clattered past him, and beneath the raised portcullis. Like a man entranced, he'd turned and followed, until the wagon stopped near the lip of a steep embankment. And one by one, the bodies had been flung over the side.

He began to tremble again, just as he had then. He wanted to shut out the memory, as he'd wanted to turn his eyes away from the heartrending sight all those years ago. And just as before, he was unable to do so. His father, his brothers, were tossed like refuse, their bodies rolling and tumbling to the very bottom of the rocky ravine. Other knights, stripped of their armor, some with the horrendous wounds of battle marring their flesh, others with no sign of injury save the telling fluid movement of their heads on boneless necks, tossed away without a prayer or a tear shed for them. Then the women. The first charred corpse was unrecognizable, until he'd glimpsed one unburned corner of the gown. His mother's gown.

"My God, Roland." Rhiannon's voice was choked, and she clutched his shoulders in her hands. She'd been inside his mind, he realized dully. She'd relived those moments of his long ago homecoming right along with him. "I had no idea," she whispered. "I'm so sorry."

"So am I, Rhiannon. Had I been at home, where I belonged, I might have prevented it."

"How? Roland, you were a boy, a boy with no knightly training when you left home. What might you have done, other than be killed yourself?"

He looked into her upturned face, and shook his head as he battled a rush of childish tears and a fierce burning in his throat. "I'll never know, will I?" He managed to swallow past the lump, and blink the blurring moisture from his eyes. "Unfortunately, I had left. I had been trained. I'd been in battle, and gained a reputation as a fierce fighter, thanks to Gareth's family. There may have been nothing I could do before the fact. But afterward—"

"If the murder of Gareth enraged you, the murder of your family and the taking of your home must have been far worse."

He nodded, remembering, experiencing it all again as he relived it for her. "It happened in an instant. I went from paralyzing shock, and unspeakable grief, to rage and a thirst for revenge that drove me close to madness. It took weeks, but I gathered an army. Some were friends of my father's. Most were knights in the employ of Gareth's family. They aided me as a matter of honor. I had avenged Gareth and their fellow knights, so they would help me to avenge my family."

"And?"

He looked into her eyes, wishing he didn't have to go on. But he did. He couldn't have stopped himself from telling her all of it now, had he wanted to.

"By my command, they gave no quarter, nor did I. Some of the Rosbrooks escaped the blade, but most died by it. Until only one remained. A younger daughter, no older than I."

He saw Rhiannon close her eyes, and assumed she was dreading what came next. "Her name was Rebecca, and she had the face of an angel. Silvery blond curls, huge blue eyes. She was an innocent. I ordered her thrown into the dungeons."

She released her breath all at once.

"Why are you relieved, Rhiannon? Because I didn't kill her outright? It would have been better if I had."

She shook her head. "I know you, Roland. After a few days, you must have realized that her father's sins were not hers, and released her."

"Released her?" He almost laughed. "No, Rhiannon. You don't know me at all. But you are partly right. In time, I regretted that she should suffer for what her father had done. I removed her from the dungeons and put her into a bedchamber on the third level. I intended to return her to her relatives, until I learned she had none left. The girl, of course, detested me for what I'd done, just as I had detested her family for the murder of mine."

"What became of her, Roland?"

He removed Rhiannon's hands from his shoulders, folded them into her lap and covered them with one of his own. He searched her face, waiting for the condemnation he was certain would appear there soon. "I decided the best I could do for her would be to wed her. To keep her in the castle and try to right the wrong I'd done by making her my bride, sharing with her my wealth and my name."

Rhiannon blinked. "Did you . . . did you love her?"

"Love is an emotion of which I am not capable, Rhiannon. Nor have I ever been, even then. Does an animal feel love?"

She parted her lips, then bit them. "What did she say to your proposal?"

"It was not a proposal. It was a command. She could marry me or return to the dungeons permanently."

She didn't flinch from his steady gaze. "Which did she choose?"

"Neither. She flung herself from the tower."

"Oh, God." Rhiannon closed her eyes, and he noted the appearance of moisture on her thick lashes.

"So, now you know." He let his chin fall to his chest. A second later, he felt her fingers threading through his hair. That she could bear to touch him at all now, amazed him. That she did so with such tenderness was beyond comprehension.

He lifted his head, and met her damp gaze. "I swear, I didn't intend to hurt you, Rhiannon. I simply lost my senses. I allowed the violent nature that is truly me, to take control. I'm more sorry than you can imagine."

"I know. As I know you were sorry after the girl's death, and more than likely, after every battle you ever fought from then on."

He shook his head. "I became a mercenary knight, a hired fighter. I left the castle in the hands of caretakers. I couldn't bear to be here, with the memories of my past mistakes haunting me in every hall."

"Ah, but now you alter the tale, Roland. For I knew of you long before you knew of me. The gallant knight who fought for a price, but always on the side of the weak, and always on the side of the just. I knew you were one of The Chosen, Roland. I was fascinated by you."

He frowned, not believing her.

"It's true," she said. "It was years after your knighting, of course, and I knew nothing of what horrors had befallen you in your youth. I heard tales of your valor and I tracked you down. For some time, I followed you and your men. God, what it did to me to see you leading them, astride that magnificent black war-horse with the eyes that seemed to blaze. To witness you in battle was worse yet. The gleaming armor, the powerful way you would wield that sword, your fearlessness."

"You saw me fight?"

She nodded. "The battle at Lorraine, at midnight, fought to free the kidnapped Lady la Claire. And the one in Normandy, when you helped the fallen men from the field, friend and foe alike. So I know you exaggerate this battle lust you claim."

He felt his jaw go slack. "Rhiannon, why did you never tell me this?"

She shrugged. "I was afraid you'd laugh at me. An immortal vampiress, smitten by a man she'd never met. But I was, you know. I wanted to come to you, even then. Never had I seen a man so strong, or so brave. I was enamored of you, Roland. Then, you heard of Bryan, Gareth's young son, that same babe you'd rescued from the wolf, a man grown by then. He was in dire need, and you rushed to his aid."

Roland nodded. "Yes. His castle was under siege and he couldn't withstand the attackers much longer. A messenger managed to slip out, and brought word to me."

"And you went there, knowing full well you were short on men, and still exhausted from the last skirmish. With little food, and weapons in need of repair, you went. By night, you went, so I was able to follow, and to watch."

He nodded. "The enemy outnumbered us ten to one," he said, recalling his shock as he'd peered at them from the cover of the forest.

"And you attacked them all the same, but only after releasing any of your men who wished to leave. Few did, as I recall. That battle was the fiercest I had ever seen, Roland. I was terrified for you. You managed to rout the invaders, but in the end, you were cut down. I found you lying in the dirt, near death. You remember?"

He nodded, recalling vividly his first glimpse of her. A mysterious, utterly beautiful lady in a flowing black gown, leaning over him, whispering that he would live, that she would not allow him to die. He remembered her tears, raining down on his face, and the way their moist warmth transcended his pain.

"Of course, I remember. I was dying. It was then you transformed me."

"Knowing full well you were worthy of the gift. More worthy than any of us, perhaps. Yet you spend eternity grieving over past mistakes and condemning yourself for a passionate nature."

Roland stood, and gazed upward at the stars. "You call it passion. I call it evil."

She was on her feet, at his side before he was aware she'd moved. She had a talent for that, moving soundlessly, as if floating. She stood before him and lifted her soft palms to cup his face. She drew it down, so he was gazing into her eyes, rather than at the starry night. Of the two, he thought, her eyes were the most lovely, the most brilliant.

"It is time for you to let the past die."

He felt his heart contract painfully in his chest. "I cannot."

"Yes, you can. There is so much for you here, in the present. So much you deny yourself. So much you could take and savor—"

"There is nothing, Rhiannon."

"There is Jamey."

He released a ragged breath, though the pain inside only grew sharper. "Yes, there is Jamey. I've been giving him a lot of thought these past days."

Her hands fell from his face, and settled upon his shoulders.

"I'm beginning to think you were right. The boy may be better off with his natural father. He needs a normal life, not one filled with danger and immortal beings. He ought to live in a suburban house, not a crumbling ruin."

She drew a thoughtful breath. "You'll still need to watch over him, even if you are able to locate his father. And there is always a chance..." She bit her lip and her eyes filled suddenly. Roland felt her wince inwardly in pain, and wondered at it. "A chance that his father will not want him," she finished. Her hands fell to her sides, and she averted her face.

"Rhiannon, what—"

"And even without the boy, you have your friends. Eric and Tamara adore you, Roland."

"They have each other." He shook his head. He couldn't tell her how terribly lonely he felt when he had to witness their happiness. It only exaggerated his own isolation.

"What about me, then?" She faced him again, gripped both his hands in hers. "Don't tell me you didn't forget all that pain when you made love to me. Don't say you didn't feel the same sheer joy of being alive, that you made me feel."

He closed his eyes. "I did not make love to you. I assaulted you."

She drew his hands toward her, pulling them around her to the small of her back. Then she left them there, to slip her arms around his neck and press her body to his. "Perhaps you will get it right the next time, then."

He didn't push her away. He couldn't. Staring down into the endless pools of her eyes, he simply couldn't. "There cannot be a next time, Rhiannon."

"There can. There will." She pressed her lips to his, parted them, swept her tongue into his mouth.

Summoning every ounce of his faltering control, he released her and turned away. "No."

"But Roland, I—"

"No, Rhiannon. You still don't comprehend it, do you?" He shoved his hands roughly through his hair. "There is so much in you that reminds me of who I once was. The impulsiveness, the passion, the way you laugh in the face of danger. Dammit, Rhiannon, it is never as hard for me to control my nature as when I am with you. Your very presence stirs in my soul the qualities I constantly fight to suppress."

She said nothing. He couldn't turn to face her. Looking at her would only tempt him anew to give in to the beast. It was ironic that the one thing he wanted most in this world was the thing that he must deny himself. It was almost as if the gods were laughing at him, dangling this prize before him just to see him pay for his sins. "Sometimes, Rhiannon, I believe you are my punishment. My curse."

He turned then, and stopped dead. The pain in her eyes was such as he'd never before seen. Yet they remained dry. Wide, and hurting, but utterly dry. Without a word, she turned and walked away, toward the wrought-iron gate.

Her rapid pace was brought up short, though, when Eric appeared just beyond it, emerging from the mist like a ghost.

"Rhiannon, thank God I've found you. Is Roland—"

"Here, Eric," Roland called. He moved forward, glancing at Rhiannon's stricken face. He'd hurt her again. Severely this time. He felt it as surely as he felt the river-moistened breeze on his face, and he had no idea how, or even if, he could remedy it.

"Excuse me," she muttered, then staggered away into the densest part of the woods.

Roland took a step to go after her, but Eric's hand on his shoulder stopped him. In the distance, he heard Rhiannon retching violently. He shook Eric's hand away and again began to go after her.

"Dammit, Roland, listen to me. Jamey is gone."

Roland halted on the dark path, his lower legs swathed in mist, river-damp air filling his lungs. An icy hand closed around his chest. He turned. "Gone? What do you mean, 'gone'?"

"He's left. Run off." Eric fished in his pocket, and pressed a folded sheet of paper into Roland's hand. "We found this in his room."

Roland glanced again in the direction Rhiannon had gone. He heard nothing now. He sent the probing fingers of his mind out to hers, but found it closed to him.

"I'll go," Eric said softly. "Read the damned note and meet me back at the castle."

Roland watched him go, then smoothed the note open with hands that were not steady, and read;

Dear Tamara,

I have to leave. Please don't try to find me. I'm a man now, and I can take care of myself. But as long as I am with Roland, he'll think he has to take care of me. Now everything is happening like it did before. Curtis is back. DPI is driving everyone crazy, all because of me. It was my fault Rhiannon got knifed at the match. And I know it was my fault she got hurt again last night. I heard you and Eric talking. I don't know what happened, only that Roland hurt her somehow, and that it was because of that stupid drug he's been taking to keep him awake. He wouldn't have been taking it if it hadn't been for me. He shouldn't have. Even I know better than to mess with drugs that way.

Tell Eric to lay off on the chemicals. He's always trying to change what he is, what all of you are. Tell him I think you're about as close to perfect as you can get. Better than any of the normal people I know, except my mom.

Don't worry about the DPI guys catching up with me. I'm not stupid. I know how to be careful. I'll write to you when I figure out where I want to stay, and get my life together, just so you'll see that I'm okay.

I really love you guys. All of you, but especially you, Tam. You've been like an older sister to me. I'll miss you, but I have to do this. Try to understand.

Love,
Jamey

Roland closed his eyes slowly, and crumpled the sheet in his fist. "Damn."

She stiffened at the approaching steps, but it was only Eric. She swallowed the bitter bile in her throat and schooled her face into an emotionless mask. Not for anything in the world would Eric see that her heart had been torn to shreds. He'd only report the fact to Roland. She would die before she'd let him know how much he'd hurt her.

His curse. Perhaps he was right, at that. She'd been her father's curse, and now Roland's. Rejected by the only two men in the world from whom she'd craved acceptance. Shut out by the only two men she'd ever loved.

Loved?

Posh, she didn't love Roland. She wasn't foolish enough to have allowed her heart to become involved in what was purely a physical attraction. She'd loved once, and once only. She'd loved her father, and his disdain had taught her well never to love again.

She lifted her gaze to watch Eric's hasty approach. She waited until he reached her.

"Are you all right?"

She lifted her palms up and glanced down at her own form. "I seem to be, don't I?"

"You were ill. I heard you—"

"Dry heaves. A reaction to too much exertion after... after what happened. No more than that, I assure you."

His eyes narrowed and she knew he didn't believe her. It was to his credit that he didn't pry.

"Go on, tell me what's happened. You didn't come charging into the woods to check on my health."

"No, I didn't. Though maybe I should have." He took her arm, his eyes scanning her face with some concern. "Come with me. I'll explain as we go."

He did, and by the time they entered the great hall, Rhiannon knew the situation was grave. Jamey, determined though he was, couldn't hope to outsmart or outmaneuver DPI. Her concern for the boy acted as a buffer against the sting of Roland's condemnation. She had a focus.

Tamara paced, her face wet with tears, her eyes as red-rimmed as a drunkard's. She whirled toward the door when they entered, and it was heartbreaking to see the disappointment in her eyes when she saw that it wasn't the boy.

Frederick sat on the floor, knees drawn as close to his bulky chest as he could get them. He looked as if he'd been crying, as well.

Rhiannon went to Tamara, and folded the slight woman into her arms. "There's no need for such devastation, fledgling. We'll find the little rat in no time."

"How? We don't even know where to begin."

"Your cat's gone, too," Frederick moaned from where he sat. "I should have been watching him closer. It's all my fault. What if those bad men get Jamey? What will they do to him?"

"No bad men are going to get Jamey," Eric intoned.

Tamara sniffed and straightened. "It's not your fault, Frederick. We were all supposed to be watching him. Jamey is too smart for us, that's all."

"I'm stupid," Frederick said softly. "If I wasn't so stupid—"

Rhiannon stepped to him, bent over and pulled him to his feet. "Freddy, you are not now, nor have you ever been, stupid. I won't hear such nonsense from you again. Jamey slipped by all of us. Do you think *we're* stupid?"

He shook his head.

"You're right. We're not. And neither are you. Now..." She turned, slowly, addressing all of them. "Enough of this weeping and wailing. I cannot stand it. You're all forgetting one important thing."

"And what is that?" The voice was Roland's. He stood just inside the doorway. She hadn't heard him come in, and his eyes sought hers now, not hard with condemnation, but desperate for help.

"Who I am," she said, her voice so low it was only a hint above a whisper, but as clear and resonant as a bell. "Rhianikki, daughter of Pharaoh, princess of Egypt. I was a priestess of Isis, studied the words of Osiris. I felt the burning sands of Egypt beneath my feet when the pyramids were still new. Within my soul is the wisdom of the ages, young ones, and there is nothing, *nothing*, that I cannot do."

She watched Roland's reaction to her speech, fully expecting to see the familiar skepticism on his face. Instead, she thought she saw relief.

There was no doubt it was hope that filled Tamara's round eyes. "What should we do, Rhiannon?"

"Not we, Tamara. You. You are the closest to Jamey. You and he had a psychic bond even before Eric transformed you, isn't that true?"

"Yes, but—"

"No buts. You need only concentrate on the boy. Seek him out with your mind."

Tamara shook her head. "I can't. I only feel him when he's trying to reach me, or—or when he's in trouble."

"You can. It takes only the power of the mind. I will show you the way, Tamara." Rhiannon turned to Roland. "We'll need a quiet room. One with no outside auras cluttering it up."

Roland frowned. "No one has used the chambers on the third level in centuries."

She nodded and turned to Frederick, who was sorely in need of something to do. "Freddy, in Roland's chambers, in the small dresser beside the bed, you'll find two special candles and a packet of incense in a silver chalice. Will you get them for me?"

Frederick limped off to do her bidding. Eric scoffed. "Incense and candles? What kind of nonsense is this? We ought to be out searching for the boy."

"Be my guest, Eric. Go and search to your heart's content. You'll only be wasting your time. We have to know where he is."

Eric shook his head. "Don't take it personally, Rhiannon. I'm a man who believes in science, not hocus-pocus."

"No doubt were you human right now, you wouldn't believe in the existence of a race of undead blood-drinkers," she retorted.

He looked at the floor.

"Eric, listen to her," Tamara said softly. She turned from him. "I trust you, Rhiannon. Just tell me what to do."

Eric threw his hands in the air and turned to Roland. "Are you going to stand still for this?"

Roland shrugged. "Unless you have a better idea, or a clue where to begin searching..."

Frederick returned with the incense and candles. Rhiannon took them and led Tamara up the stone staircase, Roland and Eric following. On the third level, she passed several rotting doors before pausing at one. She stood still a moment, then nodded. "This one."

"Why?" Roland stared at her intently.

"You object?"

She watched him for a moment as he struggled with the decision. She didn't know why, and she told herself she didn't care. He'd made his feelings for her clear enough. She wouldn't trouble herself about them any further. Her only goal now was to locate the boy. Then she would leave and never return.

Finally, Roland sighed and nodded once. "Go on."

She pushed the door open and stepped inside, Tamara behind her. For just a moment, she paused in the darkness to examine the chamber with her preternatural vision. The outermost wall curved with the shape of the tower, but the other three were flat. Two windows had been cut through the stone on that curving wall. Narrow openings, narrower without than within, that had no glass in them to block the night wind coming through. Two benches, facing each other, and carved of castle stone, sat near the windows. Ancient rushes, dry as husks, lined the cold floor, crackling beneath her steps. The tapestries that had once been brilliant works of art, hung in straggles from the walls.

Rhiannon turned to Roland and Eric. "It would be better if you waited below."

"And leave Tamara to play sorceress games alone with you? Not quite, Rhiannon. I'm staying." Eric stepped farther into the room, leaned back against the stone wall and crossed his arms over his chest.

"Eric—"

"It's all right, Tamara," Rhiannon said. "I'm fairly used to being mistrusted by males."

"It isn't that—"

She quelled Eric's protests with a single glance. "I'll need your cooperation if you insist on staying. You must be utterly silent and still, and you must make an effort to keep your mind closed to us. Agreed?"

"Fine."

She glanced once at Roland, though even looking at him brought a stab of pain so intense she had trouble keeping it hidden. "You won't know I'm here," he told her.

Oh, but she would.

She moved into the room's center, knelt down and waited for Tamara to join her. "I want you to lie down," she told her as she placed the candles and poured some of the incense into the chalice.

"I might have some matches," Roland offered.

"Silence." Rhiannon's whispered word carried a tone of authority, and Roland said no more.

Rhiannon stretched herself out on the crisp rushes, lying on her back. At her right, near her shoulder, but far enough away to be safe, was one blood-red candle. Near her waist, the silver dish, and a small mound of dried incense. Near her hip, the second candle. Beyond those three items, Tamara lay still.

Rhiannon closed her eyes. "Relax, Tamara. Close your eyes. Put all fear and worry from your mind. Feel the stone floor beneath your back begin to soften. Inhale slowly, deeply. That's it. Hold the breath in your lungs for a moment. Drain the nourishment from the air before you release it once more. Slowly...slowly. Yes, all of it. Every bit, until your lungs are utterly emptied. Now, wait... wait...and inhale once more. Fill yourself to bursting, but slowly. Yes."

She kept her voice low, even, hypnotic. "With each breath you take the floor is becoming softer. Feel it? It's like down, now. You can feel yourself sinking into it, can't you?"

"Yes."

"Good. Now, continue just as you're doing. And I will do the same. When your mind is floating free, you will know, Tamara. Reach out to Jamey then. Think of him. Put his image in front of your eyes. Surround yourself with the memory of his scent. Concentrate on the precise curl of each lock of his hair, the sound of his laughter, the warmth of his touch. In this way, you will find him."

Rhiannon began her own ritual breathing, then. She allowed herself to relax, and began sinking into the abyss of her own psyche. She would focus on Pandora, and hope for some clue through the cat.

Roland stood beside Eric, leaning back against the wall, watching the bizarre ritual. True, he'd been willing to give Rhiannon a chance, especially since he was afraid to open his mouth to object. He seemed to wound her every time he spoke to her. Why, he wondered? Why did he hurt her the way he did? He certainly hadn't intended to. God knew, she didn't deserve it. He'd shared with Rhiannon his most terrible secret, the one he'd been sure would cause her to hate and fear him. Instead, she'd offered comfort. Dammit to hell, she'd shed tears for him! And he'd wounded her in return.

She hadn't looked him squarely in the eye for more than a second at a time since she'd left him in the *cimetière*. He regretted that he'd caused her such pain. But at least now, her feelings toward him seemed to have cooled. One of them needed to remain at a distance, or he'd end up hurting her beyond repair. And looking at her slender body, relaxed in a trancelike state on the rush-strewn floor, he knew damned well it couldn't be him.

As the minutes ticked away, though, even Roland began to doubt her. What sort of witchcraft was she working here? How could lying about in age-old rushes help Jamey?

He was eager to be out and searching for the boy, and worried in case DPI should beat him to it. Then, with a small popping sound, the candles standing between the two women burst into flame. A second later, the incense in the dish began smoldering, sending a soft gray spiral of fragrant smoke upward.

CHAPTER TEN

Nothing came. Nothing she wanted, at least. Rhiannon sat up abruptly, and pinched the candles out with her fingers. She massaged her temples and sighed.

This had been *her* room. Rebecca's room. The girl who'd thrown herself from the tower to escape marriage to Roland. Images of the young, lovely creature had flooded into Rhiannon's psyche, making it impossible to concentrate on Pandora. There was something troubled in Rebecca's spirit, something uneasy. She was not at peace.

"Rhiannon?"

She glanced up at Roland, saw the question in his eyes. "I'm sorry."

"He's in a car."

Tamara's small voice startled them all. She still lay on her back, but her eyes were open. She remained motionless, as if she feared that moving would shake the images from her mind.

"He's in a small, black car. There's a blue duffel bag in his lap, with some clothes inside, and a little money. And his cleats. His cleats are in there, too." With that sentence, her voice warbled and her eyes filled.

Eric started forward, but Rhiannon held up a hand.

"Tamara, who is driving the car?"

She frowned. "I don't know him. He's very big. Like a wrestler. His hair is cut close to his head so it sticks up in bristles. It's dark. His nose is like a bulldog's." She frowned harder. "There is a tattoo on his right forearm, a cobra."

"Lucien," Roland whispered.

"Can you tell which direction they drive, Tamara?"

She shook her head. "There are mountains, with snow at the peaks." Tamara sat up slowly, and Eric bent to help her to her feet. She met his intense gaze. "It's the same man who attacked Rhiannon, isn't it? He has Jamey now."

Eric nodded.

Never before had Rhiannon seen such an expression on the fledgling's face. Always, she'd seemed so timid, so mild. Now, her eyes glowed with the fierceness of an approaching storm. She tossed her head like a lioness, her jaw tight with what looked like rage. "If he hurts Jamey, I will kill him." She spoke in a calm, level voice, leaving no doubt she meant what she said. Stiffly, she moved past Eric and out the door. Eric hurried behind her.

"Well. I've never seen her like that."

"I have," Roland said softly. "But only when the boy was threatened."

She turned in the doorway, where she'd been standing to watch them go. She was alone with Roland, she realized all at once. She swallowed the lump that leapt into her throat. "This was *her* room, wasn't it?"

He glanced around him, and nodded. "How did you know?"

"I feel her here. She did not detest you so thoroughly as you think, you know."

He shook his head. "That, I cannot believe."

She shrugged. "It's not my concern what you believe. I only thought you might like to know." She turned to go, but he caught her shoulder from behind.

"My words, in the *cimetière* were not meant to cause you pain, Rhiannon. If they did, then I'm sorry."

She stiffened. "It takes more than words to cause me any pain. Don't worry yourself on that account."

He pulled her around to face him, and she saw the regret in his eyes. "Rhiannon, I hurt you. I know I did, and believe me, I wish I could take back the words that caused that hurt."

"Why take back the truth?" She removed his hand from her shoulder with a brush of her own. "We have the boy to find, Roland. This conversation only delays his rescue."

Roland sat in the front of the rental car, map unfolded on his lap. Of them all, he was the most familiar with the area and the terrain, having traveled much of it by horseback in times long past. True, the towns and cities and roads differed. But the lay of the land was the same. And the only snowcapped mountains near enough for Lucien to have reached within such a brief span of time, were in the direction they now traveled.

Eric drove as Roland navigated. Rhiannon remained in the back seat beside Tamara. The small vehicle seemed to reverberate with the tension it held. It was Eric who finally broke the silence.

"I believe I owe you an apology, Rhiannon."

"Whatever for?"

"I didn't take your meditation seriously. I should have."

She waved a dismissive hand. "Don't give up your skepticism so easily. We haven't found Jamey yet."

"But we're on his trail. Tamara feels it too strongly for it to be a mistake. I don't doubt that."

Roland shook his head. "Admit it, Eric. She had you hooked from the moment those candles burst to life on their own."

Eric smiled and glanced over his shoulder at Rhiannon. Roland wished he could do the same, but looking at her had traumatic effects on his mind.

"He's right," Eric said. "That was a convincing display."

By the tone of Rhiannon's voice, Roland knew the exact expression on her face. That almost smile. The look in her eyes that said she knew something you didn't. Many, many things you didn't.

"A simple parlor trick for an immortal, Eric. I could teach you to do it. To be honest, I usually light the candles in a more mundane manner, but I was angry and wanted to be sure you were suitably chastened."

Roland glanced sideways at his friend in time to see the surprise on his face.

"Well, it worked." Eric frowned and adjusted his mirror for a better view of her face. "You say you could teach me to do it?"

She must have nodded, but Roland wasn't certain. "You have all become familiar with the physical strength that comes with immortality. But the dark gift brings with it a psychic strengthening, as well. It grows with age, as the physical powers do. Lighting the candles is simply a matter of focusing your mind's power on their wicks. Like a beam of light, it hits, and they ignite.

"As both the strengths reach full potential, we can learn to combine the psychic with the physical to achieve the two feats even I've not yet mastered. But I've heard of some who have."

Roland tilted his head. "Rhiannon, there are some things better left alone."

"Of course there are," she told him. "Cobras and active volcanoes are among them. This is not."

Eric grinned wider. "She's got you there. Tell me, Rhiannon. What two feats are you speaking of?"

"One is flight. And I'm actually very close to mastering that one. I can remain aloft for just under a minute. The trick is in maintaining the speed, and keeping the mind utterly focused."

Roland did turn now. "For God's sake, Rhiannon! I had no idea you were experimenting with such nonsense. You'll get yourself killed."

Her eyes narrowed. "If I do, that will be no one's problem but my own." She shifted her gaze back to Eric. "Actually, practicing is horrible. I can only go up once a night. Then I fall and am usually too broken and bruised to do more than crawl back to my lair and wait for the healing sleep."

Eric frowned, and Roland felt the glance he shot his way. "That *is* pushing your luck, Rhiannon. Suppose one night you're too badly injured to make it back before dawn?"

She shrugged. "Then I supposed I would roast, wouldn't I?"

She was trying to hurt him, Roland thought. Her words were filled with bitterness and pain; pain caused by his own careless words. She was only speaking this way to strike back. What in God's name had he said to hurt her this much?

"And the other feat?" Eric prompted.

"Ah, this will amaze you. There are some, I am told, who are able to alter their form."

"You mean, change shape? In what way?"

"Any way they wish, I imagine. The tales I've heard name only one immortal capable of such feats, and the forms he's said to have taken include the raven, the wolf and the infamous vampire bat."

Now, Roland noted with a twinge of gratitude, even Tamara's attention was caught. She'd done nothing throughout the entire ride but stare out the window into the passing night.

"You've got to be kidding," she said, eyes wide. "A vampire bat?"

"Well, I like to think he has a sense of humor, and did it on a lark. Honestly, if given the ability to be anything one wished, why would one choose to be a nasty little bat?"

"Who is this talented immortal?" Eric asked, and Roland could tell by the tone of his voice that he was fascinated by the possibilities.

"He is called Damien. He is said to be the oldest and most powerful of any of us. I never sought him out. I have no desire to meet the man."

"Why not? I'd be thrilled to talk to him," Eric said.

Rhiannon lowered her voice deliberately, Roland was sure. "You know the trick I did, igniting the candles with my mind?" Eric nodded. "Well, it is said Damien can perform the same feat on people, mortal and immortal alike. He just looks at them, and...*poof!* Living torches."

Tamara nudged her with an elbow. "You're trying to scare us." She looked at Roland. "None of this is true, is it, Roland?"

He sighed. "As far as I know, it's all true. Though I've never witnessed any of it firsthand."

Eric shot Roland an accusing stare. "Why have you never told me any of this?"

"As I said, there are some things best left alone. You think I want you out leaping from rooftops and breaking your neck? Changing yourself into a baboon and then getting stuck that way? Seeking out this man who can burn you to a cinder?"

"Honestly, Roland, you are such a—" Rhiannon stopped in the middle of the sentence, her entire body going rigid. Her hand flew to her lips. "Stop the car! Stop, Eric, at once!"

Eric slammed his foot onto the brake pedal. Tires skidded in gravel as he tried to pull to the side. Rhiannon was out the door before the vehicle had come to a full stop. Like a gazelle, she leaped the ditch and bounded into the forest.

Roland raced after her, having no idea what to expect. He knew Eric and Tamara were right behind him, but his entire being was focused on Rhiannon. He'd felt the slap of her sudden shock as if it had been his own. But she'd been so closed off to him since they'd spoken in the *cimetière* that he hadn't been able to tell what was wrong.

Then he saw her. A quivering, sobbing heap on the ground, her arms around the sleek, black body. Pandora wasn't moving. The cat's eyes were closed, and there was a sickening twist to one foreleg. Blood caked to a cut near her silken ear.

Roland knelt and pulled Rhiannon away. Eric and Tamara were there, and as Eric began to examine the cat, Roland held Rhiannon in his arms. She sobbed helplessly, her entire body quaking with each spasm. Gone was the haughty, arrogant princess. In his arms, he held a devastated child, and it tore his heart out to see her so tortured.

"She's alive," Eric said softly. "But I'm not sure we can save her. She needs a veterinarian."

"Then we'll find her one," Roland declared, his arms tightening of their own will around her shuddering body. Her tears soaked his cloak at the shoulder. "There's a town five miles east of here. It will only be a small detour." Roland lowered his head, pressed his lips to hers. "She'll be all right, Rhiannon,'' he whispered into her hair. "I promise you."

She shook her head against his neck. "She...has to be." She drew a ragged breath and lifted her head to gaze into his eyes. "I'm s-sorry." Stiffening, she pulled herself from his embrace. She bent over the cat again, carefully slipped both forearms beneath the body and lifted her. Then she turned and started for the car, her shoulders still quaking with involuntary sobs.

Roland swallowed hard. Had he so alienated her that she couldn't even accept comfort from him?

He raced ahead of her, and opened the car's rear door. Rhiannon folded herself into the vehicle, the cat still in her arms. She scooted across the back seat, cradling the huge animal's head and shoulders in her lap. Roland gently eased Pandora's hindquarters in as far as he could, and closed the door with care. Tamara squeezed into the front, between the two men.

As Eric drove, Rhiannon whispered, stroking the cat's big, still head. She spoke as if no one else were in the car, addressing the animal as if it were human. "Don't leave me now, Pandora. There is no one else, you know. Only you. If you go, I'll be alone again." Between each few words, a sob was torn from her breast.

Tamara turned in the seat, tears dampening her lashes. "You love her very much, don't you?"

Rhiannon shook her head briskly. Her hair hung over her face, still bowed to the cat's. Tears glued strands of it to her cheeks. "Don't be ridiculous." She sniffed and sobbed once more. "I'm an immortal. I don't believe in loving anything." She stroked Pandora's head. "It's just that...she has loved me. Just as I am, she has loved me. No one else ever has."

"Oh, Rhiannon—"

"I never had to prove myself to her. I was never unworthy in her huge green eyes. Never her curse."

Roland winced at her words.

"Unconditional acceptance, absolute devotion. I've never known those things in all my years of existence except from Pandora. She wouldn't dream of rejecting me as not good enough to deserve her attention."

Roland felt a stinging in the backs of his eyes, and he heard a suspicious sniff from Eric. "Rhiannon, no one could ever see you as unworthy—"

"No one but you, you mean? Ah, but you were not the first. No, that honor was reserved for the man who sired me. Don't think your indifference is so important, Roland. The greatest Pharaoh of Egypt labeled me his curse long before you did."

Eric pulled the car to a stop at an all-night service station, and as the attendant emerged, he rolled down his window and asked in French if there was a veterinarian in town. When the answer was affirmative, Roland got out and demanded a telephone and a directory. He would rouse the man from sleep, if necessary.

As he waited for the veterinarian to answer his telephone, he berated himself endlessly. He'd known nothing of Rhiannon's past. That her father had rejected her. Oh, God, and with the same words he'd used in the *cimetière*. He could not have caused her more heartache, he suspected, had he been deliberately seeking to destroy her. Could he not inhale without hurting her? How could he repair the pain he'd caused?

Rhiannon leaned over the table in the clinic that was no more than a room in the man's home. "You ought to keep her sedated until I return," Rhiannon told him. "There is no telling how she will react to strangers."

"Oui, I will take no chances, *mademoiselle."* He rubbed his balding head, and adjusted the rectangular specs on his nose. "I have treated many species, but never ze pet panther." He paused, but Rhiannon offered no explanation. After a moment he shrugged and let it go. "She was struck by ze auto, *non?"*

"I don't know. I found her in the woods like this." Rhiannon glanced up into the mortal's pale blue eyes. "If you can save her, I will build you a new clinic. An entire hospital, if you wish. I will give you more money than you can make in a year. Three years."

His smile was sudden, and genuine. He took her hand and patted it. "I adore animals, *mademoiselle.* You share zat with me, *non?* I will save her eef I can, whether you promise me the moon or bushel of apples as payment." He released her hand to stroke Pandora's silken fur.

"I believe you will." She sniffed, and swiped at her eyes. She hadn't cried so much since the guards had carried her from her father's palace, to be placed in the temple of Isis. She'd been a five-year-old child then. She was ageless now. It was ridiculous, how fond she'd grown of the cat. "I don't know when I can come for her. A few days, perhaps."

"I will care for her. Do not fear."

"Thank you." It didn't seem enough. She'd meant what she'd said. If he pulled Pandora through this, she would shower him with rewards.

Leaving the cat there felt like abandoning a babe. Rhiannon fought her tears and forced herself to go. Jamison needed her right now. She mustn't forget that.

In the car, she sat in stony silence for a time, until Tamara took her hand and held it firmly. "She'll be all right."

Rhiannon nodded. "Lucien will not."

"You think he did that to her?"

Rhiannon nodded again. "Pandora was with Jamey. Now Jamey is with Lucien, and Pandora is on a cold table. Yes, I believe he is responsible. And I believe he will wish for death long before it's granted him." She closed her eyes and sent her thoughts over the miles. *Do you hear me, Lucien? I'm coming for you, you know.*

Her eyes flew wide with surprise when she heard, echoing through her mind, the reply. *I'll be waiting.*

"It will be dawn soon. We need to seek shelter."

Tamara sighed in frustration and Roland well understood her feelings. "We'll do Jamey no good if we all sizzle in the sun, Tamara."

"True enough."

Eric continued driving, but turned onto smaller and narrower dirt tracks, in search of a safe resting spot for all of them. Finally, an abandoned barn came into view. Roland pointed to it. "We can drive around to the back, to hide the car from view. Better yet, get the door open and pull it right inside. What do you think?"

"That would be the best idea. The ground in front looks smooth enough. Why don't you open the door, and see if there's room inside?"

Roland did, wrenching the door. It gave way and slid on its rusted tracks until there was room enough for the car to pass through. The barn was empty, save for a huge mound of musty-smelling hay and a few ancient-looking tools scattered about. Roland moved a broken pitchfork and an old milk can out of the way, and waved for Eric to bring the car in.

As soon as the engine died, Roland closed the barn door, plunging them into darkness.

"This will be safe enough," Tamara observed.

"Can't be certain about cracks and crevices, Tamara. We'd best burrow into that haystack before we sleep, just to be safe."

She nodded, moving closer to Eric, who slipped his arm around her shoulders and squeezed her closer. She let her head lean onto his shoulder and closed her eyes. "What do you suppose this Lucien person wants with Jamey? He's not DPI."

Eric shook his head.

"He wants immortality, Tamara," Rhiannon told her. "He wants me to transform him. I imagine he will use Jamey's life to bargain with."

Tamara grimaced, and turned fully into Eric's arms. Roland felt his stomach clench and unclench in involuntary spasms. His arms ached to wrap around Rhiannon in the same manner. But he told himself the breach between them was a good thing. No matter how bad it felt. No matter how he longed to erase the hurt he'd caused her. It was better this way.

"He knows we're coming," Rhiannon said. "He has incredible psychic capacity for a human. He's waiting for us."

"At least we know Jamison will be kept alive in the meantime," Roland said, seeking to comfort Tamara in some small way. Unfortunately, he was about to cause her a great deal more discomfort.

"Tamara, there is something I need to tell you. About Jamey."

She turned, frowning. "What is it, Roland?"

Roland averted his gaze. She would likely hate him for this. "I've initiated a search for his natural father."

Her eyes widened. "You—but why? I don't understand. Jamey doesn't need him. He has us."

Roland shook his head slowly. "I am as fond of him as you are, Tamara. You know that. But we must think of what is best for Jamison."

"To leave the people he knows and loves? To go off and live with a stranger? You think that's best for him?"

Eric touched her face, turned it toward his. "Tamara, hear him out. If you were in Jamey's place, wouldn't you at least like to know your father, to find out something about him?"

She frowned harder, and shook her head. "He abandoned his son—"

"He never knew of the boy's existence," Roland said slowly. "You said it yourself. He deserves to be informed. Jamey deserves to be given the options, and to make his own decision."

"If you're sick of caring for him, Roland, then Eric and I will take him!"

Rhiannon shook her head slowly. "Tamara, as long as he is with us, DPI will hound him. They watch us too closely, we're too easily spotted. In a normal, mortal family, Jamey would blend in as just another human boy. He'd be safe."

"I can't believe you're all saying these things," Tamara said, shaking her head. "Especially you, Eric. How could you turn on me this way?"

Eric looked stricken. "No, Tamara. I only—"

"I don't want to hear any more!" She tugged free of his grip and raced out of the barn, through a smaller, side door, and into the night.

Eric put his head in his hands. Roland felt as if he'd been saying the wrong thing at the wrong time forever. "I'm sorry, Eric. I didn't realize how strongly she would react."

Eric shook his head. "Not your fault, old friend. She'll see that it's the right thing, given time." He glanced again toward the fading night beyond the door. "I'd better go after her."

He did, and Roland turned toward Rhiannon. "You think I'm doing the right thing?"

She sighed, and walked away from him, settling herself down on the hay. "Since when does the staid and honorable Roland de Courtemanche seek the opinion of the reckless and self-destructive Rhiannon of Egypt?"

"I would like for us to remain friends, Rhiannon." He crossed the barn, and sat down beside her in the sour-smelling hay. "And while I do think you reckless and self-destructive, I still value your opinion."

"Do you?" Her finely etched brows rose above her slanted, dark eyes.

"You know I do."

She sniffed, tilting her chin upward. "Then you'll be interested to hear that I think you are the biggest fool ever born."

He frowned, studying her perfect face, seeing the hint of sadness still lingering in her eyes. "Why?"

She stared at him intensely, as if trying to light the wicks of the candles in his mind. "You'll never have with another, what you could have had with me."

His throat went dry. "I know that."

"Then you're ten times the fool I thought you were." She turned away from him.

He touched her shoulder. "I didn't know about your father's rejection, Rhiannon. I chose my words poorly when I referred to you as my curse. It's little wonder you're so angry with me." She didn't turn to face him. "Rhiannon, I didn't mean it the way it seemed to you. It's that I want—"

She jerked away from his touch and faced him, eyes blazing. "I do not care *what* you want, nor am I interested in your interpretation of your own words."

"Rhiannon, if you would let me explain, you would see that—"

"It no longer matters, so stop hectoring me with it." She looked away once again, and her eyes cooled until they held a chill that reached out to him. "I am leaving, Roland. Just as soon as the boy is safe, and Pandora is well enough to travel. I am leaving, and this time, I will never darken your door again." She smiled very slightly, but it was a smile of bitterness and pain. "You ought to be extremely relieved. Your *curse* will soon be removed."

CHAPTER ELEVEN

Roland rose before the others, flinging the mildew-scented hay away from his face, and brushing it vigorously from his clothes. His sleep had been anything but restful.

He told himself of the many possible reasons for that: Tamara's anger at him, and the rift he seemed to have caused between her and Eric; worry over Jamison's physical well-being, compounded by concern for the boy's state of mind; the question of whether the cat would recover, and if not, what effect that would have on her owner.

But none of those things were truly what had kept his mind twisting and turning all day long. In truth, it was his own careless words and the pain they had caused in Rhiannon that haunted him. God, for the power to travel back in time, armed with the knowledge about her he now had. If he'd known that her own father had rejected her with the same decree, "You are my curse," he'd never have repeated the devastation. True, he needed to remain apart from Rhiannon, but not for his life would he wish to hurt her.

The truth was, he cared for her. A great deal more than he'd ever allowed himself to admit. It had been easily denied when she'd been far away, when her visits had been few and oh, so far between. Denying it had become more difficult with her return, but not impossible. Her reckless

ways and boisterous nature enabled him to mask irrita-
tion as dislike and disapproval.

But when he'd seen her on the dew-wet forest floor, re-
duced to uncontrollable sobbing, clutching the limp cat
like a babe in her arms, he'd been unable to deny it any
longer. Her pain had sliced into his heart. He'd suddenly
wanted nothing more than to take that pain away.

He strolled to the side door, his feet sinking in loose hay.
Three birds took flight as he passed beneath the rafters on
which they nested, their wings flapping noisily and echoing into the high barn. A feather drifted down past his
face, and he watched it fall.

Outside, onto the drying, browning autumn grass, he
moved. The air held a hint of the winter to come, but the
sky was without a cloud. Stiff weeds scraped his shoes as
he moved away from the barn, senses attuned for out-
siders. He heard only the perfect harmony of the crickets,
the occasional whir of a bat swooping and diving overhead, the unearthly whine of the wind whipping across an
ancient weather vane high atop the barn.

He didn't want Rhiannon to leave.

The knowledge made itself known to him almost as soon
as her decision had left her lips. He would be utterly alone
if he knew he'd never see her again. True, she'd never been
a steady presence in his life, but he'd always known she was
there. He'd always had the absolute certainty that if he
summoned her, she would come to him; that when he least
expected her, she'd show up unannounced. She'd drag him
into a whirlwind, whip it into a hurricane, listen to him tell
her how foolish and reckless she was, and then blow away
like an errant summer breeze.

He couldn't ask her to stay. Her presence played havoc
with his control, made him careless. He would only hurt
her, over and over, as he'd already proven.

He closed his eyes, and her face hovered in his mind. That he could ever harm her deliberately seemed absolutely impossible. For a moment, he considered the possibility that Eric had been right. That his brutish behavior with Rhiannon had been a side effect of the drug.

Then he shook his head roughly. What difference did it make? It couldn't change what he knew about himself, what he truly was. How could he ask Rhiannon to stay, knowing her presence would drive him beyond hope of recovering?

If only she would change her reckless ways, alter her wild nature, calm her impulsive mind. He could help her. She could help him. If he could convince her of it, then perhaps . . .

No. Rhiannon would never change. He was sorely afraid he'd hear of her death one day. And he had no doubt it would be dramatic and horrible.

"Roland?"

He turned at the feminine voice, knowing by its lack of depth and timber that it belonged to Tamara, not Rhiannon.

She came forward, head bowed, not meeting his eyes. She stopped when her toes nearly touched his, slipped her arms around his neck and hugged him hard. "I'm sorry I said those things to you. I know how much you love Jamey."

He returned her embrace, taking comfort in the physical closeness of another living being. "It's all right, Tamara. You're on edge. We all are."

She lowered her arms and took a step backward, her gaze meeting his at last. "I'm so afraid for him."

"We won't let any harm come to him, fledgling."

She nodded fast, squeezing her eyes tight for a moment. When she opened them again, she searched his face.

"What about you? I know you're hurting. I can see it in your face."

He averted his own gaze, shaking his head in the negative.

"Don't lie to me, Roland. You're in pain. But so is Rhiannon."

He looked at her once more. "Has she spoken to you about this?"

"Of course not. She can't even admit to herself that she's hurting. But she is. When this is over—"

"When this is over, Rhiannon will go her own way, and I will go mine. To do anything else has . . . has risks far too great to consider."

Tamara smiled very slightly. Her palm came up to cover his cheek. "Oh, Roland. How can someone as wise as you be so blind? There are no risks too great, when it comes to love."

"Love?" He shook his head as her hand fell away. "There is no love involved here. Your romantic leanings are clouding your vision."

"Your stubbornness is clouding yours."

"Everyone ready?" Eric's words accompanied the squeaky protest of the large barn door as he forced it open.

Roland looked beyond him to where Rhiannon stood, brushing bits of hay from her hair. She moved forward, yanking the car door open. Roland couldn't stop himself going to her before she got in. He reached up, as she stiffened, and took a piece of hay from the back of her head. He held it up between them. "You missed one."

Her eyes, as they fixed on his, were wide and fathomless. He scanned their ebony depths in search of some hint she would allow him to become her friend again.

Instead, he saw a glimmering tongue of flame beyond the jet, and felt an answering fire leap to life in his soul.

She still wanted him. And God help him, he wanted her, too. She licked her lips, swallowed hard and finally tore her gaze away. As she tucked herself into the car, Roland closed his eyes and swore under his breath.

"You'll work it out, old friend." Eric's hand clapped to Roland's shoulder, his deep voice, with a hint of amusement, was low and near his ear. "If you don't go stark raving mad first."

Roland shot him a scowl and rounded the car's nose to slide into the front passenger seat. He wouldn't attempt to sit beside Rhiannon in the back, though his body was demanding he do that, and anything else necessary to be close to her. He needed to focus on Jamey. All of this anguished soul-searching would wait until the boy was safe and sound once more.

Rhiannon hated herself for still feeling such potent desire for a man who'd rejected her time and time again. Still, there had been something in his eyes, something new.

She closed her eyes and shook her head. She was imagining things, that was all. The thought of leaving him, of never seeing him again filled her with such utter desolation she wondered how she would bear it. Already, the idea burrowed a fresh wound into her heart. It dug in right beside the pain she felt for Pandora, and the worry of losing her, as well. Was there to be nothing left to her?

When the car ran low on petrol, Eric pulled into a service station. He and Tamara got out to stretch their legs. Roland leapt out, as well, and she saw him head for a pay phone. He'd barely said a word to her throughout the journey, but she'd felt his eyes upon her often, and looked up to see his head turned, his gaze caressing her. And he didn't look away when she met it. He faced her and allowed her to search his eyes, to try to see what drove him now. Unfortunately, all she detected was misery, regret and confusion. No help at all.

In a moment, he returned to the car, got in and twisted around in the seat, propping an elbow along the back of it. "I phoned that vet. He says Pandora is going to pull through."

Rhiannon was stunned, and the relief that rinsed her soul with his announcement overwhelmed her. "She's all right? She's really going to be all right?"

Roland nodded. "She might have a permanent limp, but she's recovering nicely and he was able to save the leg."

Rhiannon closed her eyes and released all of her breath at once. When she opened them again, she saw that self-satisfied expression on his face. "I suppose I owe you my thanks."

He shook his head quickly. "You owe me nothing. I only wanted to see some of the worry leave your eyes."

She felt a lump form in her throat. "Why?"

"Why? What do you mean, why? I care about you, Rhiannon. To see you in pain causes me pain, as well."

The hot moisture that sprung to her eyes was rapidly battered back by her fluttering lids. She bit her lip and forced her breaths to come calmly, not in broken gasps. Was he saying he cared for her? She refused to ask. She wouldn't give him yet another opportunity to reject her.

Yet, an insane and childish hope alighted in her heart, despite her best efforts to squelch it.

Tamara returned to the car with Eric and they were off yet again, headlights bounding into the night. It was nearly dawn when they entered a tiny village in the shadows of the French Alps, and Tamara clutched Rhiannon's hand and whispered urgently, "This is it. This is what I saw."

Eric stiffened behind the wheel. "You're certain, Tamara?"

"Yes."

Rhiannon licked her lips, her pain forgotten as she began feeling the anticipation of the showdown she sensed was to come. A little shiver of unease danced over her nape, making her shudder.

"We should park the car," Roland said, his voice sure and calm. "We'll strike out on foot, and search for Lucien's automobile. We can question any villagers we meet about the black car, and describe both Jamey and Lucien to them, in case they've been seen."

"Or we might try simply asking Lucien where he is. He wants us to find him. I'm certain of it."

Roland turned to stare at Rhiannon. "But then he would be forewarned."

"He already is, Roland. He knows we're coming," she said slowly.

"But not exactly when we'll arrive."

"Not the precise moment, no. But he knows it will be by night. And he must know that tonight is the most likely possibility, simply by the distance traveled. We do not have the element of surprise in our arsenal, Roland." She licked her lips, thinking again of Pandora's twisted leg. "Nor do we need it."

"She's right," Eric said. "I think we should get this thing underway, right now, tonight. If we begin searching, we may not find them before dawn. Then we'll be forced to leave Jamey in his hands for another day."

Roland inhaled, pursed his lips and finally sighed. "All right. Since time is of the essence, go ahead, Rhiannon. Make contact if you can."

Her brows rose at his "if you can," but she settled onto the back seat and closed her eyes. *The time has come, Lucien. Where are you?*

She didn't need to try again, or to concentrate very hard at all. It was as if he'd been attuned to her already and was only awaiting her words to make the fact known.

Very good. You were faster than I'd hoped. There is a cabin, halfway up Mont Noir. I will await you there.

She frowned, disliking the confidence emanating from his mind. *Is the boy well? Is he safe? I warn you, if you've harmed him, you will pay.*

She waited. But there was no response. Focusing her being on his, she tried again. *Lucien, this conversation is not over. I wish to know of the boy.*

Again, there was no reply. Rhiannon opened her eyes, and shook her head. "A cabin, halfway up a mountain called Noir. Odd name."

"I know where it is," Roland said. "Come, we'll have to go by foot. There are no roads up that sheer face."

Eric clasped Roland's arm before he could get out of the car. "We do not wish to be trapped up there at dawn, Roland. Is there time?"

Roland nodded. "Three hours is sufficient. I'd guess we have nearer to four." Roland glanced into the rear seat, and Rhiannon bristled, sensing what he was about to suggest. "Perhaps it would be better if some of us remain behind, in case the others are somehow bested."

"Good idea," Rhiannon said quickly. "You and Eric should wait here, while Tamara and I go up and teach this foolish mortal a lesson."

Eric turned fast, then understood her motives and smiled. "I would never allow Tamara to face danger without me at her side. Unfortunately, she feels the same about me. Aggravating as all hell, but there it is." He glanced toward Roland. "You can't hate the man for wishing to protect you, Rhiannon."

"I am capable of protecting myself," she replied, her voice thin. "And him, too, if necessary. If he knows me at all, he ought to know that."

"With your recklessness and your anger over the cat, Rhiannon, I am afraid you'll charge without hesitation into whatever kind of trap the infernal bastard has waiting." Roland sent her a quelling glare that held more than just anger. "I was only hoping to keep you from an earlier than necessary demise, if possible."

She tilted her head to one side. "With you there, constantly reminding me how foolish I am, how can I help but exercise a modicum of caution? You worry for nothing."

"I worry for you!" The words burst forth on an explosion of anger as Roland jumped out of the car and slammed the door. Rhiannon got out, slamming her door, as well, and stood facing him, formulating a scathing reply.

But his hand suddenly swept a path through her hair, settling in a gentle curl around her nape. "Stay close to me, Rhiannon. And be careful. Please, for God's sake, be careful."

Again that stupid lump came into her throat, so large this time it nearly choked her. And she heard herself answer like an obedient schoolgirl. "I will, Roland."

She shook herself.

A second later, the four of them started down the narrow, twisting roads of the village, toward the mountain that loomed at its edge. A dark, hulking shape, it rose from the smaller peaks around it like an angry god among sinners. Its sheer face seemed to be barren of anything, save dark-colored granite, and its peak was swathed in dense mists.

The climb would have been difficult for mortal men. Roland winced as he thought about Jamey, being forced, perhaps brutally, to ascend the ragged-edged slope. He would have been exhausted by the time they reached the top. Cold, perhaps hungry. Frightened. Grieving for Pandora, if he knew of her fate. The poor child had no way of knowing she would recover, or even that she'd been found.

He took a moment to curse himself for not seeking out the child's father long ago, then returned his attention to the matters at hand. Rescuing Jamison. And protecting Rhiannon. He had no qualms about admitting the sudden fear for her that held him in its grip. For it was Rhiannon who seemed to be the sole focus of Lucien's obsession. She was the one he'd attacked with his nasty little blade. She was the one whose blood he seemed determined to have running in his veins. She was the one he could contact psychically, and whom he could hear in turn. The man was no ordinary human. And his interest in Rhiannon, Roland sensed, had far greater meaning than any of them yet knew.

The slope angled sharply away from the level, grassy ground. An abrupt change from the lush and fragrant area around them. The surrounding hillsides were grassy, at least at their bases, and dotted with trees and vegetation. Not Mont Noir. A fitting locale, Roland thought, for the grim battle that was to come.

In very little time, they had ascended beyond the spots where malnourished tufts of coarse grass sprouted from between the stone, and clambered their way over sheer, bare rock.

Roland's foot slid once on the surface. He caught himself, then reached behind him to grip Rhiannon's hand and help her along. The look she shot him was not one of anger, but one of puzzlement. Why should she seem so confused by his wanting to help her? Eric helped Tamara along in much the same way.

They were four dark shapes, scaling the side of a black mountain in the dead of night. To the world below, they would be invisible. Wind howled over them, buffeting them as if to send them tumbling down. Air grew thinner and crisper with every foot they gained.

Finally, they crested to a level area and in the distance, Roland saw smoke spiraling into the night. He pointed to the pale gray column, and started toward a cluster of boulders and rock outcroppings. The smoke seemed to emanate from somewhere beyond them. Though the ground was level, and much safer here, he kept his hand curled around Rhiannon's. He half expected her to pull hers free. When she didn't, he immediately wondered why.

Hurrying now, they raced over uneven, rocky terrain, rounded the cluster of stone that blocked their way and stood facing a reddish log cabin. Small windows stood on either side of a wide, plankboard door, like eyes above a toothy grin. Frilly-edged curtains, from this distance, were the lacy lashes. So cozy, this little haven on high. So innocuous in appearance. The perfect, comforting setting to disguise purest evil.

Her hand still resting in his, Rhiannon stood beside him, gazing as he did at the quaint little building. He studied the soft yellow glow of the lamplight from beyond the windows, and he felt the shudder that rippled through her.

Instinctively, he squeezed her hand. Just as instinctively, he thought, she squeezed his in return. The exchange took place in less than a second and then they were looking at each other. Eyes searching, a thousand questions in both sets. Not a single answer in either.

Roland swallowed. He released her hand and slipped his arm around her shoulders as they started for the cabin. She didn't pull away. Eric and Tamara walked abreast of them until they stood before the door.

"I'm certain he doesn't have the tranquilizer," Rhiannon said softly as she reached for the door's curving metal grip. She closed her hand around it and pushed it inward.

It swung without a sound. Glancing around apprehensively, Roland stepped in before her. A hearth on the facing wall snapped and sparked invitingly. In an overstuffed chair, the back of Lucien's head was all that was visible.

"Come in, come in," he said without turning or moving in any way. "Rhiannon is quite right. I don't have the tranquilizer. And this is no sort of a trap. It's a meeting. One I hope will be mutually beneficial."

Roland stepped farther inside, still looking about him. His senses were honed for others present, but he sensed no one. Rhiannon came in beside him, but her eyes, he noted, were only for Lucien. They were filled with hatred and anger, and he touched her arm in an effort to calm her.

She stepped forward, gripped the back of the chair and yanked it onto its back. Lucien rolled to the floor, eyes wide. But as she loomed over him, his lips curved upward slightly.

"I'm going to kill you now, you bastard," she said slowly. "I'm going to take my time about it. Are you ready?"

He shrugged. "I have nowhere to go."

She reached down for him, but Roland grabbed her arms from behind. "Wait, Rhiannon." He looked down at the man who waited expectantly for him to finish. "Lucien, where is the boy?"

A solid line of eyebrows rose. "When I tell you that, she'll be free to murder me. I'd be kind of foolish to give away my edge, now, wouldn't I?"

Rhiannon tugged, but Roland held her firm. He was surprised to see Tamara leap forward, grip Lucien by the front of his knit sweater and haul him to his feet, though she had to lift her arms above her head to do so. Seeing such a small figure exert so much brute strength was impressive, and strange. "If you don't tell us where he is, then I will kill you, anyway, so you don't have much choice."

Again, the dark brows rose. "Such tempers on you immortal women." He pulled his sweater from her grip and stepped backward, smoothing the fabric. "I have a proposal to make. The least you can do is hear it before you make a decision."

Eric had vanished. Vaguely, Roland knew he was searching the cabin to ascertain for himself the presence of anyone else, including Jamey. He emerged from a room then. "Jamison isn't here."

"No. He isn't here. If you want to know where he is, you'll listen to what I have to say."

Rhiannon glanced over her shoulder at Roland, the look in her eyes assuring him it was safe to let her go. He released her arms, giving her a slight nod, then focused on Lucien once more. "Say your piece, *monsieur.* But know that if we dislike what you have to tell us, you'll not live to finish the sentence."

Eric came to stand close to Tamara. "And you'd best begin by telling us about Jamey. Where is he? Is he safe?"

Lucien drew himself up, though he already towered above all of them and fairly bulged with muscle. "The boy is in perfect health and quite likely to remain that way...so long as you cooperate. His location, I'm afraid, is something I cannot reveal to you just yet."

Tamara drew a shaking breath. "Tell us what you want, Lucien. Let's stop playing games and get to it."

"A woman who thinks like me. I like that." Lucien walked brashly past them, bent and righted his easy chair. He circled to the front of it and sat down, waving a hand to the other seats nearby.

Rhiannon took the rocker nearest the fire and pulled it forward, directly in front of Lucien. She sat down, her gaze glued to his unshakably. "We all know what you want, Lucien. The dark gift. Immortality. But I don't believe you realize how foolish it is to ask it."

"Why foolish?" He leaned forward. "Isn't eternal life what every man longs for in the depths of his soul? Hasn't it been that way from the beginning of time?"

"Do you know how the change is accomplished?"

He nodded. "You will drink from me. Then I from you. When our blood mingles, I will be one of you."

"You will never be one of us," Tamara snapped.

Rhiannon's eyes seemed to pierce the very space between them. "What is to stop me from draining you dry once my teeth are embedded in your muscled neck, you fool?"

He smiled, his gaze unwavering. "There is a letter in the hands of my lawyer, in which the boy's location is revealed. The letter is addressed to Curtis Rogers, of DPI. My lawyer has instructions to send a facsimile to Rogers tomorrow night at midnight."

Rhiannon blinked, and Lucien's smile widened.

"On the other hand, fair Rhiannon, if you transform me without mishap, I will reveal the boy's locale to you, giving you ample time to reach him first."

For the first time, Roland saw uncertainty in Rhiannon's eyes. She broke eye contact with Lucien, and sought Roland's gaze, instead.

"Do not trust him, Rhiannon. There would be nothing to stop him draining you dry, either. You'd be weakened by the act. You know that."

"A risk you'll have to take, my dear, if you want the boy safe. On the other hand, you can refuse and see him become a subject for live study by some of the world's most unscrupulous scientists." He leaned toward her still farther. She didn't back away. "I understand you have firsthand knowledge of just how much...*discomfort* they can impose on a living being."

Tamara caught her breath. Roland closed his eyes, knowing her memories of that horrific lab must be the stuff of Rhiannon's deepest nightmares.

"Here is how generous I can be," Lucien went on. "I'll give you time to think it over. Come back at sundown tomorrow. If you agree, we'll make the switch, and you'll have the boy back before the fax goes out. Or, you can kill me, try to find him on your own, fail and regret it for the rest of eternity. The choice is yours."

Rhiannon blinked slowly. "It seems we *have* little choice."

"One thing, Rhiannon. You come to me alone, tomorrow evening. I don't trust them for a minute. You come alone, or the deal is off."

Roland felt a blade twist in his chest. "Absolutely not," he said in a low voice. "I won't allow it."

Rhiannon acted as if he hadn't spoken. "I hope there will be time, Lucien. The gift of endless night isn't given as simply as you seem to think. There is a ritual involved."

Roland frowned, wondering what on earth she was up to.

"I care nothing for your rituals. I only want the blood."

She shrugged. "Well, if you don't want the full extent of the strength, then we can dispense with the meditation. I supposed..."

Lucien frowned, licking his lips. "How long does this...ritual take?"

"Several hours."

He tilted his head. "You won't need more than thirty minutes to get to the boy before Rogers does."

Rhiannon's brows arched. Roland thought he might be the only one who saw the triumph in her eyes. "Then there *is* sufficient time."

"Rhiannon, you can't do this," Tamara cried.

"I must, fledgling," Rhiannon said softly. "Think of Jamey." She turned, and fixed Tamara with an intense stare. *"Think of Jamey."*

Tamara blinked, and averted her eyes. "I—I will."

Rhiannon tossed her hair over her shoulder as she got to her feet with fluid grace. "Until tomorrow evening, then. Of course, you know you must fast from now until then. No food, no drink. Otherwise, you won't cross the threshold. You will die upon it."

Roland frowned again. It was absolute nonsense. Not that he intended to allow her to go through with it.

"And you mustn't sleep tonight, or tomorrow, either," she went on, crossing to the door. "If the conditions are not just right, you will die. Do you understand?"

Why was she spouting such drivel?

"You seem to take great care with the life of a man you despise, Rhiannon." Lucien's voice was laced with the shadows of suspicion.

"I would kill you as soon as speak to you, Lucien. It is the boy's life I'm taking care with. If you die before you tell me his whereabouts, he'll fall into the hands of devils. That, I cannot allow."

CHAPTER TWELVE

Well before dawn, they'd taken refuge in a dilapidated house several miles outside the village. Rhiannon boldly built a fire in the ancient-looking pot-bellied stove, using bits of the rotted shutters for fuel.

"You take many chances, for a being so sensitive to flame, Rhiannon. The chimney is likely in as sad condition as the house."

Roland again, admonishing her as always. "Stop worrying. There will be no direct contact between my flesh and the flames. And I'll see it's well doused before we rest."

Eric and Tamara had gone down into the basement to seek a resting place, and, she suspected, to spend some time alone. She suppressed her jealousy of them and tried to focus on more practical matters. Frankly, she wished she'd brought a huge, fluffy comforter along to wrap herself in. Sleeping in a mound of mildewed hay had been bad enough; this pile of refuse would be worse yet.

"Rhiannon, it's time."

She fed another bit of wood to the burgeoning fire, careful to keep her hand from the flames, closed the iron door and brushed the black soot from her fingers. "Time?"

"To tell me what you have planned for Lucien."

"So you can tell me how foolish and risky it is?" She shook her head quickly, and crossed the room to gingerly examine an ancient-looking sofa. "Thank you, no. You, Eric and Tamara can spend your time looking for Jamey. I'll keep Lucien busy... alive, but busy, until you find the boy."

"Thus the talk of a lengthy ritual?"

She nodded. "He wants power. He craves it the way a drunkard craves liquor. It's a weakness to want something that badly. I'll use that weakness against him. If he believes my *ritual* will give him more strength, he'll take part in it."

She thumped the ratty cushions repeatedly, watching for some creature to skitter forth. When none did, she turned and sat down.

Roland came and sat beside her. "And what of your admonition that he neither eat nor rest?"

His shoulder touched hers, he sat so close. His thigh pressed to hers, but he didn't even try to rectify matters. She wasn't sure whether she should do it herself. She knew she didn't want to.

"Deprivation of food and sleep weakens the mind. It's used by all the most successful cult leaders, you know. I only wish I could make him fast longer before I face him."

She didn't move away. If Roland didn't mind the closeness, why should she deny herself the supreme pleasure of it?

"Face him in what way, Rhiannon? You make it sound like a battle."

Sighing, she leaned back against the gray-colored stuffing that poked out from the ragged upholstery, her arms crossing over her chest. "It will be a battle, of sorts. A battle of minds." She closed her eyes and tried to see her hastily concocted plan clearly. She wanted it to seem like a sound course of action when she explained it to Roland, not like the ravings of a careless, reckless child.

"While Lucien *meditates,* Roland, I will be working on his mind. I will entrance him, as I've done to countless humans when the need has arisen. I will bring him completely under my control."

Roland half turned, so he faced her. She avoided his eyes, but he would have none of it. He caught her chin in two fingers and turned her face to his. "You are well aware this man is no ordinary human. His psychic abilities are strong. He is able to conceal his mind from yours." His eyes sparked with emotion, but she didn't think it was anger. His jawline tightened. His full lips thinned.

"He will be weakened and tired. I will be strong and ready for the fight. The incense and candles that distract him will help me to focus."

His hand dropped from her chin, to settle on her shoulder. "If this works, and you are able to get him under your power, what then?"

She resisted the impulse to tilt her head sideways, and brush her cheek over his hand on her shoulder. Barely resisted it. "I'll scan his mind and learn where the boy is. I'll relay the information to you and the others, and you will rescue him."

"You make it sound so simple."

"Because it is."

"And if you fail? If his mind is too strong?"

"That will not happen."

"It could, Rhiannon."

"It won't." She reached up with one hand to cup his face. "Just this once, Roland, try to believe in me. Look beyond all my faults and see the strength that is mine. I can do this."

His frown came suddenly, and left just as fast. "I've never doubted your strength. I do believe in you, Rhiannon. That's never been a question. But I fear—"

"That I will bungle it and cost Jamison his life." She lowered her hand and shrugged his from her shoulder.

"No, little bird. That you will save Jamison and risk your own existence in the process." Roland stood abruptly, reached down and gripped both her hands to pull her to her feet. "Lucien nearly killed you once, Rhiannon. I have an uncanny feeling that is his intent, even now."

"The risk is not important. Getting Jamey back is."

"I'll go with you," Roland said hoarsely. "I'll stand watch over this entire exchange, and if he lifts a hand against you, I will kill him before he draws another breath."

She shook her head. "You can't. He wants me alone—"

"I'll go along, or you will stay away. Your choice, Rhiannon." Like chips of glassy coal, his eyes glittered.

She sighed and turned away. "Why must you be so difficult?"

A hand of steel closed on her shoulder, turning her so she collided with his chest. At the instant of impact, another arm snapped around her waist, as firmly as a padlock's hasp. His breath bathed her face as she turned it up, and then his lips caught hers in a merciless hold. His tongue fought its way through the barricades of her lips and plundered every part of her interior within reach.

In seconds, she went from shocked victim, to willing partner. Her mouth opened wide and the sensual dance began. They took turns lapping each other's mouths, suckling each other's tongues, nipping each other's lips. Rhiannon's arms twisted around his neck. Roland gripped her buttocks in his eager hands, and pressed her hips to his, moving them back and forth to rub her against his bulging arousal.

When his mouth left hers at last, she felt the shudder that rocked through him. He lowered his face to her hair, and his lips moved against it. "That's why I am so difficult, reckless one. Because this planet, without you among its inhabitants, would be as grim a place as…as this house. And as empty."

Rhiannon closed her eyes at the sweet agony those words inflicted on her soul. She could feel the thunder of his heartbeat against her chest, his breath in her hair. "But you want that emptiness. You want my disturbing presence removed from your life."

His hold on her tightened. His words came on a voice gone gravelly with feeling. "No, Rhiannon. It's not what I want, but what is necessary. It's not you I want out of my life, but the monster that lives within me. How can I make you understand?"

The breath she drew was halting and shallow. "I don't want to understand. I only want you." She lifted her head from his shoulder and looked up into his eyes. "I swore I wouldn't give you the chance to reject me again, Roland, yet here I am offering myself up for your scathing words. When Jamey is safe, and I am far away, I'll have nothing but sweet memories of your touch, your kisses. The ghost of that single time will never be enough to sustain me, I fear."

His dark eyes fell closed, and she saw his lips tremble.

"Give me one more memory to cling to, Roland. I'll ask no more of you, I promise. Make love to me now."

He opened his eyes again, and the fire in his gaze burned into her heart. She lowered her forehead to his chest, unable to face him as he pushed her away from him, yet again.

"Go on," she whispered. "Tell me to leave you alone. Remind me that no lady would say the things I've said. Let me feel your disapproval one more time. Perhaps then I will finally get it fixed in my mind that I'm not worthy of your..." She stopped herself as her throat closed off. Love. She'd been about to say love. God, what was happening to her senses?

"I'm sorry, Rhiannon."

She bit her lip, bracing herself for his rejection. He brought his hands slowly upward, his palms skimming her spine, his fingers brushing over her nape. He cupped her head, and tipped it up, staring down into her eyes.

"It is not you who are unworthy, it is I. I ought not allow myself even this embrace, after my loss of control the last time..." He lowered his face to hers, until his lips barely brushed over hers as he spoke. "But I cannot turn you away. My desire for you burns away my will."

His mouth covered hers, his palms still pressed to the sides of her head. He kissed her as he never had before. Gently, slowly. Every sweep of his tongue was a tender exploration, every shifting of his lips, a caress. His fingers dived into her hair, raking through it again and again. And then he drew himself away, as she rose from the sofa, shivering with passion.

"Undress for me, Rhiannon. Let me see you clothed in nothing but your stunning beauty."

She nodded, and lifted unsteady hands to the silk blouse she wore. His gaze held hers captive as she slowly freed the buttons. But when the blouse fell away, and her breasts stood unclothed before him, he broke contact with her eyes to stare fixedly at her chest. She didn't flinch from the intensity of that stare. She felt her nipples harden in response to it, as if reaching out to him.

He drew a sudden breath, and moved his gaze lower as she released the fastening of the denims, and drew down the zipper. Without shame or hesitation, she pushed the jeans down, and the panties with them. She stepped out of the garments and kicked them aside.

Roland came toward her, one arm reaching out. She stepped away just as quickly, and when he sent her a quizzical glance, she smiled. "Now you."

Her smile was answered with one of his, and he quickly removed his shirt, dropping it to the dusty floor.

She let her gaze roam freely over the expanse of skin revealed to her, the dark swirling mat of hair that invited the exploration of her fingers, her lips. "I've always adored your chest, you know. So broad, so . . ." Unable to resist, she moved nearer him, and ran her hands over the crisp hairs and firm muscled wall. She lowered her face to its center, and inhaled his scent.

When she lifted her face away, she ran her hands upward. "And your shoulders," she whispered, surprised at the hoarse quality of the words. "And your arms. One would think you a bodybuilder by the shape of you."

"The only weight I've hefted was that of a broadsword, as well you know."

She pressed her lips to his shoulder. "Then I'm glad you hefted it." She kissed a trail toward his neck and up it, savoring the taste of his skin. Her hands slipped downward, fumbling to open his trousers, then eagerly shoving them downward. "Hurry, Roland."

He chuckled low, and helped her divest him of his remaining clothes. Then they stood, bodies pressed together, flesh against flesh. The hairs of his chest rubbed over her breasts. The hard length of his arousal stood rigid against her abdomen. She ran her hands over the curve of his back, down to his buttocks, which flexed in response to her touch.

Roland's hands rested at her waist and he kissed her deeply, hungrily. As one, they sunk to the floor. Rhiannon pushed gently until Roland lay back. She stretched out atop him and lavished his neck and shoulders with kisses. She moved her lips over his chest, and ruthlessly caught one small nipple between her teeth. He gasped in pleasure or surprise. She wasn't certain which, until his hands closed on her head to hold her closer. She sucked at the hard little nub, then licked a path down his sternum, across his belly, around his navel.

His body shuddered its response to her ministrations. His breaths came faster as she continued tormenting him. When she touched the tip of his arousal with her tongue, he groaned like distant thunder. When she closed her lips around him, his hips arched upward. His fingers twined in her hair. In moments, he was panting, and his hands sought to move her away. But she persisted in worshipping the core of him with her mouth until his panting became a helpless plea, and the hands fighting her, gripped her, instead.

He cried her name in a strangled voice, and his entire body went rigid as his essence spilled into her.

Slowly, he relaxed, still shuddering with her touch. She lifted her head and slithered up over his body. She held his gaze, and licked her lips. Instantly, his hardness pressed to her thigh and she shifted, settling herself over him, poising herself to receive him.

His hands shot down to her hips and he drew her down hard, sheathing himself inside her. Her head fell backward and her eyes closed. He filled her, more than filled her, and not just physically. Being with him this way filled some barren cavern in her soul. An unexplored place no one had ever entered.

She felt his hands glide over her back, and press to her shoulders. He drew her downward, lifting his upper body, and capturing one of her breasts in his mouth. Gently, he suckled her, then harder, the pressure of his mouth increasing with the pace of his upward thrusts.

Rhiannon felt him pushing her quickly toward that place she'd just taken him. She lifted and lowered her hips, urgently racing to that place. She cradled his head to her breast as she approached it, feeling the skim of his teeth just as the world exploded around her. She shook with the force of her release, even as he continued moving inside her. He held her hips in place, and kept the pace frantic. He nipped and tugged at her nipple until she cried out, and pulled away.

Then he lay still, staring upward into her eyes, and she knew he hadn't completed the journey with her. He pulled her down to his chest, holding her there. Her face was buried in the kinky curls, and her body still trembled with the aftermath.

Clutching her tight to him, he rolled them both over until she was beneath and he was above. He tipped her head upward and kissed her long and hard. She was breathless, and somehow, still hungry for more of him. He seemed to know for he began again, in a slow, tormenting rhythm she thought would surely drive her out of her mind. Her nerve endings seemed to have been rubbed raw, for she felt every sensation as if it were magnified a thousand times. The size of him, and her own flesh stretched around him, the whisper of his crisp triangle of hair meshing with her own, softer one, the lash of his tongue inside her mouth, the friction of his chest against hers.

As the fires inside her blazed anew, she lifted her legs to encircle him, hooking her ankles behind his back. His reply was to slide his arms beneath her, cup her buttocks, lift her hips more tightly to him and spear her more deeply than before. His pace increased as her body grew taut. His tongue lapped a path from her mouth to her ear, and then his teeth closed on its lobe.

It was she, this time, who was made to pant helplessly as his body drove hers higher and higher. But it was both of them who cried out in sweet, anguished joy as their juices met and mingled. She felt the slow throb of his body and her own convulsing around him.

Gradually, the room came back into focus. Rhiannon looked around her, then into Roland's jet eyes. "We are fortunate Eric and Tamara have not walked in before now."

His smile was slow and enticing. "They won't. I have it on good authority that they are hidden away somewhere, doing the same thing we are."

She nodded with understanding, her envy of their happiness striking her anew. For her, this would be the last time. Already the pain of that knowledge began to engulf her in misery. "Perhaps we ought to find a place to rest before dawn."

"We have an hour until dawn, Rhiannon." He lifted a hand to stroke her hair. "An hour I intend to fill in some most interesting ways."

The pain faded. "What ways?"

"Let me show you."

As dawn approached, they took refuge in a darkened closet on the second floor. They lay down in the narrow space, still naked, bodies twined together.

Already, Rhiannon slept. Her head rested on Roland's shoulder, her silken hair covering his chest like a blanket. He held her close and listened to her breathing.

He hadn't lost control. He hadn't become a raging beast, not even for a moment. Instead, he'd become one with her, and found a joy beyond anything he'd ever known in the joining.

Perhaps there was hope for him yet, he thought, finally facing the idea which had nagged him from their first kiss. He was no longer sure he had the strength to let her go.

Let her go? He shook his head slightly. There was no certainty in his mind that he could convince her not to go. Always before, she'd flitted in and out of his life with all the predictability of a cyclone.

But that was before, he thought in troubled silence.

Before what? What have we shared, beyond the consummation of a long-lived mutual lust? The fevered coupling of two willing bodies?

No. There was more to it, surely. Not love, for he knew himself incapable of such a tender emotion. He'd believed himself in love once before.

Like a blade, the memory of that other time sliced through his mind. Rebecca, so young and innocent. He'd fancied himself in love with her for a time. But his actions, his need to control and command her, had resulted in her suicide. His love, or, what he'd thought of as love, had been poison to her.

Would it be the same to Rhiannon? Was he not, already, searching his brain for ways to change her, to transform her into some meek-willed creature who'd be content to live the solemn life he preferred? Would he, in time, kill her spirit the way he'd killed Rebecca's?

He looked down at her, sleeping so peacefully in his arms. No, he couldn't do that to her. It would be a crime beyond murder to try to stifle Rhiannon. Perhaps he could convince himself to let her go, after all. Perhaps he could keep his thoughts to himself until she was free of him.

He owed her her freedom, if nothing else. It was, after all, the only gift he had to give.

* * *

Just after dusk, the two of them made the trek up the side of Mont Noir, to the quaint-looking cabin that held within its cozy walls an unmeasured evil. Lucien. Who was he? Rhiannon wondered. Why had he singled her out, of all the undead who walked the night in this twentieth-century world? There were many. Few older than she, but some. The infamous Damien, for one. Why had Lucien not sought him out to demand the dark blessing?

Rhiannon nearly laughed aloud at that notion. Even among vampires, the name of Damien was whispered with wariness. Lucien would not dare to try his games with such a creature.

She stumbled on a protruding rock, and Roland's arms came around her. She leaned gratefully into his embrace. Too soon, she would leave him. Too soon. She shook her head at the thought. Never would be too soon.

"Something troubles you."

She faced him, sighing. She was rapidly growing weary of guarding her thoughts from Roland. The venture was an exhausting one, for he seemed constantly to be probing her mind with his questioning one. He'd always been the one being with whom she'd felt most able to relax. She'd always allowed him to roam her mind at will.

Sad, how things had to change.

"I was only thinking of Tamara," she lied with unease. "She is so new to these games of the mind. I hope she is able to locate the boy."

Roland nodded, still holding her close to his side as he maneuvered around a bed of loose stone. "It would be helpful if Jamison were trying to reach out to her."

"Do you think he will?"

Roland's lips thinned as he shook his head. "Not if he thinks doing so would lead her into danger. I suspect he's learned the trick of guarding his thoughts from us. Otherwise, we'd have tracked him by now. He's a stubborn one, that boy."

Rhiannon nodded, thinking again of Tamara and Eric. She'd left them sitting upon the moss-covered ground in a small clearing of a nearby wood. Candles and incense burned between them, and Tamara's eyes were closed as she sent the fingers of her mind out into the night, in search of her beloved Jamey. If anything happened to the boy, Lucien would die, there was no question of that. For if Rhiannon and Roland didn't finish him themselves, Tamara would do so.

A small smile tugged at Rhiannon's lips. "Eric's fledgling has a dark side to her."

Roland glanced sideways at her. "Don't we all?"

"I suppose we do. But with her, it's well concealed. Like the leaves of the nightshade vine, and its wine-colored berries. Beautiful, harmless-looking, but containing a deadly nectar."

"I'd hardly classify Tamara as deadly."

"We all have the capacity, Roland, given the right motivations. I believe most humans do, as well." She licked her lips and watched his face as she spoke to him. "This notion you have that you are somehow more monstrous than the rest of us is born either of ignorance or conceit. I've not yet decided which."

He halted, turning to face her, a frown digging a ditch between his brows. "Are you angry with me, Rhiannon?"

She blinked. He'd hit on it, precisely. She was angry with him. Furious, in fact. Because of his foolish notions, she would be miserable for longer than she cared to think about. But rather than voice this newfound knowledge, she only shrugged, and pointed. "The cabin is just around those rocks, as I recall. I ought to go on alone from here."

Roland set his jaw. "I'll come a bit farther."

"He'll be able to see you. Just wait here, in the shadow of these boulders. As soon as he is assured I've come alone, you can come nearer. But do take care, Roland."

His eyes seemed to scan her face for a moment. "I can barely believe what I'm seeing. You're excited about this encounter! You're looking forward to it!"

She lifted her eyebrows, and shrugged. "I've always enjoyed facing a challenge." She knew the remark would infuriate him. She also enjoyed doing that, though she'd never quite understood why.

She glanced down at her attire, gleaned from some of the tourist shops in the village below. Close to her skin, she wore tight black leggings, and a form-fitting bodysuit of that wonderful fabric called Spandex. This would enable her to move as freely as possible, should the need arise. Her shoes were flat, and shiny black, but the soles had good treads for climbing the sheer rocks.

However, she'd covered the practical, contemporary garments with a flowing kimono of deep blue satin, which, when she freed it, would cover her feet. At the moment, it was bunched up around her waist to ease her travel. Roland had added his own black cloak as a finishing touch. It was warm, and added an air of magic to her every movement as it gleamed around her like the wings of a raven. It had neither collar nor ties, only two buttons to hold it in place at her throat.

Roland nodded in approval. "Every inch the enchantress, Rhiannon. He'll shudder in fear at the sight of you."

"Don't make light of it," she chided. "Every advantage I can use is needed, and if my clothing can help to intimidate him, that's all the better."

"I know. I wasn't." He caught her shoulders, and held them firm. "Be careful, Rhiannon." His eyes conveyed much more meaning than his words. He was truly worried for her safety. "At the first sign of skulduggery, summon me. Don't hesitate."

"I won't." Something inside her urged her to move forward, to press her body to his just once, to lift her lips to his, and wait for his parting kiss. She fought the feeling, hoping it didn't show in her eyes, averting them in case it did. "Now, let me go, before I lose my nerve."

"The gods would lose their wisdom first," he said, but his hands fell away.

She turned and hurried toward the cabin.

CHAPTER THIRTEEN

Rhiannon halted a few feet from the cabin's little door, closed her eyes and silently composed her thoughts. She could not afford to be distracted now by worry about the boy, or even by her extreme sadness over the parting that would follow this ordeal. She must concentrate only on Lucien.

Before she was prepared, the door opened, and the object of her thoughts filled the entrance. "Come in, Rhiannon. I trust you've kept your word and come alone?" As he spoke, his beady eyes swept the area around her, and she knew he searched with his mind, as well. He would find no hint of Roland there. He could guard his presence from this man without much effort. Despite his powerful mind, Lucien was only a human.

"Of course. Did you think I'd risk the boy, or that I'd be so afraid of you I would bring reinforcements?" His gaze came back to her, and altered slightly as he took in her attire. "Don't fool yourself, Lucien. I fear no mere mortal."

He stepped aside as she strode into the cabin. She made her steps broad, kept her head high. He would see no faltering in her entrance.

"No? Not even Curtis Rogers?"

Was that remark supposed to shake her? "Him least of all. He is a weakling, blinded by his hunger for vengeance. I could kill him with as little effort as you would swat a fly. But that is neither here nor there, is it?"

Lucien shrugged and closed the door. Rhiannon focused her mind on the house, finding it empty save for the two of them. She stepped nearer the hearth, allowing the fire's warmth to spread over her.

"You're dressed quite differently from the way you were last night. Is there any significance to it?"

She turned a surprised glance upon him. "I thought you knew all about me. Can it be your research is lacking, after all? Do you not recognize the robes of an Egyptian priestess?"

He said nothing, only eyed her up and down. "May I take your cloak, at least?"

"You may not. I've grown rather fond of it."

"Suit yourself."

She studied his face. His eyes appeared slightly slack-lidded. She detected darker circles beneath them. "You have followed my instructions?"

"I have. No sleep, no food, no drink. I'm thirsty as a sand dune right now, to tell the truth."

"It will pass," she told him. "How is the boy?"

"Fine. Safe, for the moment, at least. I've no doubt your friends are out looking for him."

She only lifted her brows. "Think what you will."

"It doesn't matter. They won't find him." He crossed the room toward a closed door, and opened it. He stood aside, and waved a hand for her to enter.

Rhiannon moved forward, the cape swaying with every step, the kimono brushing the floor. Pausing in the doorway, she saw a small room, a bedroom, perhaps, but devoid of any furnishings, save a table and a glowing kerosene lamp.

"Let's get on with it." Lucien stood close behind her, his voice cold on her nape.

She stepped inside, and he followed. From a pocket inside the cloak, she pulled a small sack. Lucien's gaze took in every movement.

"What's that?"

She loosened the drawstring and removed several candles, a packet of incense and a silver dish, placing them on the floor in a small circle. "Nothing to be afraid of, Lucien. You see?"

He knelt and picked up a candle, studying it, sniffing it. Then he lifted the packet of herbs and examined that, pouring a bit into his palm.

"Incense," she said. "It goes in the dish, in the center of the circle of candles."

He shot her a wary look, then poured as she had instructed. "You want me to light them?"

He was nervous. She saw it in the way he kept licking his lips, in the constant darting movements of his eyes. "No. We'll take care of that in a moment. Douse the light, if you please."

He frowned, but stood. Cupping a hand over the far side of the glass chimney, he blew into the lamp. The room fell into inky darkness. She could see him clearly. He could see nothing, though he tried to keep her in focus. Right now, he was squinting like a mole.

"Now sit, cross-legged upon the floor."

He did as she told him. Rhiannon rounded the circle of unlit candles and lowered herself opposite him. Tentatively, she probed his mind with her own, as a test. She found it completely closed to her.

"You must concentrate, Lucien. There must be nothing on your mind except the candles. Focus upon their wicks.

Think of nothing else. Envision flames, leaping to life at your command. Do it now.''

She saw him staring hard at the candle just in front of him. She aimed the beam of her own thoughts there, and in a moment a small pop sounded, and the wick flared to life.

Lucien jerked as if slapped.

"Very good," Rhiannon purred. "Your mind is strong, for a human." Again, she sought his thoughts and found nothing. "But you are not concentrating hard enough. Focus your mind."

He did. His eyes picked out another candle, and she let him stare at it awhile before she caused it to light. One by one, Rhiannon lit the candles, as Lucien's guard was slowly lowered.

His eyes widened in amazement, his face now glowing in the soft light of the tiny fires. "Now the incense. It's a bit more difficult. Concentrate."

She watched him as he stared at the silver dish, but she did not ignite the herbs it held. Instead, she probed his mind, seeking knowledge of Jamey in its foggy depths.

For a moment, she saw the boy, lying upon a cot, with a wool blanket tossed over him. But the image vanished as Lucien looked up at her.

"It isn't working."

"You're not concentrating. Try again."

He did. It was laughable the way he contorted his face with the effort. The fool grated his teeth. Again, Rhiannon searched his mind, this time seeing a bit more. A room, in utter darkness. A shuttered window. Smoky cobwebs in the corners.

She glanced at the incense and it began to smolder. Fixing her mind more firmly inside his, she tried to see the locale of Jamey's prison. It was near. Very near, but not in this cabin. Ah, there. Another cabin, similar to this, but in sad disrepair. Upon the mountain? she wondered. No. Below it, but not in the village.

A wall seemed to lower itself around his mind all at once. "You're trying to trick me, aren't you?"

He knew she'd been snooping. She met his accusing glare. "Our thoughts must mingle as well as our blood, Lucien. This will not work unless you cooperate."

Give yourself over, she chanted in silence. *My will becomes yours, Lucien.*

She saw his eyes begin to cloud.

"You must relax. Breathe deeply. Like this." She demonstrated, and he mimicked her for several long moments. His lids drooped slightly. She almost smiled in triumph.

"Much better. Now focus on nothing. Try to free your mind from your body until you feel as if you are floating."

The lids drooped a little farther. His deep, regular breathing came on its own now, without her instruction.

"Imagine yourself as a spirit, if you will. Feel the chains of your physical self falling away."

Your will is mine, Lucien. You have no desire except to do my bidding. You have no thoughts, save those I will give you. Surrender to me, Lucien. Surrender.

Slowly, his eyes fell closed. His breathing deepened still further, and came in long, drawn-out turns. His head hung downward on a neck gone limp.

Where is the boy?

Roland's entire being was focused on Rhiannon inside the cabin. He waited as long as he could stand it, then started forward, toward the tiny structure. He would go around until he located a window through which he could see what was happening. She was so involved in her efforts with Lucien that he could feel no hint of her thoughts, had no clue what was happening.

His every thought on Rhiannon, Roland stepped out of his concealment beyond the rocks. The shot came out of the darkness. Something stabbed into his chest.

His hand came up to clutch the object that pierced his flesh with a burning pain. He tugged it free, but his mind was slipping away. A black haze slowly coated his consciousness as he stared down at the blood-slicked dart he'd torn from his chest.

He fell to his knees, lifting his gaze. Curtis Rogers stood only yards from him, an evil smile lurking about his lips. Damn! Roland had been so determinedly focused on Rhiannon, he'd failed to continue scanning the area for another presence. He'd failed . . . he'd failed Rhiannon.

His mind whispered a warning he prayed she would hear, just before he fell forward, into darkness.

Rhiannon's thoughts were interrupted by a sudden bolt of knowledge. Something had happened to Roland.

In her moment of distraction, Lucien broke the hold she'd had on his mind, and gave his head a shake. Then he glared at her, leaping to his feet. "I know what you're trying to do. I should have known I couldn't trust one of your kind."

She stood, as well. "Do not tempt me, Lucien, or you'll die here and now. Tell me where you've hidden the boy."

"You never had any intention of keeping your side of the bargain. Why should I keep mine?"

"Because you will die if you don't." She stepped around the candles toward him, but froze when the door behind Lucien swung wide, and Curtis Rogers stood there, pointing some sort of weapon at her.

"You!"

"Ah, we meet again, Princess."

She took a single step and no more. The dart plunged into her shoulder and she cried out in sudden pain. She closed her eyes, certain the dart contained the tranquilizer, certain her time had run out. With her final moments of consciousness, she sent her thoughts to the fledgling, Tamara, conveying all she had learned, begging her to find a way to save Roland and the boy. She fell forward, catching herself on a wall, then slipping slowly downward as her legs folded beneath her.

"Her friend was outside," she heard Rogers saying, though his voice echoed as if far away.

"Will you take him, too?" That was Lucien.

"No. I've learned from my mistakes. I don't want to deal with two of them at once. One at a time, from here on. He's not going anywhere. Let the sun take care of him."

She felt her neck muscles melt as her head fell forward. It was jerked up again by a cruel hand in her hair. Lucien's twisted face hovered before her. "Before you go beddy-bye, there's something I want you to know. The scientist you killed all those years ago, Daniel St. Claire's partner, was my father. And I won't rest until I see all of your kind pay for his death."

She tried to make her lips form words. "B-but ... you ... you wanted ..."

"To become one of you? Yes. The strongest one of all, so I could eliminate the rest with ease. So I could live to see the last of you die in agony."

"You," she whispered with the last bit of strength she possessed, "are the one . . . who will die."

Nearly dawn.

Roland felt the approach of morning with every cell in his body, and still he could not move. He'd managed only to pry his eyes apart. Now he could watch the horizon slowly paling, from deepest black, to midnight blue, to varying and ever-lightening shades of gray.

The cabin was empty now. There was no sense of Rogers, or Lucien . . . or Rhiannon. He knew they must have taken her. Again, she would be subjected to their cruel torments. Because of him.

Roland grimaced in pain at the thought of Rhiannon in Rogers's hands. He had to live—if only to free her.

Summoning every muscle to do his bidding, grating his teeth with the effort, he slowly, painstakingly, clutched at the earth and dragged his body forward. He couldn't wait for Eric to come to his aid. There might not be time, or his friend, too, might be disabled or in trouble. Again, Roland dug his fingers into the dirt and stone. Again, he hauled his body a few inches forward. At this rate, he wouldn't make it to the cabin's door before noon. Still, he had to try.

Away from the shelter of the rocks, he dragged himself. Halfway into the clear, level area, with no kind of shelter from the rising sun. Halfway to the cabin. Again, he clawed and pulled his way, glancing toward the east, where he could see the pale orange glow just touching the edge of the sky. Sweat beaded on his forehead and ran, burning, into his eyes. He clutched at the ground again, and grunted with effort as he struggled onward.

From the opposite direction came the sound of padded feet, running toward him. He turned his head, and then released his breath in a rush. To his left, the sun. Now, to his right, a wolf the size of a Saint Bernard, but with muscles rippling beneath its sleek coat instead of fat. If the one didn't kill him, the other surely would. He had no strength left to fight either enemy.

Recalling his last experience with a wolf, Roland wished the sun would hasten its arrival. Then the beast was upon him, and he knew it was too late.

But what was this? Not a snarl came from the wolf, not a bared fang did the animal display. Instead, it stopped at his side, lowering its huge head, nudging its way beneath Roland's all but useless arm.

In shocked wonder, Roland could only stare as the wolf pushed and shoved at his body. It only stopped when Roland's right arm and shoulder were supported by the animal's strong back. Having no clue what was happening or why, or whether this was some dream he was having in the throes of death, Roland fought to bring his other arm around the front of the animal's neck, until he could link his hands together. The moment this was accomplished, the wolf started forward, not even straining under the tremendous burden of Roland's limp weight. Roland's upper body was carried, the rest of him dragged, but in the wrong direction.

He could have screamed in frustration. If only he could command the wolf to drag him to the cabin, the way Rhiannon could command Pandora. He tried, but found the wolf a poor listener. He forced his head up, to look ahead, his cheek brushing the soft, deep fur at the wolf's throat, his nostrils filling with the animal's scent. Then his jaw fell open. The wolf had brought him to a small cave, dug into the side of a sheer stone wall. It was barely visible with the overlapping rock above, and the outcrop jutting from the sides. He'd never have known of the cave's presence.

The beast dragged him inside, then along the cool, uneven floor, around a sharp bend and all the way to the back. The sun would never reach here, Roland suspected. He released the wolf's magnificent neck, and lowered himself to the floor.

The wolf stood over him, staring down into his eyes for just a moment. There was a wisdom in those eyes, the likes of which had no place there.

"I know not what you are, wolf—" a memory of Rhiannon's tales about ancient ones who could alter their form, about Damien, hovered in his fogged mind "—but I thank you," Roland managed to say. His eyes were heavy and he could barely form words. "Meager reward...for saving a life. I know."

He'd expected the beast to turn and lope away. Instead, it lowered itself to the stone floor a few feet from him, and its eyes fell closed. In a few seconds, Roland's did, as well. His last thoughts were of Rhiannon. Where was she as the cruel sun rose into the sky? Was she safe? Sheltered from the burning rays?

When next Roland awoke, he was alone. He glimpsed the stone walls around him, wondering whether he'd dreamed the entire incident with the wolf.

It was night again. He felt strong, and he hurried out of the cave with one thought on his mind. Rhiannon. He must find her, now, before even another minute passed.

He strode toward the cabin. He'd begin there, to search for a clue.

"Roland!"

The shout brought him up short, but he knew an instant later it came from Eric. He faced his friend, accepted the harsh embrace. "Roland, what's happened? We've been out of our minds with worry."

Roland's soul felt as empty, as hollow as he knew his words sounded. "Rogers. He got me with one of those darts of his, then left me for the dawn to find."

"And Rhiannon?"

Roland felt his throat seal itself off. He closed his eyes. "I . . . I don't know."

Eric grasped Roland's arm and both men approached the cabin. Eric flung the door wide, so hard it smashed into the wall, and the two went in different directions, searching the place with methods none too gentle.

In the small, empty room, Roland stopped, his heart twisting as he eyed the circle of candles and the dish of incense. It's exotic scent still tinged the air. Then he saw the bloody little dart, lying on the floor in a corner. In a voice gone hoarse with pain, he called to Eric, and pointed. "They've taken her," he whispered.

"We'll get her back."

Roland nodded, then scanned his friend's face. "Where is Tamara?"

"She's taken the boy back to the castle, Roland. They're in no danger, now. Jamey was suddenly released last night. It was never him they wanted, only Rhiannon. Once they had her, they let him go. If they need bait to lure the rest of us, they'll use her."

Roland nodded, for the explanation made perfect sense.

"I'd have been here to help you, Roland, but Jamison was turned loose in a forest, and left to find his own way. We spent most of the night searching for him, and I had no idea what had occurred up here—although I think Tamara did."

Roland cocked a brow. "How?"

Eric shrugged. "She heard something from Rhiannon...it was what led us to that particular patch of woods in the first place. Then she heard no more. She kept saying she was certain something was wrong, but she didn't know what." He shook his head. "I was damned afraid for you, Roland. How did you manage to escape the sun, with that tranquilizer in your blood?"

Roland thought again of the wolf, of the knowledge in its eyes. "I'm not certain." He shook himself. "It doesn't matter now. We have to find Rhiannon."

As the drug's effects waned, the day sleep took over. Rhiannon roused only very briefly between the two. In a fogged, floating kind of state, she glanced around her, knowing she was in a chilly place with no windows or doors, no light of any kind. She sat hunched on a cold floor, with another cold surface at her back. And when she moved her arms or legs, there was the sound of metal clanking against metal.

Then she slept again, so she thought it must be day. When the sleep evaporated, she knew it was night. Or was it? For with the setting of the sun would come the rush of tingling energy, and the zinging awareness in her every nerve ending. With night would come strength, and power.

Why did she still feel as if her limbs were made of lead, and her head stuffed with wet cotton?

Lucien's face loomed above her, grinning lasciviously. "Don't fret, Rhiannon. It's only Curt Rogers's handy little drug making you feel so weak. I gave you a half dose just before sunset. Looks as if it was enough."

Vaguely, her brain began to function. She felt the damp chill of the stale air around her, smelled the stench of stagnant water, and rodent leavings. "Rogers ... told you he'd never ... give you the drug."

"Rogers didn't have a choice in the matter. Did you really think I'd let him drag you off to some sterile laboratory and hold you under military guard before I had what I wanted from you?" He laughed low in his throat and shook his head. "He had no more intentions of keeping his promise to me than you did."

Her body weak, Rhiannon struggled to her feet, only to realize that iron manacles encircled her ankles, with chains that were bolted to the stone wall. Her wrists were likewise imprisoned, with longer lengths of chain. She turned her head to one side, then the other, testing the strength of the chains with an experimental tug. The cold iron bit into her flesh.

"I'll keep you weak enough so you won't be able to tear them free, Rhiannon. Don't doubt that."

She faced him, feeling her anger well up inside her. "What has become of Roland?"

"Your friend who was lingering outside the cabin? Curtis shot him with a dart, like you, and left him there for the sun. He's probably dead by now. No hope of rescue there."

His words were like the lashes of a whip across her heart. She closed her eyes against the flood of tears.

"Oh, how touching," Lucien said, gripping her chin and lifting it. "Now, unless you want to follow him, *after* you watch me kill the boy, you will transform me."

Her eyes flew open. "You still have Jamey?"

"Of course."

She studied his face, wondering if he was telling the truth. She'd awakened with the sense that Jamey was well and safe. Had it been a dream? Wishful thinking? Or had someone been attempting to reassure her?

"I can keep you here indefinitely, Rhiannon. I have plenty of the drug, and all the time in the world. If the boy's life isn't incentive enough to convince you, we can try using pain as an impetus. I know how much you dislike that."

Her neck was so weak she had trouble holding her head up when he took his hand away from her chin. Her memories of the time this man's father, and his partner, Daniel St. Claire, had held her captive, loomed in her mind in an attempt to drive her from her senses. She pushed it away with effort. "And if I capitulate? If I initiate you into the world of unending night, what then? Am I to suppose you will release me, when I heard you admit you live only to see me die?"

"Suppose what you will. I'll free the boy if you do as I say. If not, you both die. The choice, fair Rhiannon, is yours."

She lowered her head until her chin rested upon her chest. It was hopeless, then. She had no need to fight the fear, for her grief overwhelmed it.

"I have things to do. I'll return for your decision in an hour." With that, he left her, his steps echoing in the darkened, stone dungeon.

Yes, dungeon. Where on earth had he brought her? A dungeon suggested a castle, and a castle likely meant they were still in France. Perhaps even in the Loire valley where thousands of medieval castles dotted the landscape, Roland's among them.

Roland.

Just the thought of him brought a stab of pain to her soul. She called out to him, sending her mental voice into the night like a mournful wail. Again and again she called to him, but she heard no reply.

Could he truly be dead? Gone forever before she'd managed to tell him the truth she'd kept locked away for so long?

"I love you, Roland de Courtemanche, baron, knight, immortal, man. I love all of you," she whispered. She lifted her head skyward, as if to cry out to the gods. "Return him to me, and I swear I will become what he wants. No more will I seek out danger and flaunt myself in its face. No more will I live recklessly, walking an unsteady line along the very edge of sanity. I'll become the staid and quiet woman he wants, anything he needs. Never will I leave his side, if only I am given one more chance!"

Her words died on a broken, ragged cry, and she let her head fall forward once more on a neck gone limp. Her sobs racked her body, and only the lengths of chain kept her from falling. For she knew in her heart, her chances were gone. Roland had not answered her desperate cries. He'd been taken from her, torn from her heart before she'd realized he'd made his way into it.

Her grief paralyzed her, and she sobbed endlessly, wellsprings of tears pouring from her eyes.

Still, she knew that if Roland would ask anything at all of her from beyond the grave, it would be to do what was necessary to protect young Jamison. The last gift she could ever give to him would be the boy's life. She had no choice but to do as Lucien asked. He'd kill her when the deed was done, there was no longer any doubt of that. She could only hope it would be swift and clean.

Halfway down the mountainside, her cries reached him. Roland's head came up, and his stomach clenched in a tight knot at the anguish in her voice.

Eric's hand clamped down on his shoulder like a vise. "Don't answer her."

"Are you insane? Listen to her—"

"I am. No doubt, Lucien is, as well. If you answer, he'll be ready and waiting for us. He already has too many weapons in his arsenal, Roland. That drug, Rhiannon's life, Curt Rogers's aid. No use giving him fair warning, as well."

Roland swallowed hard. Rhiannon's cries kept coming, and he heard her grief, her tears, her pain. God, but he'd never been aware how much she truly cared for him. No wonder his careless words had hurt her, time and again. He cursed himself now, for having to hurt her once more, and swore on the graves of his family that he would never, in all eternity, ever cause her pain again, even if it cost him his life.

He closed his mind off, for her pleas were driving him to near madness, and his rage added to that still more. He focused only on honing his mind to her location, and then pointed himself in that direction.

He and Eric sped through the night until all at once, Eric skidded to a halt, gripping Roland's arm. "I was mistaken in that list of Lucien's advantages. Look." He pointed down a steep embankment.

Far below, a smoking wreck was all that remained of Curt Rogers's Cadillac. Roland sent the fingers of his mind into the wreckage, and saw the vision of Rogers's charred body, twisted grotesquely behind the wheel.

"This was no accident," Roland said softly. "He died by Lucien's hand."

Eric nodded his agreement. "Then Lucien has no intention of turning Rhiannon over to DPI once she's transformed him."

"No." Roland's voice was grim. "He intends to kill her."

CHAPTER FOURTEEN

They circled the ruined fortress twice, in search of guards or watchmen, before leaping the crumbling wall. They crossed the barren courtyard, Roland's palms itching to feel a steel hilt, his shoulder aching for the butt of a crossbow. A moat, filled with green brackish water that appeared thick with filth and stunk to the heavens, surrounded the castle. The drawbridge was raised.

In days of old, they'd have fashioned a bridge of a freshly cut tree, a battering ram of another. Today, matters were much simpler. The two leapt the moat, side by side, and edged around the square stone shape of the keep, in search of a way to enter quietly. Both were careful to guard their thoughts, even from each other. A steel wall had been lowered around their minds. Lucien must not know of their approach.

It was difficult, for Roland knew that somewhere within these decaying stone walls, Rhiannon was imprisoned. Weakened, perhaps in pain. Were she well, she'd have torn the place apart by now, and Lucien along with it. Her patience would have found its end.

They finally came to a small opening in the stone, a window, which had never seen glass. Roland clambered through, and stood, looking around him while Eric followed. The place was in ruin, no question. The very walls were crumbling. The stone floors had spider webs of cracks, and huge gouges. It was black as pitch within the cold walls of this castle, but with his piercing night vision, he made his way slowly forward, along decrepit corridors, his mind on Rhiannon.

His heart grew heavier with every echoing step he took. Surely these weak stone walls could not hold her in her normal state. How he wished to see her, enraged, bringing Lucien to his knees with the sheer force of her anger. He closed his eyes for a moment and shook his head. That he'd ever thought to tame her spirit was a joke. It was untamable, as she was. It was what made her Rhiannon.

After trekking through endless corridors and passages, they came to the top of a set of stone stairs, crumbling as they spiraled downward into what seemed the hub of the earth. The smells of dankness and decay assaulted him as they descended. The sounds of water trickling, of rodents scratching, and of their own steps, echoed in his ears. She was here, in this hell, more than likely believing him dead.

Each step was placed with utmost care, as silently as possible. Roland scarcely dared draw a breath for fear he would alert Lucien and incite the man to harm Rhiannon. God, the very thought of her here was enough to drive him mad. Was she imprisoned in some freezing, tiny cell? Was she, even now, shivering with the cold and with her grief over his own supposed demise? Was she drugged, weakened to the point of helplessness in the face of Lucien's brutality?

Had the bastard harmed her? Had he touched her?

He'd die if he had, Roland vowed. He would die either way, he amended. The beast was loose, and Roland, for once, welcomed its presence. He'd tear Lucien limb from limb and take great pleasure in the tearing.

Eric touched his arm, and inclined his head. Only then did Roland hear the sounds of voices, echoing softly through the cavernous underworld. Like ghosts wandering aimlessly, the voices filtered toward them.

"Are you ready, then?"

"I'm ready, Lucien." Rhiannon's voice was weak, conveying the state of her body, and of her mind. The sound of it was a torment such as Roland had never known. He crept nearer.

"Remember, no tricks. If any harm comes to me, the boy will die where he is. You understand that?"

"Yes."

"Good."

"So I will bide my time, Lucien. And you will pay."

There was the sound of grim laughter. "I knew you'd be furious about the cat. The animal gave me no choice, Rhiannon. When it bounded in front of my car, the temptation was just too great for me." There was a pause. "From the boy's reaction, you'd have thought I'd killed his dearest friend."

Roland stepped closer, still unable to see them, but he could hear more clearly. He heard Rhiannon's labored breathing, and then her voice, with the barest hint of her former spirit making her words quiver with rage. "You didn't kill the cat. And when the boy is safe again, you might well become a snack for her."

"The cat survived? Then why are you still so angry?"

"Bastard!" Rhiannon drew a deep, ragged breath. The argument seemed to be taxing whatever strength she still possessed. "You know...the cause of my anger. What you did to Pandora pales...beside your other crimes." She paused, breathing deeply, brokenly. "You...you've taken from me...the only man I have ever loved." The final words were barely whispered, and the evidence of tears was clear in her voice.

Roland stood stock-still when those words floated toward him through the darkness. He closed his eyes as a horrible pain washed over him, and only stirred again when Eric's voice urged him on.

"Steady, my friend. You'll get used to the idea."

He swallowed hard, and began moving silently forward. The shock of Rhiannon's admission faded as his rage, again, began to build.

"I will avenge Roland, Lucien," she whispered. "Make no mistake."

"You leave me no choice but to be sure you never get the chance, Rhiannon. One would almost think you had a death wish."

"Take care." Her words were weak and faint. "For I have nothing left to lose."

There was the sound of chains rattling. Then a strangled gasp. "Feel the tip of this needle in your side, Rhiannon? If I get the slightest notion you are trying to bleed me dry, I'll depress the plunger. There's a large enough dose to kill you in seconds."

They rounded a corner, and Roland saw the nightmarish scene laid out before him, illuminated only by the harsh, flickering light of a single torch. Rhiannon, all but limp, supported more by the chains at her wrists, than by her own power. Her eyes were hooded and moist with pain, without light of any kind. Desolate. Her hair hung over one side of her face. The hem of the deep blue kimono was dampened and dirty.

Facing her, his back to them, Lucien stood with legs planted apart, his fist gripping the hypodermic that was jabbed into her side, right through the flowing kimono she wore. He gave it an evil twist and she whimpered, too weak to cry aloud.

Roland lunged, but Eric gripped his arm. "If you attack now, he'll kill her." The words were whispered harshly into Roland's ear. "We have to get him to remove that damned needle before we touch him."

The sight of Rhiannon suffering riled him, but he knew his friend's words to be true. He glanced around, seeing in all directions in the inky blackness. Far above, more chains dangled from a towering ceiling. Roland could guess at their torturous purposes there. He nudged Eric, and pointed.

Eric nodded. "Can you get up there without a sound?"

"I'll know in a moment. Can you get Lucien's attention without costing Rhiannon's life?"

"I'd better, hadn't I?"

Roland drew a steadying breath and leapt upward, gripping a protruding stone high above, and anchoring the toe of one shoe in a chip in the wall. He glanced below, saw Eric watching, and gave him a single nod.

Eric stepped forward, out of the shadows, into the red-orange torchlight. "Pardon me, Lucien, but you forgot to tell her a few things, didn't you?"

Lucien whirled, tearing the syringe from Rhiannon's waist as he did. Her face contorted in pain. Her cry brought a convulsion to Roland's stomach.

"Marquand, isn't it? Rogers told me about you." Lucien lifted the needle like a weapon, clutched in a beefy fist, and started forward.

"Before you killed him, you mean?"

Roland waited. He needed a bit more space between Rhiannon and the point of that needle.

Lucien glanced over his shoulder at Rhiannon. She only hung, all but limp in her chains, hopelessness etched into her face like chinks beaten into old armor.

"Shut up, Marquand."

"Afraid I'll spill the beans, are you? Once she knows, she won't be so cooperative, will she?"

Roland nodded in approval. Lucien would lose if Rhiannon were to learn Jamey was safe and sound. He would be forced to silence Eric.

"Knows...what?" Rhiannon's head came up slowly. Her eyes focused on Eric.

"Why, that Jamey—" He stopped, sidestepping Lucien's charge with all the grace of a matador dodging a bull. Roland launched himself from the toehold in the wall, soaring above the stone floor, catching the dangling length of rusted chain. It swung with the force of his momentum, carrying him swiftly onward. He let go a second later, and plunged downward, onto Lucien's broad back. Both men crashed to the floor, Lucien landing facedown with Roland's weight atop him.

Lucien's hand, still gripping the hypodermic, twisted and turned, straining backward in a doomed attempt to stab Roland. Roland rose, one knee pressed into the center of the much larger man's spine. He clamped a hand on Lucien's wrist, and squeezed until he felt the subtle cracks of bone giving way. With a shriek, Lucien released his hold on the syringe. And even then, Roland didn't let the bastard up. The beast within wanted vengeance, and it was on the rampage.

A little more pressure and you can break his spine just as easily. Snap it in two. Just press the knee a bit harder...

"Roland?"

He lifted his gaze from the quivering heap of flesh beneath him, and saw Rhiannon staring as if she were seeing a ghost. The beast within seemed to dissolve in that instant. He no longer thirsted for vengeance, only for her.

For her touch, the feel of her lips beneath his, the sight of her half smile and the mischief in her eyes.

He stood, aware that Lucien rolled to his back and clutched his shattered wrist with his other hand. He paid no attention, knowing Eric would see to the bastard. His only concern was for her as he moved slowly forward. Her eyes widened. Her lips parted slowly and she mouthed his name again, though no sound emerged this time.

He reached her, then, and his arms went around her. Oh, to feel her, living, breathing, her strong heart pounding against his chest! He cradled her head to the crook of his neck, threading his fingers in her silken hair, words tumbling from his lips without thought, or even order. Here was where she belonged. In his arms, her body pressed to his. He felt he could never release her.

She lifted her head and her eyes moved over his face with such intensity he could nearly feel their touch. "I . . . I thought . . ." Her hands came then, following the path of her eyes, touching his face as if not believing it was real. The chains jangled with her movements.

"I know," he whispered. "I know. I dared not answer you, knowing that one's psychic strength." He caught one of her wrists in his hands, drew it downward, away from his face, and easily snapped the manacle. As it clattered down, slamming into the wall, he reached for the other. "Has he hurt you, Rhiannon? Has he touched you?"

"Nothing . . . could hurt me . . . more than believing . . . I'd lost you."

Their eyes met for a long moment, and Roland wondered how he'd failed before to see the love in hers. He must have been blind.

Unsure what to say in the face of such powerful feelings, uncertain what this meant to either of them, Roland dropped to one knee and snapped the shackles at her ankles. Her arms came to his shoulders, and then her weight when she tried to step away from the wall. He scooped her up with minimal effort. Her head fell limply to his shoulder, and he closed his eyes in exquisite agony. God, but it was sweet to hold her again.

Eric tossed the now-unconscious Lucien aside, and came to stand beside them.

"I should have killed him," Roland muttered, gazing toward the man on the floor of his own dungeon.

Eric lifted one brow, and tilted his head toward Lucien. "Go right ahead, my friend. He can't even resist, at the moment. I'm sure, beast that you claim to be, it won't bother you in the least to lean over and crush his larynx. Only take a moment. Go on. I'll take Rhiannon for you."

Roland glanced down at Lucien once more, then at the woman in his arms. He couldn't murder a man in cold blood. In battle, yes. He'd take great pleasure in fighting Lucien to the death. But not like this. He eyed Eric, and sighed. "I suppose there is a lesson in there somewhere, my friend. But all I wish now is to take Rhiannon out of this place."

He started back through the dungeon, and then up the crumbling stairs, leaving Lucien to his own devices. Likely a mistake, but there it was.

She rested in his gentle, unfaltering embrace, sometimes conscious, sometimes not. She knew little of the exact process by which they'd arrived, only that in what seemed little time at all, they were entering the great hall of the Castle Courtemanche, to the cries and embraces of Tamara, and Jamison, and Freddy.

A low snarl drew Rhiannon's gaze downward. Pandora limped through the little gathering, her foreleg wrapped in a plaster cast. She rose on hind legs, her good forepaw on Rhiannon's chest, and nuzzled her mistress's cheek with a cold nose.

Rhiannon stroked the cat's face. "Pandora, my kitty, you're home. Yes, yes, it's good to see you, too, love." She kissed the cat's muzzle, before Roland shooed her away.

"We picked her up on the way back," Tamara said softly, crowding forward much as the cat had, to stroke Rhiannon's hair away from her forehead. "I wanted her to be here to greet you when Roland brought you home." The young one frowned, her gaze concerned. "Are you all right?"

Rhiannon smiled her assurance that she was, though she felt far from all right. She was rapidly growing weary, resenting the powerful effects of the drug. She sought out Jamey's face, and reached out to him. "Jamison. I was so afraid for you."

He looked at the floor. "I'm sorry. I almost got you killed . . . again."

She shook her head, but Roland turned away from them, striding down the vaulted corridor toward his chambers, with her in his arms. "We'll all have time to talk later. She needs rest now." As he spoke, he looked down at her face.

She searched his, wondering at the uncertainty, the endless questions in his eyes. He seemed almost afraid of something. A most unusual state of being for one so valiant. Moments later, he was lowering her onto the bed, tucking her beneath the brilliant yellow comforter, propping her head and shoulders with the pillows she'd purchased such a short time ago, but seemed like aeons.

"Roland." She reached up to cup his face in one unsteady palm. "I have much to tell you."

"Shh. I want you to rest. By tomorrow evening, you'll be feeling like your old self again, I promise. We can talk then."

"My old self?" She blinked slowly, recalling her promise to whatever gods might be listening. She would lose him unless she could keep her vow. She knew that beyond any doubt. "No, Roland. I'll never be—"

He hushed her with a gentle finger upon her lips. "Rest, little bird. We'll talk later."

"Yes." She let the heaviness of her eyelids pull them down, no longer wishing to fight off sleep. "Yes, we can talk later."

But she was not herself again when she rose the following evening. Nor did she return to normal in the following days. Stronger, yes, Roland observed in the great hall. There was no longer the film of drug-induced stupor covering her diamond-bright eyes. But the mischief wasn't there, either. Or the taunting, or the come-hither gaze he'd half expected to see. She was like a shadow of her former self. Quiet, exceedingly polite, refusing to argue, no matter what stupid remark he made to incite her.

Roland leaned sideways, elbowing Eric's middle. "Do you suppose there are lingering side effects to Rogers's tranquilizer?"

Eric cocked one eyebrow. "Why do you ask?"

"Look at her. She's quiet, almost . . . timid. She's been like this damn near a week now." As he spoke, Roland glanced again toward Rhiannon. She sat in an oversize chair Roland had hauled down from one of the storage rooms above, staring into the flames of the huge hearth, seemingly absorbing the fire's warmth in the chill room. She absently stroked the head of the cat that lay at her side.

Eric shrugged. "I suppose she might still be a bit shaken . . ."

"Rhiannon doesn't *get* shaken."

"Hush, she'll hear you," Tamara whispered, crossing the room with Jamey at her side. "And this is no time to upset her. Jamey's father will be here any minute. We don't want him walking in on one of her indignant speeches, do we?"

"I'd pay to hear one of her speeches, right about now," Roland muttered, but they moved as a group nearer the fire, and the various chairs situated around it.

"The great hall looks much nicer, Rhiannon. You've done wonders."

Rhiannon looked up, smiled softly and continued stroking the cat.

"Yes," Eric said, picking up where Tamara had left off. "All the candles and lamps soften the harsh stone, and the curtains and rugs are in perfect taste. Don't you agree, Roland?"

Roland only nodded, watching Rhiannon's face, a frown tightening his own.

"I still think it would have been better if you'd let her hang your paintings, Roland," Tamara said.

Roland shrugged. He did, too. He'd only refused Rhiannon when she'd asked because he'd been sure she would argue and fuss and fight with him until he conceded. He'd been looking forward to fighting with her. He missed it. Instead, she'd only nodded in acceptance and not asked again. He felt like screaming at her.

He watched her, watching him. "It's lovely, yes. And a shame we won't be able to remain here longer. But with

Lucien still alive, and knowing our whereabouts, it will be better if we all move on.'' He studied the way her fingers tightened around the stem of her glass. At last, he thought, as her knuckles whitened in evidence of her fierce grip. "I can think of no other solution. Can you, Rhiannon?"

For an instant, the fire flared in her eyes, so brilliant he feared sparks would leap out to burn holes in her new rugs. "The solution," she said, back stiffening, chin lifting, "would be to find that sniveling worm of a man and..." She blinked rapidly, looking at each of them in turn. Then she sunk back into her chair like a balloon slowly deflating, and shook her head. "Whatever you decide to do is fine with me, Roland."

Roland pressed two fingers to his forehead, while Tamara shot Eric a concerned look. Eric only shook his head.

A heavy knock sounded throughout the room, and Rhiannon rose with her ever-present grace. Her long skirt billowed around her, touching no part of her legs or giving any clue to her shape as she moved. Its waist was cinched, but the blouson bodice drooped over the waistline. The neck was high, and buttoned all the way. Worst of all, her hair, her glorious, raven's wing hair, was twisted into a sleek knot at the back of her head.

Give her a pair of wire specs and some button-up shoes and she'd be the picture of a nineteenth-century school mistress.

She touched Jamey's arm. "You know Roland only did this for you."

"I know." Jamey touched his pocket, the one Roland knew held the letter from his father that had been waiting here upon their return from the mountain. He hadn't expected his solicitor to find the man so easily, or that he would reply so soon. "I'm not angry. I think . . . I think I need to do this."

Rhiannon stroked Jamison's hair, then hugged him to her. A second later, Tamara rushed forward to do the same, while Rhiannon opened the door.

The man who stood there was six inches shorter than she. His build suggested an active life-style, but his dark hair was short, and thin, and he wore round glasses perched on his nose. His eyes were the kindest Roland thought he had ever seen, and they focused only briefly on the beauty at the door, danced once around the great hall and the people within it, then homed in on Jamey, and glowed with emotion.

For a long moment, the two only stared at each other. Several letters and phone calls had been exchanged by now, so they were not quite strangers. Roland had to respect James Knudson's easygoing methods. He hadn't tried to convince Jamey to become his son overnight. Instead, he'd invited the boy to spend a few weeks at his home in California. To get to know his stepmother, and half brother. And Jamey had agreed.

Roland felt his throat tighten when Jamey moved forward. He stopped before his father, and for a moment the two simply stared at each other. Then the man clasped the boy in a fierce hug, and they clung for a time. When they stepped apart, James Knudson removed his glasses and pressed a thumb and forefinger to his eyes.

It hurt to know he would lose the boy to his father. But it was right, and Roland had known it for some time now. The man was a junior varsity soccer coach, for God's sake. What more could a boy wish for?

Jamey turned and met Roland's gaze. "F-father, this is Roland. He's saved my life . . . more than once, now."

Jamey bit his lip. "And this is Eric, and Tamara, and Rhiannon." He faced each of them in turn, his eyes dampening.

James cleared his throat, obviously a bit confused by the eccentric setting, and the formal clothing all but Tamara wore. But he stepped forward and shook each hand firmly. "I know how much you all mean to...to my son." He shook Roland's hand last, and longest. "I'm more grateful than I can tell you. If you hadn't searched for me, I might never have known I *had* a son."

Roland nodded. He couldn't have replied had he wished to. His throat was too tight.

Tamara stepped forward, speaking in his place. "Remember, we love him, Mr. Knudson. And that this is only a trial run. The decision to stay with you must be entirely Jamey's."

He nodded. "I would never try to force myself on him, Miss, uh, Tamara. I love him, too."

She met Jamey's gaze, then hugged him once more. "You know how to reach me if you need anything, kiddo."

"I know." Jamey hugged her in return, then released her and faced Roland. "I'm, uh, I'm gonna miss you."

Roland's heart trembled in his breast. "No, young man. I'll visit so often there will be no chance of that."

Jamey held out a hand, and Roland gripped it firmly and pumped twice.

The boy turned toward Pandora, who'd been sleeping near the hearth, and up until now hadn't made a sound. Jamey went to her, bent over and wrapped his arms around her neck. The cat's tail swished, and she rolled, pulling the boy with her. He sat up laughing, and the cat placed a paw upon his knee.

"Take care of them, Pandora."

The cat's green eyes seemed to assure him she would. Then Jamey rose and returned to his wide-eyed father. When the man could tear his eyes from the black panther, the two moved to the door, and stood in its opening.

"We'll be watching out for you, Jamey," Rhiannon said softly.

Eric nodded. "If you get into any danger, we'll know. You can count on it."

"Curt's gone now, so there will be no more harassment from him," Tamara whispered.

"And Rhiannon's computer-expert friend is going to erase all of your files from DPI's systems. It will be as if you never existed, to them." Roland stepped nearer Rhiannon as he spoke, needing someone close for this painful parting. "You can enjoy yourself the way a fourteen-year-old ought to, with no more worry about cloak-and-dagger nonsense."

Jamey opened his mouth, then closed it. Instead of words, he moved back toward Roland and hugged him hard. Then he turned, walking quickly toward the door, and his father. "I'm ready now."

His father clapped an arm around Jamey's shoulder. He glanced back at the others. "I hope you'll stay in touch."

"Rest assured, we will," Roland said.

The pair stepped out into the night, and the door swung slowly closed behind them. Eric folded Tamara into his arms. Roland wished he could do the same to Rhiannon, but he hesitated. She'd shown him no hint of encouragement since the incident with Lucien, and he knew her well enough to know she would have, if she wanted him.

Perhaps his hard heart had finally killed the love she'd once felt for him. Why now, when he wanted it so desperately?

CHAPTER FIFTEEN

Amid glowing candles, Roland put the finishing strokes to the canvas before him.

In a week, he hadn't seen this woman. Oh, Rhiannon was here, as he'd prayed she would be. She'd mentioned no more about leaving him forever. But she wasn't really Rhiannon. She was a dim shadow of the vivacious, slightly vain princess of the Nile. He wanted her back again, as wild and flighty and unpredictable as before. He missed her. The entire castle seemed empty, like a tomb, without her boisterous presence filling its every corridor. He wondered why he'd never noticed the emptiness before.

His eyes traveled the image of beauty before him. His brush had captured the texture of her skin, the glow of devilment in her dark eyes, the waves of her satin hair. He longed for her as much as ever, perhaps more. But she seemed almost indifferent to him now. Where before, she'd driven him to frustration with her constant flirtations, now she barely sent him a longing glance. It was maddening.

"So that's what you've been doing up here." Eric's voice came from the trapdoor in the floor's center, just before his body followed it up.

He stood, brushed himself off, then eyed the painting, arms crossing over his chest. "Roland, it's breathtaking."

"It's Rhiannon. How could it be otherwise?"

Eric smiled, giving his head a swift shake. "Have you told her yet that you're madly in love with her?"

Roland scowled. "She'd likely laugh me out of the castle. You know Rhiannon's views on silly, human emotions."

"Her views might have changed these past weeks, my friend."

"They wouldn't be the only thing to have changed, then."

Eric studied Roland's face for a long moment. "You know, you might stop to consider that she is only conceding to your requests."

"What kind of fool notion is that? I never asked her to become a piece of the furniture."

Eric shrugged, thrust his hands into his pockets and slowly paced away from Roland. "You've constantly reminded her how reckless she is, how impulsive. You've criticized her love of attention, her need to attract notice wherever she goes, her outrageous behavior. More than once, in my presence, you've asked her—no, ordered her—to behave like a lady. Now, you're complaining because she's doing as you wished."

Roland frowned hard, and looked at the floor. "Do you really think that's what she's doing?"

Eric shrugged. "It's as good a guess as I can come up with at the moment."

Roland dropped his brush into its holder, and kept his gaze focused on it. "So what do I do about it?"

Rhiannon held the sunny, yellow pillow in two fists, pulling in opposite directions until the fabric gave way with a horrible tearing sound, and fluffy white stuffing snowed down onto her feet. She gave a little growling shriek and spun in a circle.

"Ah, Rhiannon, there you are. Where've you been hiding these past few days?"

She faced the fledgling and bit her lips. She hadn't meant for anyone to witness her release of temper. "I don't know what you're talking about."

"Ha!" Tamara came into the room, bent and picked up two handfuls of stuffing, flinging it in the air. "What's this, then? You planning to restuff all the pillows to impress him?"

Rhiannon batted aside the falling fluff. "I don't need to impress anyone."

"Of course, you don't. I only wondered if you were aware of it, that's all."

With a little snarl, Pandora leapt off the bed to pounce on the wads of stuff as it landed, batting awkwardly with her plaster-encased paw.

"You make no more sense than my cat does," Rhiannon said softly, kicking more of the stuffing aside and walking into the living area.

"How long do you think you can keep this up, Rhiannon?"

She turned to Tamara, who followed on her heels. She was about to shout a denial, but saw the wisdom in the young one's eyes. "Not much longer. Oh, Tamara, I simply wasn't created to be meek. I'm ready to claw my way up the walls. What's more, it doesn't seem to be having the desired effect at all. He's barely looked at me since that night he carried me home."

"Oh, he's looking, all right."

Rhiannon frowned, but the fledgling seemed reluctant to say more. "Out with it, vampiress, or leave me in peace."

"Some peace, tearing apart innocent pillows when it's really him you'd like to rip in two."

Rhiannon sighed, her patience as thin as her temper. "Say what you've come to say, young one."

Tamara smiled. "Eric and I are leaving tonight. I only came to say goodbye."

"Leaving?"

"Oh, don't worry. We'll come back again soon. It's just that I want to be close to Jamey, in case he needs me. And you and Roland need to be alone, I think, to work this out."

Rhiannon looked at the floor and shook her head. "I fear there is nothing to work out. He knew I meant to leave as soon as the boy was safe. I've not kept my word and no doubt, he's wondering why."

"Well, before you do, take my advice and talk to him. Tell him everything. Don't hold anything back, not anything. Get things straight between you, once and for all, Rhiannon. If you don't, you'll never forgive yourself."

Rhiannon blinked. Then she tenaciously lifted her arms and put them around Tamara's shoulders. She hugged the little thing to her chest. "For one so young, you give good counsel, fledgling. I will miss you."

They gathered that night, the four of them, round the hearth in the great hall once more. Roland watched Rhiannon's eyes, noting with some satisfaction the spark that had finally returned. She wore the black velvet gown she'd worn that first night, and she toasted them all with her blood-red nails gripping the glass she lifted.

"When next we meet, it will be someplace different," Eric said softly. "I'll miss this drafty old castle."

"Oh, I don't know," Tamara said. "Roland might not have to give the place up, after all." Her eyes held a secret, and Roland almost grinned at the childish amusement she seemed to take in knowing something the others didn't.

"Go on, fledgling, say whatever it is that's on your mind."

"Yes, Tamara. You've had that look in your eyes all evening, ever since you made those phone calls to be sure it was safe for us to return to the States," Eric said. "What on earth makes you so smug?"

She shrugged. "I spoke with my friend, Hilary. The one who's still with DPI. It seems they're investigating the disappearance of a powerful psychic, suspected of murdering Curtis Rogers."

"What?" Roland's hand gripped his glass more tightly.

Tamara shot Rhiannon a knowing glance. "The last they heard of him, he was at an emergency room in Paris, having a crushed wrist set. He vanished from his hospital bed in the middle of the night, and no one's heard from him since."

Roland slanted a glance at Rhiannon, noting that Eric and Tamara were looking at her, as well. She sipped her beverage, and pretended not to notice.

"Rhiannon, what do you know about this?"

She met his gaze and shrugged delicately. "I haven't a clue what you're talking about."

"Rhiannon . . ."

She sent him a silencing glare. He was so relieved to see her acting haughty again that he let the matter drop. He could see she either didn't know what had become of Lucien, or had no intention of saying.

When they'd said their farewells at the front door, Roland closed it and faced Rhiannon. The time had come, he decided, to tell her the truth. He would bare his soul to her, once and for all, risk her ridicule and her ire, admit he'd been wrong all along and ask her to forgive him. True enough, he'd driven poor Rebecca to suicide, and that was a pain from which he'd never recover. But he thought Rhiannon was too strong a woman to allow him to hurt her the same way. At least, he hoped so, because there was no way in hell he could let her walk out of his life. Not ever.

What he saw in her eyes stopped him cold. The arrogant daughter of the Pharaoh was back, indeed. She glared at him for a single moment, then started up the stairs.

"Come with me, if you will, Roland. I, too, am prepared to take my leave, but there is something I must discuss with you first."

"Leave?" He hurried after her, trotting up the worn stairs. When she proceeded right up to the tower room, he thanked his stars he'd covered the painting before he'd left it. "You're leaving? Rhiannon, I—"

"No. I've given you ample time to say your piece. You haven't so much as whispered a word of it, so my turn has come." She went to the ladder at the room's center, up it and out onto the very top of the keep.

Roland followed. When he emerged on the top, she was leaning against the uneven layer of stone that created a short wall, gazing out over the rolling field, through the night, to the junction of the two rivers. The night wind whipped her hair, until strands of it came loose from the bun at the back of her head. She turned to face him, her hands going to the knot of hair, angrily tearing pins free, and tossing them over the side with an exaggerated flourish.

When her hair whipped loosely around her, she sent him a defiant stare. "So dies your wallflower."

Thank God, he thought. But he said nothing.

She turned from him once again. "I cannot leave here until you learn the truth, because I will, in all likelihood, never see you again to tell you how your beloved Rebecca really met her demise."

Roland frowned. "I thought we had come here to discuss . . . you, and me."

She licked her lips, and averted her gaze. "On that subject, it seems there is little to discuss. But there is much you don't know about Rebecca." She drew a breath as if to steady herself. "You told me you never loved her, but you know you cannot lie to me. I sense your feelings . . . most of the time. I know how very much you cared for her."

"And what it drove her to," he muttered, glancing beyond Rhiannon, to the ground, far, far below. Remembering the way he'd found Rebecca there. The pain came to life inside him, the guilt.

"The room where I took Tamara to meditate, it was Rebecca's room. I've been back there, you see."

Roland frowned. "Why?"

"Her aura has remained. She hasn't been at peace, Roland, not in all these centuries, because of your guilt. She needed you to know."

He shook his head, not wishing to hear this.

"Tonight she will rest at last, for tonight I will tell you what she made known to me in that room."

Roland closed his eyes. "I do not wish to discuss Rebecca. Not here." The image of her body plunging over the side haunted him even though he squeezed his eyes tight to shut it out. "She loved you, Roland."

He opened his eyes all at once. "She despised me."

"She wished to hate you for what you'd done, but she found herself falling in love with you, all the same. She came here, to this tower, only to try to decide what to do. She was racked with guilt at her feelings. She felt she might be betraying her father's memory by them, but she intended to accept your marriage proposal all the same."

He released a sudden whoosh of air. "You lie. Why are you saying these things, Rhiannon? To try to erase the burden of guilt I've carried for ages? It's no use. I know what I did to her."

"She wore a golden crucifix, on a leather thong around her throat."

Roland inhaled quickly, looking into Rhiannon's eyes. She didn't seem to be seeing him. Instead, it was as if she were looking beyond him. Her hand rose, in a fist, to the spot where the cross had rested upon Rebecca's throat.

"How do you know that?"

"It was fashioned for her by her father, and she cherished it." Her hand came away, palm opened. Her gaze searched her empty hand. "But the thong came loose, and the gold cross fell."

Roland frowned, unable to speak. Rhiannon turned, and leaned over the wall. "It became caught in a crevice of the stone. She could see it, and she tried to reach for it."

Roland gripped Rhiannon's shoulders. Her stance, the way she leaned over, was precarious at best. He turned her toward him, astonished to see tears in her eyes. "But she was small, like Tamara. She couldn't hope to reach it, could she, Roland? And she fell. Poor, innocent, silver-haired angel. She fell, and the cross remains." She stepped aside, pointing one finger downward.

Stunned, Roland stepped to the wall, and leaned over it. At first, he saw nothing. Then a glimmer caught his eye.

There, wedged tightly between two rough-hewn gray stones, the small crucifix glinted a reflection of the moon above. He shook his head in wonder, as an incredible burden seemed to dissolve from its longtime place upon his shoulders.

"She didn't take her own life," he whispered.

"No, Roland. It was an accident." Rhiannon returned to the trapdoor, and stepped onto the ladder. "So now you may live your life without the guilt you've been feeling. It is my parting gift to you."

Roland whipped himself around to face her. "Wait!"

Despite his bark, her head vanished as she stepped down the ladder. Roland leapt through the trapdoor after her, catching her shoulders, and turning her to face him before she could reach the next door.

"I said wait."

She blinked rapidly, but her gaze didn't flinch from his. "For what?"

He shook his head. "There…are still things we need to discuss, Rhiannon. You know it as well as I."

"It no longer matters, Roland. It makes no difference now."

"Why?"

"Because, you fool, there is nothing more I can do. Nothing more I *care to do* to make myself desirable to you. For years, I've sought to show you I was worthy. These past weeks have been one escapade after another. Yet all I did to show you my strength only served to anger you further. The more I endeavored to make you want me, the more averse you became to the notion."

He felt his lips pull upward in a smile, and reached out to her, but she pulled away, turning her face from his eyes. "Rhiannon, I—"

"No. Listen to me for once, Roland. I will say this now, or never feel moved to again. You might as well know all of it. When Lucien held me in that hole, he told me you were dead. And I howled my grief to the gods. I swore I would be the meek-willed creature you wanted me to be, if only they would return you to me. Can you believe it? Me, Rhiannon, bargaining for a chance to please a man."

He closed his eyes, and shook his head slowly, but she rushed on.

"I've tried to do as I promised, Roland. For days, I have whispered around these walls like a withering primrose. And what has it accomplished? You pay less attention to me now than before. And it wouldn't have mattered if you had, because I cannot convert myself to suit you, or anyone. I've learned that only recently. I am who I am. Rhiannon, born Rhianikki, daughter of Pharaoh, princess of Egypt, vampiress, immortal woman."

She turned, and gripped his shoulders in her hands. "Look at me, Roland. Do you not see it in my eyes?"

The only thing he saw in her eyes, just then, was a sudden, glittering flood of tears.

"I love you," she whispered. "You can search the world, sift the deserts, comb the seas, and you will never find a love like mine for you. It is endless, boundless, and will never fade. I've fought it for most of my existence, and still it remains. Yet you choose to throw such love away, just as my father did before you. You are a fool, Roland, to let me leave here. But I am equally a fool for throwing myself at your feet one last time before I go. Step on my heart and end this agony, once and for all. At least now, you can have no doubt what you will be missing."

Roland bit his lips. He wouldn't shout at her, though the temptation was great. "Rhiannon, are you finished?"

She nodded. "Yes. I'll keep my promise and leave you now."

"No. Not quite yet. I believe there are a few things left unsaid between us. Will you listen?"

"No."

He searched her face, but she turned it away. "Why not?"

Her voice came hoarsely. "I don't wish to compound my humiliation by crying like a child in front of you, when you reject me this one final time."

He sighed as she stepped away from him. "At least hear this, Rhiannon. All this time, all the risks you've taken, the recklessness you've shown, you haven't been trying to prove your worth to me."

She turned slowly, her gaze fierce. "Haven't I?"

"No, nor to your father." He stepped nearer, and gripped her shoulders. "You've only been trying to prove it to yourself. Your father's rejection, and then mine, made you question your own worth, Rhiannon."

She blinked, and he saw the fresh moisture that sprung to her lashes. "Perhaps . . ."

"Question it no longer. Your heroism, your courage, are beyond those of any knight I've ever known, Rhiannon. You are a woman beyond any who has ever existed, nor ever will. Believe that."

She sniffed angrily, and tugged away from him, averting her eyes. "Let me go. I've no wish to cry in front of you."

"Is that what telling you I love you will do, make you cry?"

She swallowed hard, and turned to him, eyes wide with disbelief.

He took her hands in his, and brought them to his lips. Rhiannon, just hear what I will tell you, please. I've ought my love for you from the night when you found me, early dead on that battlefield, and took me in your arms. h, I thought I had reasons. I was an animal, unworthy of uch a goddess as you. I told myself my love was poison, hat it would bring you only misery as it had everyone I ad loved before. I resented the way you would come and o at will, leaving me longing for your return, and con- nced myself I didn't care if you stayed a day or a month ith each visit. But I did, and I died a little inside every me you left me alone."

He turned toward the covered painting, and took one orner of the cloth in his hand. "This time I swore I'd keep small part of you with me, for always." He tugged the bric away, and heard her sharp intake of breath.

He looked at her as she stared at the image of herself on e canvas. Her hand trembled as it moved from her lips, the painting. She touched it, and tears rolled from her es, down her cheeks. She shook her head. "This... n't...can't be...me."

"It is the very essence of you, Rhiannon. But I'm afraid ve changed my mind." He met her startled gaze. "I won't t you go this time. I won't be satisfied to gaze at this inting. I want to gaze into your eyes. And I want to see em alight with life and mischief the way they've always en. Not dull with the effort of reining in your own na- re. I came to love you just the way you are, Rhiannon. nd I will fight with you through all eternity if ever you try change."

He fell to his knees at her feet, clutching her hands to his art. "Stay with me for always, goddess among women.

Be my mate, my lover, my friend. Never leave me alone long for you again."

She dropped to her knees, as well, her hands threadi[ng] through his hair. "I adore you, Roland. But I'm not su[re] I can exist in seclusion, live this life of a hermit the way y[ou] do."

"No, I would not ask it of you. My sentence is at an en[d] Rhiannon. You've given me the keys that set me free."

She smiled, then, and it held all the mischief and dev[il]ment he'd missed these past days. "Tell me again."

"I love you, Rhiannon."

He rose, and his arms crept around her waist. He[r] slipped over his shoulders. He kissed her mouth deep[ly] thoroughly, as if he were tasting her for the first time.

"Your father was so wrong, Rhiannon. Do you kn[ow] that yet? You are a treasure, one so rare, so p[re]cious...one that can be sought, and found, but nev[er] owned. Only held for a while."

"Then hold me, Roland. Hold me for a very lo[ng] while."

* * * * *

ETERNAL LIFE, ETERNAL LOVE

Twilight
Memories
MAGGIE SHAYNE

Darkly handsome Roland de Courtemanche had rejected Rhiannon's affections for centuries, banishing her to exist alone for all eternity. Yet now that the man she loved and the boy in his care were in danger, Rhiannon knew staying away was impossible.

Discover the dark side of love in *Twilight Memories* by Maggie Shayne, book two of WINGS IN THE NIGHT, available in April from Shadows.

Take 4 bestselling love stories FREE

Plus get a FREE surprise gift!

Special Limited-time Offer

Mail to Silhouette Reader Service™

3010 Walden Avenue
P.O. Box 1867
Buffalo, N.Y. 14269-1867

YES! Please send me 4 free Silhouette Shadows™ novels and my free surprise gift. Then send me 4 brand-new novels every other month, which I will receive months before they appear in bookstores. Bill me at the low price of $2.96 each plus applicable sales tax, if any.* That's the complete price and—compared to the cover prices of $3.50 each—quite a bargain! I understand that accepting the books and gift places me under no obligation ever to buy any books. I can always return a shipment and cancel at any time. Even if I never buy another book from Silhouette, the 4 free books and the surprise gift are mine to keep forever.

200 BPA ANRN

Name _____ (PLEASE PRINT)

Address _____ Apt. No. _____

City _____ State _____ Zip _____

This offer is limited to one order per household and not valid to present Silhouette Shadows™ subscribers. *Terms and prices are subject to change without notice. Sales tax applicable in N.Y.

USHAD-94

©1993 Harlequin Enterprises Limited

And now for something completely different from Silhouette....

In May, look for MIRANDA'S VIKING (IM #568) by Maggie Shayne

Yesterday, Rolf Magnusson had been frozen solid, his body perfectly preserved in the glacial cave where scientist Miranda O'Shea had discovered him. Today, the Viking warrior sat sipping coffee in her living room, all six feet seven inches of him hot to the touch. His heart, however, remained as ice-cold as the rest of him had been for nine hundred years. But Miranda knew a very unscientific way to thaw it out....

Don't miss MIRANDA'S VIKING by Maggie Shayne, available this May, only from

IT'S OUR 1000TH SILHOUETTE ROMANCE, AND WE'RE CELEBRATING!

JOIN US FOR A SPECIAL COLLECTION OF LOVE STORIES BY AUTHORS YOU'VE LOVED FOR YEARS, AND NEW FAVORITES YOU'VE JUST DISCOVERED. JOIN THE CELEBRATION...

April
REGAN'S PRIDE by Diana Palmer
MARRY ME AGAIN by Suzanne Carey

May
THE BEST IS YET TO BE by Tracy Sinclair
CAUTION: BABY AHEAD by Marie Ferrarella

June
THE BACHELOR PRINCE by Debbie Macomber
A ROGUE'S HEART by Laurie Paige

July
IMPROMPTU BRIDE by Annette Broadrick
THE FORGOTTEN HUSBAND by Elizabeth August

SILHOUETTE ROMANCE...VIBRANT, FUN AND EMOTIONALLY RICH! TAKE ANOTHER LOOK AT US! AND AS PART OF THE CELEBRATION, READERS CAN RECEIVE A FREE GIFT!

YOU'LL FALL IN LOVE ALL OVER AGAIN WITH SILHOUETTE ROMANCE!

CEL1000

Fifty red-blooded, white-hot, true-blue hunks
from every State in the Union!

Look for MEN MADE IN AMERICA! Written by some
of our most popular authors, these stories feature fifty
of the strongest, sexiest men, each from a different state
in the union!

Two titles available every other month at your favorite
retail outlet.

In April, look for:

LOVE BY PROXY by Diana Palmer (Illinois)
POSSIBLES by Lass Small (Indiana)

In May, look for:

KISS YESTERDAY GOODBYE by Leigh Michaels (Iowa)
A TIME TO KEEP by Curtiss Ann Matlock (Kansas)

You won't be able to resist MEN MADE IN AMERICA!